> "I had a purpose in bringing you to my aunt's house," Sin said.

A look of wariness entered Rose's blue eyes.

His lips brushed the delicate shell pink of her ear and she shivered. "If I'm to be condemned for seducing you, then I should be granted the pleasures of that seduction, not just the pains."

"The pleasures?" Her voice was breathless.

Sin smiled then, his first genuine smile of the day. His hips held her soft body captive against the rungs of the ladder, making him instantly aware of how much more he wanted from her. "Oh yes."

She blinked as realization slowly settled on her face. "You're going to *seduce* me?"

"Oh yes, my little Rose. You've owed me that pleasure for six years, and the time has come for you to pay."

"Hawkins always delivers delightfully humorous, poignant, and highly satisfying novels."

—*RT Book Reviews*

*Turn the page for rave reviews of
more enchanting romances by Karen Hawkins . . .*

"Couldn't put it down. . . . Ms. Hawkins is one of the most talented historical romance writers out there."

—*Romance Junkies* (5 stars)

"Charming and witty."

—*Publishers Weekly*

"An adventurous romance filled with laughter, passion, and emotion . . . mystery, threats, and plenty of sexual tension, plus an engaging premise which will keep you thoroughly entertained during each highly captivating scene. . . . *One Night in Scotland* holds your attention from beginning to end."

—*Single Titles*

"With its creative writing, interesting characters, and well-crafted situations and dialogue, *One Night in Scotland* is an excellent read. Be assured it lives up to all the virtues one has learned to expect from this talented writer."

—*Romance Reviews Today*

and Karen Hawkins

"Fast, fun, and sexy stories that are a perfect read for a rainy day, a sunny day, or any day at all!"

—Bestselling author Christina Dodd

"Humor, folklore, and sizzling love scenes."

—*Winter Haven News Chief*

"Always funny and sexy, a Karen Hawkins book is a sure delight!"

—Bestselling author Victoria Alexander

Also by Karen Hawkins

Available from Pocket Books

KAREN HAWKINS

How to Capture a Countess

Pocket Books

New York   London   Toronto   Sydney   New Delhi

Pocket Books
A Division of Simon & Schuster, Inc.
1230 Avenue of the Americas
New York, NY 10020

This book is a work of fiction. Names, characters, places, and incidents either are products of the author's imagination or are used fictitiously. Any resemblance to actual events or locales or persons, living or dead, is entirely coincidental.

First Pocket Books paperback edition October 2012

POCKET and colophon are registered trademarks of Simon & Schuster, Inc.

For information about special discounts for bulk purchases, please contact Simon & Schuster Special Sales at 1-866-506-1949 or business@simonandschuster.com.

The Simon & Schuster Speakers Bureau can bring authors to your live event. For more information or to book an event, contact the Simon & Schuster Speakers Bureau at 1-866-248-3049 or visit our website at www.simonspeakers.com.

Designed by Jacquelynne Hudson

Manufactured in the United States of America

10   9   8   7   6   5   4   3   2   1

ISBN 978-1-4516-8517-6
ISBN 978-1-4516-8519-0 (ebook)

To my daughter, Kym Hawkins, an amazing poet and wordsmith.

I dedicate this book to you.
I expect you to return the favor one day.

Dear Reader,

How to Capture a Countess is set at Floors Castle, a beautiful castle built in 1721 for the first Duke of Roxburghe. Floors was built on a natural terrace overlooking the River Tweed. On the opposite bank is the ruin of Roxburghe Castle, which was once considered the strongest fortress in the Borders region. Interesting to note, too, is that an ancient fort once located on the Roxburghe estate is one of the rumored locations for King Arthur's Camelot.

Floors Castle is the largest inhabited castle in Scotland. Known for its beauty and elegance, Floors is open today for tours. Since it first opened for tours in 1977, over a million visitors have passed through its magnificent front doors.

Most of the castle you see today is the result of renovations that took place between 1837 and 1847. Drawing inspiration from the Heriot's Hospital in Edinburgh, architect William Playfair remodeled the castle to include a roofscape of turrets, domes, and spires, lending a fairy-tale feel to an already beautiful building.

If you'd like to read more about Floors Castle, visit my website at www.karenhawkins.com. And be sure to check into Hawkins Manor, where you can play games, win free books, help a Regency lord and lady select their clothing for a ball, read about fascinating real-life people who helped define their time period, find recipes to make Regency-era dishes, and more!

Prologue

The Palazzo Albrizzi
Venice, Italy
June 11, 1806

From the Diary of the Duchess of Roxburghe
At the urging of my husband, Roxburghe, I put pen to paper in the hope that this diary may undo some of the unkindnesses posterity will attempt to attach to my name. There are truths . . . and then there are untruths.

For example, it's *true* that I've thus far outlived four husbands and am now married to a fifth, my beloved Roxburghe. It's also *true* that each man I married was fabulously wealthy and older than the last. However, it's patently *untrue* that I married for wealth and wealth alone.

Call me a romantic, but I could never marry without love, for that—and family—are the cornerstones of a worthy life.

But despite my many marriages, it is the one sadness of my life that I am childless. Thus I have dedicated myself to the happiness of my only sister, the Dowager Countess of Sinclair, and her grandchildren. I've three handsome great-nephews, scattered across the hills and vales of England and Scotland, two of whom I've now seen safely married.

Sadly, the eldest, the Earl of Sinclair, has become a cause for concern. I've never been certain why, but Sin finds the concept of matrimony odious. At one time I thought him merely obstinate, but lately I've begun to wonder if far more lurks behind the bored visage he keeps turned to the polite world . . . Is it truly boredom, or is it icy disdain caused by some unknown hurt?

Sadly, he is not one to share his thoughts and, in an attempt to keep the world from knocking upon his door, he's growing more and more willing to engage in socially reprehensible behavior. This very morning I received a disturbing missive from my sister reporting that my beloved great-nephew Sin has been embroiled in a scandal of some sort.

My sister is a known stoic, but I recognize her cry for help, and so I must hurry back to Scotland. I wish we could find our way there quicker, but passage must be secured, carriages found, trunks packed, and—oh, a thousand details.

I fear that in the month it will take us to return to our home, the damage will be done. I can only hope that it will not be permanent . . .

Lady MacAllister's Annual Hunt Ball
Two weeks earlier . . .

Lord Sinclair stood at the edge of Lady MacAllister's ballroom and wished to hell that he'd never come. The evening had been one disappointment after another. First, cajoled by his grandmother to provide her with a ride to the ball, she'd surprised him by bringing with her not one but two unmarried hopefuls—a Miss MacDonald and some other woman whose name he'd already forgotten. The two had spent the entire ride to the ball alternately staring at him and giggling. It had been enough to make Sin ill to his stomach.

His second disappointment had been the absence of Viscount Throckmorton. Sin had come to the ball for no other reason than to corner the viscount and persuade him to sell a certain high-stepping bay that Sin had seen on the streets of Edinburgh last week. Apparently Lord Throckmorton's plans had changed, for he was nowhere to be seen.

Sin's third disappointment had been with his hostess, Lady MacAllister. Known for being notoriously tightfisted even among the Scots, she had scrimped on the refreshments to the point that by the time he'd arrived, every drop of port and whiskey had already been consumed, leaving nothing but cloyingly sweet sherry and painfully dry champagne.

But the crowning indignity was the realization

that the sporting people with whom Sin usually bandied words had wisely decided to forgo Lady MacAllister's brand of amusement for events that were, Sin suspected, genuinely amusing. Even worse, the ball was awash in young, doe-eyed, annoyingly eager innocents. It was becoming all too obvious that his grandmother's casual mention that she'd heard that Viscount Throckmorton was to attend Lady MacAllister's ball had been nothing more than a ploy to trick Sin into attending an event filled with what she considered "marriageable young ladies of quality."

Sin hated the cloak of respectability society had draped over the most soul-deadening, avaricious aspect of life—that of getting married. Oh, let others talk of love; it was a mere sop to the sad truth: love didn't exist; the need to breed heirs did.

He knew what would happen the second he began a conversation with any young lady present tonight: they'd fawn and smile and pretend they were interested in every word he had to say, but he knew better. They were all pasty-faced clinging vines who saw him as nothing more than a fat purse and a coveted title. He hated such events as these, designed to truss up every available male and deliver them to a room full of hungry-eyed women where, bound by propriety to smile and converse and dance, they might slip and end up committed to a life of boredom.

It was a bitter situation, and yet here he was, sober

as a priest and denied even the relief of dickering for horseflesh with Throckmorton.

He ground his teeth against this onslaught of disappointments. As soon as his grandmother was safely ensconced at the side of one of her bosom-bows, Sin made his escape to the library where a slew of bachelors could be found in hiding.

Desperate for some amusement, he engaged young Lord MacDoonan in a card game. Twenty minutes later, MacDoonan's silver engraved flask, half full of fine Scottish whiskey, was neatly tucked into Sin's waistcoat pocket. Sin stayed another half hour, hoping to pass the time until his grandmother was ready to return home, but Lord MacDoonan was not a merry loser, and he whined incessantly about the loss of his flask until Sin had had enough. Bored, Sin left the library and made his way to the refreshment tables, which were empty but for a few crumbs, a sadly wilted flower arrangement, and a stack of unused punch glasses. He pocketed a glass, paused behind a palm, and filled it with whiskey.

Fortified, he rejoined the company and had just lifted the glass to his lips when he accidentally caught the eye of a young lady wearing a pink ball gown. The second their eyes met, she hurried forward as if invited.

Bloody hell, they're like leeches.

He turned his back on her, only to find himself being eyed by two other damsels in similarly atrocious gowns. Though they didn't lick their lips at the sight of him, their predatory gazes made him think of his hawk as it dove for a plump hare.

That was it; he was leaving. He'd leave the carriage for his grandmother and order a hackney to take him home.

Jaw tight, Sin turned and almost tripped over a slight bit of a girl who'd apparently been hovering at his elbow. For a nerve-wracking moment, he juggled his precious glass of whiskey.

As the glass settled back into his hands, he scowled at the chit who dared impede his departure. She was slight of stature, unusually tanned, with a smattering of freckles across a snub nose in a small face framed by wildly curling black hair barely held in place by a profusion of ribbons. Worse, she wore a dowdy white gown that was far too large for her, the style and color doing little to enhance her dank skin and too-slender figure.

"H-how do you do?" She offered a hurried curtsy with a desperate smile.

He tamped down the desire to curtly wish her to the devil. "Pardon me," he said in an icy tone and started to walk around her.

"Oh, do wait!" Her hand gripped his arm.

A jolt of heat raced through him.

Sin stopped dead in his tracks and looked down at her gloved hand. He'd felt that zap of attraction through three layers of material as surely as if she'd brushed his bare skin with her fingertips.

He found himself looking directly into her eyes. Pale blue and surrounded by thick black lashes, they showed the same shock that he felt.

Her gaze moved from his face to her hand and back. "I'm sorry. I didn't expect—" She shook her head, color flooding her skin, tinting the brown an exquisitely dusky rose.

Are her nipples that same dusky color? It was a shocking thought, but plain and loud, as if he'd said it aloud.

She jerked back her hand as if it burned. "I didn't mean—I'm sorry, but I—" She gulped as if miserable.

His irritation returned. "I'm sorry, but do I know you?"

She looked crestfallen. "I saw you at the Countess of Dunford's luncheon only a week ago."

"Did we speak?"

"Well, no."

"I don't remember." He'd been far too in his cups to remember much of that day at all, anyway.

"We also met a week and a day ago at the Melton house party."

He'd spent most of that evening in the library with the men, planning a hunting party for the next day. "I'm sorry, but I don't—"

"The Farquhars' soiree?"

He shook his head.

"The MacEnnis Ball? The Earl of Stratham's dinner party?"

He shook his head at each.

She looked even more crestfallen, which set off an unusual flash of remorse in him followed by annoyance. Bloody hell, he couldn't remember every chit who spoke to him, much less feel sorry for them all.

But then, none of them have ever caused such a reaction by merely touching my sleeve.

A footman came by and his companion captured a glass of champagne from the man's tray. To Sin's surprise, she took a deep breath and tossed it back, swallowing it in several fast gulps.

She caught his surprised gaze, and flushed. "I know that's unladylike, but—" She scrunched her nose and regarded her glass with disgust. "It's so horrid I didn't wish to taste it."

He had to laugh and his irritation disappeared. *Who is this girl?* He sipped his whiskey and regarded her over the edge of his glass. "So you like champagne, then? *Good* champagne, that is?"

"Yes, but there's not a drop of *good* champagne to be had, so . . ." Without the slightest hint of embarrassment, she eyed an approaching footman and, with a slight move to her left, managed to replace her glass as he passed by and grab another, which she disposed of as neatly as the first. "At least it's cold," she said in a pragmatic tone.

Sin burst out laughing. She looked so incongruous, this innocent-looking chit, with her freckled nose and black curls and wide blue eyes, snapping back flutes of champagne with a calm disdain for society's concept of propriety. Sin didn't know when he'd been so charmed.

When he'd first seen her he'd thought her a youngster, sixteen at most. But now as he met her gaze and caught a decided twinkle in her blue eyes, he realized he'd misjudged her because of her minute size. She was obviously older—and far more interesting—than she'd first appeared. "Tell me, Miss—?"

"Balfour. Miss Rose Balfour."

He boldly looked her up and down. He wasn't usually a fan of women without curves, but there was something appealing about Rose Balfour. Suddenly, the ball didn't seem so boring. "Your name suits you."

"It's not my real name. My mother was a great lover of ancient mythology so she named me Euphrosyne."

"Ah. One of the three graces." At her surprised look, he shrugged. "I read, though I've forgotten which grace Euphrosyne is. Joy? Splendor? Mirth?"

"Mirth." She made a droll face. "I'm afraid I have a very unruly sense of humor."

A naughty one? he wondered, his interest quickening even more.

As if she could read his mind, she laughed. The deliciously husky sound held a shimmery excitement that he could almost taste. This was more to his liking: a woman who refused to arm herself with faux innocence in an effort to lure one into a gossamer net, and boldly expressed her thoughts and desires.

He leaned a bit closer. "Miss Balfour, what brought you to this ball? The company doesn't seem to suit you any better than it suits me."

Looking into Sin's handsome face, Rose couldn't have disagreed with him more: the company was perfect. *He* was perfect. And given another glass of the forbidden champagne—Aunt Lettice was fortunately busy in the card room—Rose was certain she could drown in Sin's beautiful sherry-brown eyes.

She couldn't believe that those very eyes were now focused on her. She'd dreamed about this moment for so long, when the handsome, dashing Earl of Sinclair would finally see her—*really* see her—and realize that they were meant for each other.

It was a silly dream and she knew it, and yet she couldn't help but have it every time she saw him. There was something about him that made her knees quiver and her heart race. It wasn't just that he was so tall and broad shouldered, though he easily dwarfed everyone in the room. Nor was it because he was incredibly handsome, though his brow and strong jaw were carved as if from a Greek statue. And she didn't think it was because he was golden, as if kissed from the sun with hair of gold, threaded with brown.

His only imperfection was the faint broken line of his nose—a childhood break, perhaps? Or a sporting accident of some sort? She only knew that it added a heady, rakish, devil-may-care air to his already commanding appeal.

All in all, Lord Sinclair was every woman's dream, especially Rose's, and she was determined to grab this precious moment when his attention was actually hers. *All* hers.

His smile faded a bit and her heart thudded sickly as she realized with a rising sense of panic that she hadn't answered his question about what had brought her to the ball. *I can't allow him to get bored, or he'll leave and my chance will be gone. But what will interest him?* She knew that he enjoyed horses, and wagers, and boxing. And whiskey, too, and lobster in cream sauce, and that most of his waistcoats were blue, so that must be his favorite color.

She also knew that he'd dance the waltz, but never the country dances, and never with anyone who wasn't either married or a good bit older than she was. She knew, too, that every time he was in a room, her sixteen-year-old heart thudded like that of a bird newly caught in a cage.

It was beating like that now, but she knew better than to let him see her nervousness. Lord Sin usually spoke only to older, more worldly women. Women who moved with a self-possession and outspokenness that earned them the scowls of other women, but the admiration of men like him.

And suddenly, that was the exact sort of woman Rose desperately wanted to be. She gestured with her empty champagne glass to encompass the entire room and said with what she hoped was disdain, "It's a very boring party." She looked back at him. "Or it was until now."

Her champagne-fueled confidence shocked Rose as much as it seemed to delight her companion, for his gaze narrowed and he moved closer—so close that his chest brushed her arm and sent an odd heat flickering through her. Rose suddenly realized that her fingers were so tightly clutched about the champagne flute that it was a surprise the glass hadn't splintered. She uncurled her fingers, wanting nothing more than to toss the glass and her inhibitions away and to throw her arms around him, a feeling made stronger by the two glasses of champagne. "It's too bad we're at this ball now. There are other things we could be doing instead." Like riding through the park, for she loved horses as much as he did. Or, if they could escape her aunt's vigilant eye, walking through the gardens, where they might slip away and share a kiss. Her heart fluttered at the thought.

"*Other* things, Miss Balfour?" He returned her smile, an odd glint in his eye. "I would like that, too."

She smiled widely as she gazed into his eyes, completely lost. He might not remember every time they'd met, but she did. She remembered every time he'd smiled, how his dark blond hair fell over his brow and the way his eyes crinkled when he laughed. She knew far too well how his deep voice could rumble over one and leave one's heart thudding like a hummingbird—

"Miss Balfour, you are out of champagne. Shall I fetch you more?"

"Oh no, my aun—" She clamped her lips over the rest of her sentence. *Worldly women don't answer to their aunts.* "I mean, yes, I would love another glass of champagne."

He looked over her head and scanned the room. "Where is a footman? There were two hovering near just a second ago."

Rose took the opportunity to stare openly at him, admiring the strong cut of his jaw, the decidedly patrician line of his nose, and the sensual way his mouth curved just so—

His gaze dropped to hers and for a second, their glances clung.

Rose hid her gulp behind a dismissive wave at the room. "Th-there are quite a lot of people here tonight, aren't there?"

He shrugged, a flicker of disappointment in his face that she felt as keenly as the cut of a knife. "It's a ball," he said shortly.

A sense of urgency arose in her. *Blast it, if I bore him, he will leave.* She looked around, searching for inspiration. "I hate these events."

"And why is that?"

She could answer that honestly. "Everyone dresses up in so many ribbons and bows and buttons that we all look like trussed-up codfish."

He laughed, the deep sound rolling over her and making her heart sing. "Codfish?"

She practically glowed that she'd made him laugh.

"How do you entertain yourself at these sorts of events, Lord Sin?"

His smile disappeared. "Lord Sin?"

She blinked. "That's what people call you."

"People who know me, perhaps."

Rose peeped at him through her lashes, as she'd seen a widow do to him once. "If you don't wish me to call you Lord Sin, I won't, but few words trip off the tongue like 'Sin.'"

She had to fight to keep from gawking at her own temerity. *Goodness! Where did* that *come from?*

Wherever it had, he apparently found it worth noticing, for his gaze was suddenly intense. "You enjoy sin, my dear Miss Balfour?"

"Who doesn't?" she retorted, getting more and more drunk off her own bravery. She borrowed a line from the church service she and Aunt Lettice had attended last Sunday. "We're all sinners in one way or another, aren't we?"

"So we are, my lovely Rose." His smile became as wickedly inviting as ever her dreams had made it. "By the way, my name is Alton, although if you pre-fer Sin"—he offered a small bow, and his closeness brought his eyes level with hers—"you may call me Sin, if you wish."

"Sin it is, then." Whoever had named him Alton hadn't felt the effect of his warm brown eyes as they traveled across her as if he could see through her silks and laces. An odd shiver traveled over her, prickling her skin and making her more light-headed than the champagne.

His gaze found her empty glass. "I almost forgot your champagne."

"Oh, that's quite all ri—"

"Here." He reached out to grasp a flute of champagne from a footman and pressed it into her hand.

"Thank you," she said, eyeing the glass with trepidation.

"You're welcome." He removed her empty glass and placed it on a nearby table.

The last thing she needed was more champagne; she was already tipsy from her own temerity and the other two glasses she'd had. But she caught Sin's gaze and realized that he expected her to drink it just as she'd drunk the first two. And right now, she'd do anything to keep his attention—and admiration—on herself. She lifted the glass in a toast, and then tossed it back.

He looked so pleased that her misgivings instantly disappeared.

Indeed, as the champagne coursed through her, the last silly worry about her actions flew away like an irritating bee before a brisk wind. And in its place was the sudden realization that this was her one and *only* chance to fix her interest with the earl. He was here, he was paying attention to her, and—more astonishing—Aunt Lettice was nowhere to ruin the moment.

Rose knew it wouldn't last. In a half hour or sooner, her champagne confidence would be gone, Sin would be bored, and Aunt Lettice would arrive to "save" her. She didn't want to be saved. She wanted . . . Oh dear, what *did* she want? She tried to swallow, but her throat was too tight. Her gaze traveled over him, across his face to his lips, and there she lingered, suddenly certain of her goal. She wanted nothing less than a kiss. A *real* kiss, one that would sear the memory of this moment into her soul so thoroughly that if she lived ten score years plus one, she'd never forget it.

Rose glanced around the ballroom, and the answer to her predicament came in a bubble of champagne clarity. *The terrace doors lead to the garden. A worldly woman would entice Lord Sinclair into the garden and, once there, she'd boldly kiss him.*

Rose fixed a seductive smile on her lips. "Lord Sin, when you arrived, I was just going to repair a tear in my gown."

He looked at her perfect hem. "Your gown is torn?"

"In the back, where you can't see. I may trip if I don't fix it soon. I thought I might find a seat in the garden and pin it, if you'd care to escort me there?"

His gaze locked with hers and something passed between them. Rose didn't know what it was, but suddenly her skin tingled and she couldn't breathe. As she always did when very nervous, she laughed softly.

Sin gave a muffled curse, removed her empty glass from her hand and placed it on a nearby table, tucked her hand in the crook of his arm, and instantly bore her toward the terrace doors.

That was easy! Feeling as if she were in charge of the world, she allowed him to sweep her along. Within seconds they were through the terrace doors and out into the cool night air, the noise of the ball left behind. Rose's heart tripped along, happy and euphoric from a growing sense of awe and pride at her boldness. Sin's hand was warm over hers, the faint scent of his cologne mingling with the jasmine and lilies that filled the lantern-lit garden. *Could this night be any more perfect?*

Sin led her down the stone steps and to a path dimly lit by colorful paper lanterns. They passed a couple here and there, but Sin was careful to stay out of direct sight of anyone.

He turned down a broader path and finally led her into an open space where a large, low fountain bubbled. In the center of the fountain Aphrodite poured water from a jug, a small Cupid playing at her feet. Green lily pads floated all around, and the glowing paper lanterns reflected in the water like colorful stars. "This is beautiful," Rose said. *The perfect place for my first kiss.*

As if he read her thoughts, he led her to the fountain. A red paper lantern hung overhead and cast a seductive light across Sin's face. Rose couldn't believe she was here, alone with him, his warm hands now sliding about her waist as he tugged her close.

It's exactly the way it was in my dreams. Heart pounding, she placed her hands on his chest and lifted her face to his. She closed her eyes, swaying slightly from the champagne, and offered her lips.

Sin tightened his hold on her slender waist. And to think he'd been about to leave the ball. His body was aflame with desire for this little fancy piece, and he was determined to have her. He bent and captured her mouth with his, teasing her soft lips until they parted, and then flicking his tongue over her teeth. She gasped against his mouth and wiggled against him.

He almost groaned with relief at her wanton signal. That was all he needed. He slipped his hands to her ass and cupped her against him, rubbing his hard cock against her, showing her how she affected him, how she—

Her eyes flew open. For a frozen second, they looked at each other. And then, with a small cry, she shoved him as hard as she could.

Sin reeled backward, the back of his leg hitting the low lip of the fountain, and he fell in with a splash.

If shock hadn't already killed the intense flood of desire, the icy water would have done so. He gasped as he struggled to right himself, coughing water as he grabbed the statue for purchase. Aphrodite, apparently disgusted with the whole display, continued to pour water from her vase directly upon his head.

Sputtering and furious, he moved away from the statue and glared at Rose.

She stood at the edge of the fountain, her eyes wide, her fingers over her mouth, which was formed into a shocked "O." She regained her composure quickly, though, and held up a hand. "Don't move!"

"Like hell; I'm not staying here." He pushed his wet hair from his eyes and tried to wring some of the water from his coattails.

"Someone must help you out of that fountain and—I'll fetch someone now." To his astonishment, she lifted her head and yelled in a loud voice, *"Help! Someone, please help!"*

"No, don't!" He lunged across the fountain, trying to reach her. "You're going to draw atten—" His foot caught in a lily pad and down he went again, into the net of lily pads.

He came up cursing, grabbing at the slimy tendrils and yanking them from his face and neck. "Damn it!" Water and something green dangled before his face. He snatched at it, and found a lily pad perched upon his head. He threw it into the pond in disgust . . . and realized that Rose and he were no longer alone.

A dozen or so ladies and their escorts stood gawking at where he stood, water pouring from his evening clothes, another lily pad in his hand. An assortment of astonishment, shock, and the growing suspicions of mirth could be seen in each face.

Grinding his teeth, he turned toward Rose. She was facing him with a wide, astonished look, her gloved hand pressed to her mouth.

She pointed to his shoulder. "I-I beg your pardon, but there's a lily p-p-p—" To his chagrin and fury, a faint giggle erupted from her kiss-swollen lips. Instantly, Rose's giggle trickled through the crowd and, like dry tinder, they burst into laughter.

The wave of it hit him like freezing water and his jaw tightened until he feared his teeth would crack. Rose's laughter was now reflected in every gaze . . . except one. His grandmother didn't look a bit amused. If anything, she looked as if she wished he'd return to the lily pad net and drown himself.

Lord MacDoonan, obviously recovered from the loss of his flask, chortled merrily. "Lud, Sin, look at you!"

Sin shot a baleful glare at Rose. Her laughter died as her gaze locked with his, and for an instant, he thought he caught a glimmer of something . . . Remorse? Fear? Whatever it was, it wasn't enough.

"Sinclair," his grandmother said, looking furious. "Get out of that fountain!"

A tiny woman wearing a puce gown, her white hair adorned with a ridiculous amount of flowers, scurried up. "Rose! Good heavens! What are you doing here? I've been looking for you everywhere and—" The woman's gaze fell on Sin, and she gasped and jumped as if he were a loch monster. "Oh dear!" Face red, she gathered Rose. "Come. We are leaving *immediately.*"

"But, I—" Rose began, but she was no match for the tiny lady, who seemed to have grown arms as strong as a bear baiter's.

"*Now*," she said, marching Rose down a path and away from the growing crowd.

"But Aunt Lettice, let me at least tell S—" Rose's voice faded down the path.

Even though she was gone, the memory of Rose's laughter still stung Sin's ears as he waded to the edge of the fountain and stepped out. How *dare* she? He would n—

"Lord Sin!" Miss MacDonald, who'd tried so hard to charm Sin on the carriage ride to this atrocious ball, snickered behind her hand. "Something's in your pocket."

Sin looked down. His front pocket was moving slightly. As he looked, a small fish jumped out of his pocket and into the puddle at his feet.

"It appears that yet another waterlogged creature has escaped the fountain." Miss MacDonald's eyes lit with malice. "Wouldn't you say, Lord *Fin*?"

A wave of unrestrained laughter met her sally.

Sin sent an icy look at each guest. Instantly, the laughter faded and an awkward silence arose.

Sin sent a stiff bow to his grandmother, then turned on his heel and left. He couldn't believe that he—*he*, of all men—had allowed himself to be misled by a pair of wide blue eyes and a pert nose covered with freckles. Good God, how could he—he, who knew better than most men—have allowed such a thing to happen? *Damn it, that little wench tricked me. She played to my weaknesses and teased me with her sense of humor, and I followed her like a lamb to slaughter.* He wasn't certain why she'd done it—perhaps he'd dismissed her at some event, snubbed her when he'd been in his cups, or some other inconsequential thing—but for whatever reason, Rose Balfour had successfully orchestrated his very public humiliation.

Hands balled into fists, Sin passed through a gateway into the drive where, dripping steadily, he curtly ordered a wide-eyed footman to fetch his carriage. *Blast you, Rose Balfour! You will regret your actions this evening. And believe this: I will show no mercy.*

One

Floors Castle
September 12, 1812

From the Diary of the Duchess of Roxburghe
For the last six years, my great-nephew, the Earl of Sinclair, has done naught but drive his grandmother to distraction with his antics. Oh, we thought him a wild one before The Incident, but we were wrong. Since then, he has shown us what "wild" truly means, and it seems that every day brings a new report of his lascivious lifestyle.

The fault, of course, is with my sister. At the tender age of seventeen, after his parents were killed in a carriage accident, Sin was left with titles and estates and the care of his younger brothers. Though several of us advised otherwise, my sister pushed to give the boy all of the weight of those responsibilities instead of appointing an executor until he was of a more appropriate age. My sister meant no harm, and thought that the boy would mature as he assumed the mantle of responsibility. He did so, of course, but at a very high cost.

Without parents to guide him, or a partner to share his burdens, and left solely responsible for the care of his younger brothers, he became arrogantly conceited with his own independence. Though he now possesses what all women desire in a husband—excellent birth, a handsome visage, a charming manner (when he wishes), a respected title, and a growing fortune—he torments my adored sister by refusing to fix his attentions upon a woman of genteel breeding and instead openly cavorts with Notorious Undesirables.

The time has come for me to take matters into my own hands; my poor sister now regrets her lack of trust in my earlier judgment, and has made a desperate plea for help.

And desperate times call for desperate measures . . .

The butler's sedate knock was met by a cacophony of barking. Over the yips and yaps, a feminine voice called for him to enter. MacDougal sighed regretfully for his polished shoes and well-ironed breeches, then opened the large oak doors to the sitting room.

A small herd of yapping pugs met him, a mixture of brown and silver fur, flat wet noses, and curly pig tails. The dogs jumped upon him, their little nails ruining his careful creases and marring his well-tended shoe leathers.

Even so, he couldn't resist the charms of the large brown eyes now fixed upon him. "There, there, ye wee bairns. Stop yer yappin'; 'tis naught but me. Did I no' feed ye bacon jus' this mornin'? 'Tis fine treatment ye're givin' me now."

Six curly tails wagged in unison. The Roxburghe pugs were as famous throughout Edinburgh and the surrounding countryside as their mistress, the notorious Duchess of Roxburghe, a woman well into her sixtieth year (though none were certain how far) and the icy-eyed mistress of Floors Castle for the past ten years.

The dogs sniffed MacDougal's breeches and shoes as he edged through the pack and then crossed the many rugs to the two women seated before the fireplace at the far end of the cavernous room. Unable to maul his legs while he walked, the pugs had to be content with trotting and tumbling after him, puffing and wheezing as they pretended to herd him along.

As he reached the small circle of settees, Lady Charlotte looked up from her knitting. After a quick motion for silence, she pointed to the duchess, who was reclining upon the settee opposite, a kerchief soaked in lavender water covering her eyes.

Ah, yes. Her grace had played whist last night and, as usually happened when the vicar came to visit, she'd enjoyed her evening libations a wee bit too much. It showed not only in the fact that the duchess was hiding her eyes from the sunlight, but also in the way her fashionable gown of blue muslin was crinkled and her red wig was slightly askew.

Lady Charlotte leaned forward to whisper, "Her grace isn't feeling well this morning."

"Aye, me lady," he whispered back with a kind smile. The youngest daughter of the late Earl of Argyll and a distant cousin of the duke's, Lady Charlotte Montrose was a short, rather mousy woman sadly given to wearing lace mobcaps in the French manner, a fashion that did not suit her plump face. MacDougal had been made aware of this fact only this morning by that secret fashionmonger Mrs. Cairness, the housekeeper, who—when not wearing the starched black gowns as befitted her station—often dressed better than the duchess herself.

"Perhaps you should return in an hour," Lady Charlotte whispered. "Once her grace is through with her nap."

MacDougal nodded. Lady Charlotte knew her grace better than most, as she'd made her home at Floors Castle for the last eight years. It was widely held that she'd come to stay with her cousin Roxburghe after an arranged marriage to some wild hobnob of society had fallen through. Whatever the reason, she'd never left and was now as much a part of Floors Castle as the duchess herself.

MacDougal bent closer to Lady Charlotte. "Perhaps 'twould be best if I left the post fer her grace to read when she awakens? There's a missive I think she moight wish to—"

"Oh, for the love of—" The duchess moaned as if her own words caused her pain. She pressed a hand to her covered eyes, an assortment of rings flashing with the movement. "Pray stop your infernal whispering. You sound like a pack of nuns planning a murder."

MacDougal hid a smile. "I'm sorry, yer grace, but I thought ye might wish to see a certain missive tha' just arrived."

The duchess peeked out from under a corner of the lavender-water-soaked kerchief, revealing a large hooked nose and one brilliant blue eye. "He answered?"

"Aye, yer grace, much to the surprise of us all." If there was one benefit to serving as part of the duchess's household since one was a mere lad (well before she'd married Roxburghe and become a duchess), it was the privilege of occasionally speaking one's mind. MacDougal was careful not to overuse the privilege, though. He was far too fond of both the duchess and his position to do so.

The duchess tossed off the cloth and sat up gingerly, pushing her wig back in place with a well-practiced shove.

MacDougal held out the silver salver, where a small note had been set aside from the stack of cards and letters. "From Lord Sinclair, yer grace."

"Thank you." She opened the note.

Lady Charlotte watched with a bright gaze, distracted only when a small silver pug attacked a skein of yarn in her basket. "Stop that, Meenie," Lady Charlotte admonished. "Don't touch my yar—"

"Demme!" The duchess crumpled the note into a ball.

Lady Charlotte looked up, disappointment on her round face. "He's not coming."

"No, blast it all." The duchess tossed the note into the fire. "My great-nephew will attend neither my house party nor my Winter Ball. As a sop to his weak conscience—if one can call it that—he's offered to visit me on his return from his sojourn, almost a month *after* the scheduled festivities."

"How disappointing."

"How rude! To offer to visit on his way back from some low amusement, I have no doubt. Balderdash!" She threw herself back onto the settee, her eyes ablaze. "I won't receive him. *That* will teach him to refuse my invitations."

Knowing a little something about the Earl of Sinclair, MacDougal rather doubted that.

Apparently Lady Charlotte felt the same, for she said in her soft voice, "Chances are, he will merely shrug and go on his way. I don't mean to say anything ill about Lord Sinclair, but he's not the sort of male one would call accommodating."

"No, he's not. He's a fool is what he is, demme

him." The duchess tossed her kerchief back over her face and slumped down like a limp rag doll.

While it was very poor of Lord Sinclair not to accept his great-aunt's invitation, MacDougal felt that someone had to make the peace. He cleared his throat. "Yer grace, I'm sorry aboot the inconvenience of Lord Sinclair's answer, but perhaps he is busy. He must have a mountain of dooties takin' care o' his estates and such—"

"Ha!" her grace said, the puff of air sending the corner of her kerchief aflutter before she snatched it off and threw it to the floor, where four of her pugs pounced upon it and began a mad tussle. Ignoring their growls, the duchess said, "My great-nephew is very busy indeed—busy trying to sleep with every married woman in England. I daresay he'd attend my party if I invited some scantily clad opera singers, or a house full of painted harlo—"

"Margaret, my dear," Lady Charlotte said in a breathless tone, sending a quick glance at MacDougal, which he wisely pretended not to notice. "Perhaps our passions would be better served if, rather than lamenting Lord Sinclair's failings, vast though they are—"

"Like the bloody ocean," the duchess muttered.

"Like the *vast* ocean," Lady Charlotte agreed. "But perhaps rather than focusing on Sinclair's shortcomings, we would be better served by finding a way to get him to attend your ball, especially as you've invited every eligible woman of standing within miles."

"He's so stubborn." The duchess tapped her fingers on the arm of the settee, a thoughtful expression on her face. "I wish I could believe that Sin was merely too busy to attend my ball, but he's been in sole charge of his estates for over fifteen years now and he finds the daily administration no more taxing than selecting a waistcoat, especially now that his brothers are grown and married. Sadly, he values his freedom far too much."

"Too many cares as a youth, perhaps?"

"And so I warned my sister, when she decided to place the full weight of— But I'm not going to rehash old decisions; it will serve no purpose. The truth is that Sin's not coming to my ball because he's realized my purpose in bringing him here: to encourage him to find a suitable wife and settle down."

Lady Charlotte tsked. "It is a dreadful coil. Perhaps a little afternoon tea would help us think our way through this situation to a solution."

"Perhaps," the duchess said absently, reaching down to scoop up a very roly-poly pug and plop it into her lap, where it snuggled into a ball. "MacDougal, please bring a tea tray."

"Aye, yer grace. I shall place the rest of the post upon yer secretary." MacDougal crossed to the small rosewood desk and placed the letters in a neat stack on one corner. He paused to straighten them, taking his time in doing so.

The duchess leaned back, patting the pug with one hand while she absently tapped her long fingers on the arm of the settee. "Maybe I should hire some men to abduct him and have him shackled in the pantry until my ball?"

MacDougal wondered if there was anything strong enough in the pantry that the earl could not overturn. The man was several inches over six feet tall and was a fine physical specimen, made so by his many sporting pursuits.

"Yes," Lady Charlotte agreed blithely. "That would be so much easier than trying to reason with him, though I fear someone could get hurt."

"He wouldn't come quietly, would he?" The duchess's voice was heavy with regret. "And Sinclair is the devil of a good boxer."

"He's good with his pistols, too. He's never lost a duel."

"Very true, demme it." The duchess's fingers never stopped tapping as the two subsided into silence.

Lady Charlotte, her knitting needles clicking softly, said, "A pity he's not a woman. If he were, one could just invite him over for tea and have a nice cozy talk and resolve everything."

"Well, he's not a woman, so that thinking is of no use. The boy is as stubborn as his father, who was a fool." Her grace scratched the ear of the fortunate pug that occupied her lap. It stretched under her ministrations before curling into a ball again for a snooze. "The late earl was a pompous ass and a rakehell, and he passed those unholy traits to his son."

"But Lord Sin hasn't always been such a ne'er-do-weel."

Her grace's expression darkened, a flicker of sadness on her expressive face. "No, he hasn't been the same since The Incident, which—"

Lady Charlotte cleared her throat and flicked a glance at MacDougal, who hurried to knock the stack of letters off the secretary so that he had to bend down to collect them once again. Lady Charlotte lowered her voice, though MacDougal heard her plainly enough when she said, "Sinclair has changed."

"Yes, six years ago . . ." The duchess's voice trailed off, an intent expression coming into her eyes as she slowly sat up in her seat, her eyes fastened on some vision mortal eyes could not see.

MacDougal held his breath and leaned forward. He knew that look. *Poor Lord Sinclair.*

Lady Charlotte stopped knitting, her eyes widening. "You've thought of something!" Her voice was almost breathless.

"I might know a way to get Sinclair to attend my Winter Ball *and* the house party for the preceding three weeks."

"To *both*?"

"Yes, and if we do this right, he'll think it was all his own idea, too." The duchess rubbed her hands together in apparent glee. "Charlotte, this might just do the trick!"

MacDougal wondered if there was Borgia blood

somewhere in her grace's family. He'd wager an entire month's wages that there was.

"I'm all ears," Lady Charlotte said, leaning forward.

The duchess smiled as she patted the pug sleeping in her lap. "Sin changed six years ago. Before that he was a known Corinthian, a sporting man. He had already made it clear to the family that he would not accept a tame marriage, but he was not a scoundrel."

"Until The Incident."

"Since then, he's been rakehelling his way across England, as if bound and determined to prove the naysayers right."

"People did talk."

"And why wouldn't they? He'd been lording it over everyone, the most eligible bachelor in all of England, too busy with his races and prizefights to exchange pleasantries or attend social events. When he did bother to come to someone's ball, he barely danced, spoke only to a few people, and usually left long before anyone else."

"Insufferable."

"Yes. So when he was made to look a fool by a mere nobody, people were pleased. So they talked more than they might have had it been someone else. It changed Sin in some ways. I thought it was because of the gossip, but now I wonder . . ."

The duchess looked at MacDougal, who quickly

whipped out his kerchief and pretended he'd found some dust on the desk.

Her grace leaned toward Charlotte. "After The Incident, Sin moved heaven and earth trying to find that gel who embarrassed him. I suspect he wished for vengeance, but he never managed to find her. Her family had tucked her away somewhere and after a while, he stopped trying." The duchess pursed her lips and then said in a thoughtful tone, "She's the only woman who's ever eluded Sin. And for a sporting man . . ."

Lady Charlotte's eyes widened with a dawning respect. "Margaret, you may be on to something with that."

"If Sin thought she'd be at my house party, he'd reconsider coming. I'm sure of it. All we have to do is find out who she is and invite her here." The duchess's smile faded. "If she's respectable."

"She is," Lady Charlotte said. "Quite respectable, in fact."

The duchess sent an irritated glance at her companion. "Have you become a seer?"

"Of course not. But I—that is—*you* have been in correspondence with her for years. Since the year she was born, in fact."

The duchess blinked. "I have?"

"Of course. You send her a present every Michaelmas, and a nice letter on her birthday." Charlotte's knitting needles ticked on. "Her name is Rose Balfour and she lives with her father at Caith Manor, outside Aberdeenshire."

The duchess looked as astounded as MacDougal felt. "How do you know that?"

"Because you're her godmother."

MacDougal almost gasped, but managed to swallow it.

The duchess stared at Lady Charlotte. "Am I?"

Lady Charlotte nodded, her lace cap flapping over her ears. "Oh yes, though I suppose it's not surprising that you don't know it. You and Roxburghe were out of the country when The Incident occurred, and by the time you returned home, no one would speak of it in front of you."

"But they spoke of it to you."

"Frequently. At the time, I thought the name sounded familiar, but I couldn't place it. Months afterward, I was writing the Michaelmas letters and there she was on your godchild list: Miss Rose Balfour."

"Why didn't you tell me?"

Lady Charlotte blinked owlishly. "Because you said you didn't want to hear her name—*ever*."

MacDougal couldn't smother his chuckle this time, which earned him a sharp glance from her grace. He quickly pretended to cough.

She turned back to Charlotte. "You *should* have told me anyway."

"I'm sorry," Lady Charlotte said meekly.

"Still, this is to our advantage." The duchess tapped her fingers on her knee, her gaze narrowed. "So I'm Miss Rose Balfour's godmother."

"You're the godmother of all three Balfour sisters."

"All three? Lud, I'm the godmother to far too many people."

MacDougal almost nodded. Every year, he assisted Lady Charlotte in sending out the numerous requisite packages and letters to her grace's many godchildren, and every year it seemed that the number doubled or trebled.

"So I've said for ages," Charlotte said with some asperity. "You've so many godchildren now that—Here, I'll show you the list." Lady Charlotte put her knitting aside and rose, moving between the dozing pugs to the secretary.

MacDougal began dusting a nearby side table. Fortunately, a small amount of dust puffed up as Lady Charlotte passed him, so she merely gave him a sharp look before she opened the secretary and pulled out a lengthy list that contained well over fifty names. She carried it to the duchess and pointed to a line halfway down the second page. "There."

The duchess held the list at arm's length, and looked down her nose at the slanted writing. "Ah. Rose, Lily, and Dahlia Balfour." She lowered the list. "Good God, are they flowers or women?"

"Sir Balfour is a noted horticulturalist, so perhaps he is the one who gifted his daughters with such nicknames."

"Nicknames? What are their real names, then?"

"I don't recall, but they are quite overpowering."

"Remind me again—how did I become their godmother?"

"That information is under their names on the list."

The duchess held the letter back at arm's length. "Their grandmother was—" She squinted. "Miss Moira MacDonald. Ah, Moira! I haven't thought of her in years. We went to boarding school together and I always liked her." The duchess handed the list back to Lady Charlotte and looked a little guilty. "I hope I've been a good godmother?"

"Oh yes. As I said, you've sent them a small gift every Michaelmas, as well as on every major birthday."

"Charlotte, I'd be lost without you."

Lady Charlotte smiled serenely and carried the list back to the secretary, where she tucked it back in its pocket before she returned to her seat and collected her knitting once again. "So you think to use Miss Balfour as bait to entrap Lord Sin into coming to your house party and Winter Ball?"

"Entrap? There's no need to put it in such bald terms. I prefer to think of it as 'assisting.'" The duchess tilted her head to one side as she leaned back.

"Now, all I have to do is find a subtle way to let Sin know that this gel is my goddaughter."

"And then what?"

"And then he will do the rest."

Lady Charlotte didn't look convinced. "How can you be certain?"

"Because I know enough about my great-nephew to know he cannot refuse a challenge. And this gel, whoever she is, has challenged him."

"And if he doesn't?"

Her grace's brows lowered. "He must. He is the earl. It is his responsibility to marry well and have an heir."

MacDougal tried to keep his attention on his dusting, but it was difficult. Even though he understood the importance of a man of wealth and title marrying to carry on the family name, he almost felt sorry for Lord Sinclair.

"I do hope Lord Sinclair will be amenable." Lady Charlotte's tone said she thought he would be anything but.

"For the love of Zeus, Charlotte! What is all of this nay-saying?"

"I'm sorry," Charlotte said. "I was just thinking that Lord Sinclair and Miss Balfour might hate each other and—"

"Lud, pray stop thinking, for it's giving me a headache! I don't care if Sin and Miss Balfour deal well with each other or not. All I want is to get my nephew to attend my ball. Once he's here, hopefully one of the eligible chits I've invited will appeal to him and thus my sister's problems will be solved."

"Oh. I thought you meant to attempt a match between Miss Balfour and Lord Sinclair."

"No, although if they ever chanced to meet under better circumstances, one never knows what might . . ." Her grace's gaze unfocused and once again she seemed to be staring at something no one else could see.

"Margaret?" Lady Charlotte asked.

"Yes, dear. I was just thinking. Perhaps I will amend my guest list for the house party a bit."

"But why? You said you'd invited the liveliest young men and women you could think of."

"So I did." The duchess leaned back in her chair. "But we must do what we can." Her gaze landed on MacDougal. "MacDougal, forget the demmed tea. Bring a decanter of port."

"But yer grace, 'tis only eleven in the morning and the doctor says ye should not—"

"I know what Doctor MacCreedy says, but I need port. Lady Charlotte and I have some very important letters to write and a new guest list to draw up, and we'll need inspiration."

"Yes, we will." Lady Charlotte smoothed a knot from a strand of yarn. "A *lot* of inspiration."

MacDougal bowed and returned to the door, the pugs trotting behind him. He had to gently shove several of the more determined mutts out of the way before he could close the door.

In the vestibule, he shook his head. "She'll ne'er quit scheming until they put her in the ground. And mayhap no' even then."

"I beg yer pardon, sir?" asked one of the footmen who'd sprung to attention when MacDougal had appeared. "Was her grace in a mood this morning?"

"Aye, a scheming one. God help those as come into her path, fer she willna show them any mercy." Shaking his head, he left to fetch the port.

The sixth Earl of Sinclair glanced in the mirror and gave his cravat a few deft touches. After a silent study, he nodded. "That will do."

His valet, a small man named Dunn with silver hair and a dapper air, gave a sigh of relief. Dunn never allowed anyone but himself to touch his lordship's clothing, preferring to press and mend it himself. He was especially vigilant with his lordship's boot blacking, using a special mixture known only to him that included such mystical ingredients as champagne and beeswax. Belowstairs, he was known in respectful tones as "Mr. Timothy Dunn, a true stickler for fashion."

He placed upon the bed the two freshly starched cravats that he'd been holding at the ready and turned to regard the earl's efforts. "A brilliant knot, my lord. The gentleman with whom you'll be playing faro tonight will be blinded by your efforts."

"I wilt beneath your approval," Sin said drily.

"You've earned that approval, my lord," Dunn said, not acknowledging Sin's sarcasm. "That's the most beautiful cravat knot you've accomplished yet. It's a pity no one of worth will see it."

"What's wrong?" Sin asked, amused at his nattily dressed valet. "Is the company too low for you?"

Dunn sniffed.

Sin grinned. "There will be one or two people 'of worth' at Lord Dalton's." Especially fair Lady Jameston. Her husband was in London dealing with the weighty question of the Regency, as were many other lords. Their absences had opened many opportunities.

"My lord, pardon me for saying so, but I find both Lord Dalton *and* his company rather low."

Sin shrugged. "He's a bit common, but he welcomes any and all to his house. He's a generous host."

"Generous hosts do not try and strip all of the coins from their guests' pockets at games of chance."

Sin smiled in acknowledgment. He turned to the silver tray on the dresser and selected a cravat pin. As he did so, two letters that had been placed to one side fell to the floor.

Dunn instantly retrieved them. "I'm sorry, my lord, but I almost forgot to tell you; these came this afternoon while you were hunting. One is from Lady Ross, and the other from your great-aunt, the Duchess of Roxburghe."

"Thank you." Sin turned his attention to the placement of his cravat pin. "Put them on the dresser."

"My lord, aren't you going to read them?"

"Why? I already know what they say. Lady Ross wishes me to attend her in Edinburgh, as Lord Ross has been called out of the country on a diplomatic mission."

"Ah. I take it that we've tired of Lady Ross."

Sin shrugged. He and Sarah had enjoyed a mutually beneficial arrangement for the past two years, but lately she, and everything else about his life, seemed boring.

It was petty to be bored when one had so much, but he somehow couldn't dislodge the feeling. Even being away from the bustle of Edinburgh for the last two weeks to enjoy some hunting and to view a prizefight had left him feeling listless. Sin raked a hand through his hair, ignoring the valet's look of disapproval. Damn it, he had no right to feel anything other than pleased with life; he had so much—excellent brothers with whom he was close, a grandmother who, for all of her faults, had never ceased to offer her love and support, an estate that was more profitable every year, a time-honored title, manors filled with treasures of every conceivable kind, an assortment of friends and acquaintances, so many in fact that he was rarely alone—he had everything he could possibly want, and yet . . . and yet something was missing.

He met his gaze in the mirror. *Something has always been missing. But what?*

As usual, no answer came. He scowled at himself, unhappy with the maudlin turn of his thoughts. "Yes, Dunn, we're tired of Lady Ross. Very tired."

Nodding, Dunn placed the letter from Lady Ross upon the dresser, but held on to the other missive. "And your great-aunt? What do you suppose she wishes? Or should I ask?"

"What do you think?"

Dunn sighed. "She wishes for you to attend her ball and house party, fall in love with one of the hundred of young ladies she's invited for that purpose—as she does every year—and get married."

"So now you know why I'm not going to bother reading her missive."

The valet pursed his lips. "The duchess has been quite kind to you, my lord."

Sin didn't answer.

"It wouldn't hurt to at least read it." Dunn paused. "Shall I do so while you're getting ready?"

Sin met the valet's gaze in the mirror. "If I say no, you're going to continue to torment me about it, aren't you?"

"Yes, my lord."

"Then read the damn thing and be done with it."

"Very good, my lord." Dunn opened the letter. "Your great-aunt writes, 'Sinclair, I hope this missive finds you—'"

"Dunn, I said that *you* could read the missive, not that you could read it aloud to *me*."

The valet's thin lips folded in disapproval. "Shall I at least summarize what the letter says?"

"Providing it doesn't mention marriage or her confounded Winter Ball and house party, yes, although I'd be surprised if Aunt Margaret talks of anything else."

The valet sighed and returned his attention to the missive, his lips moving silently a few moments. Finally he said, "The duchess is sorry that you didn't accept her invitations, but she's resigned herself to your stubborn refusal to enjoy civilized company."

"Good for her. Of all my relatives, Aunt Margaret is the easiest to stomach."

"She's refreshingly honest."

"Annoyingly so."

"She says that it's quite fine with her that you won't be coming to her events, but not to expect to use her lands for hunting before you return to Edinburgh as you'd requested, for she's had a change in her schedule and is planning some amusements for various goddaughters."

"Goddaughters? I didn't know she had any."

"She must have quite a few, for she names seven and says they are the first batch she will be inviting to Floors Castle."

"Batch? Bloody hell."

"Just so, my lord." Dunn tilted the letter toward the window to catch more light. "The duchess says she's forced to entertain her goddaughters because of you."

"What?"

"Yes. She says that as it seems unlikely that you will ever marry and produce an issue for her to dandle upon her knee, she will have to rely upon the kindness of her godchildren to do what her own blood family will not."

"Dandle upon her knee? Does she really say that?"

"Yes, my lord. Dandle."

"Ridiculous. What about my brothers? They're both recently wed, thanks to her meddling, and either could be in the family way any day now."

"It appears she's forgotten your brothers, my lord."

"That's because she's too busy trying to leg-shackle me to some empty-headed chit."

"The duchess can be determined."

"This time she's bound to face disappointment. Let her invite her hundreds of goddaughters; I can always hunt at my brother's new estate outside Stirling. Stormont's asked me to visit for months now." Sin picked up his coat and prepared to put it on.

"My lord!" Dunn dropped the letter upon the bed. "Please, allow me. You'll crease it if you shrug into it." He came to help Sin into his well-fitted coat.

After the coat had settled on Sin's shoulders, Dunn took up a bristle brush to capture any infinitesimal bits of lint. With nothing to do, Sin absently looked down, his gaze drifting over his great-aunt's letter. His eyes locked upon a name that was scrawled in the middle of a sentence, a name he'd thought to never see or hear again—*Rose Balfour*.

Instantly, his jaw clenched. "Damn it!"

Dunn turned a surprised gaze Sin's way. "My lord? What's wrong?"

Sin unclenched his hands and picked up the letter.

> *Since you will not oblige the family with an heir, I must assuage my desire to dandle children upon my knee by cultivating my godchildren. It pains me to take this step, but you've left me with no choice and your annual hunting party will have to be postponed. During that week, I plan on inviting my seven favorite goddaughters: Lady Margaret Stewart of Edinburgh, Miss Juliet MacLean of Mull, Miss Rose Balfour of Caith Manor in Aberdeenshire . . .*

He turned to Dunn. "Pack our bags."

The valet blinked. "Now?"

"Yes. We're leaving immediately."

"May I ask why?"

"No."

"Then where?"

"To Floors Castle."

"To visit the duchess? But you said you'd never attend her house party or ball."

"I've changed my mind. I will attend them both *if* she'll amend her invitation list." Sin looked at the letter now partially crumpled in his hand.

Dunn looked even more bewildered. "My lord, I don't understand."

"You don't need to understand. I'll go down now and make my apologies to Lord Dalton. I'll use Aunt Margaret's letter as an excuse to tell him a family issue has arisen, and we'll leave as soon as the phaeton is brought around."

"Very well, my lord. I can have your portmanteaus and trunk ready within thirty minutes."

"Good." Sin tucked his aunt's missive into his pocket and left, hurrying down the hallway. Blood thundered through his veins. Thanks to this new development, his earlier ennui was not only gone, but forgotten. *Finally, after six years, I've found you. Rose Balfour, your day of reckoning is at hand.*

Two

From the Diary of the Duchess of Roxburghe

It worked far better than I'd expected. Sin answered my letter in person and *demanded* that I invite Miss Balfour to my house party and Winter Ball.

Naturally, I protested that I didn't know the gel well, and had just realized that she was one of my goddaughters. I pointed out that she might not be presentable and oh, a thousand other quibbles and qualms, but he would have none of it. "Invite her," he demanded. "Today."

I reluctantly agreed, although in truth I'd already invited Miss Balfour and she's already accepted. Of course, that isn't surprising; the gel was ruined after the little contretemps with Sin, and this represents an unusual chance to reestablish herself. I only hinted at that in the letter I sent, of course, but I'm sure it was foremost in her mind. Her enthusiastic note accepting my invitation indicated as much.

Thus far, my little scheme is working very well.

Sin's fervent insistence was promising, and I'm rather glad of the changes Charlotte and I made in the guest list. I think they will serve quite well.

The well-sprung coach rolled off to the stables, leaving Rose standing with her scuffed trunk and worn portmanteaus at her feet. She watched as the coach disappeared down the drive, the Roxburghe crest with its distinctive unicorn and threatening arm holding a scimitar disappearing from sight as liveried footmen appeared to collect her luggage. *This is it, then. I'm here.*

The main part of the castle rose before her, flanked by wings that extended forward on each side. Four stories tall, it was decorated with exquisite stonework, and the wide flagstone courtyard featured an ornate portico that could easily cover ten carriages.

She felt as if she had just stepped into the pages of a fairy tale. Though she had yet to go inside, she was certain that the castle didn't suffer from the smoking fireplaces, threadbare rugs, creaky stairways, drafty windows, and sagging floors of Caith Manor.

Her throat tightened. As beautiful as the castle was, all she wanted was to have the groom saddle a horse, and ride across the moors until the pressure in her stomach disappeared.

But that was not to be. Although she hated wearing anything other than her serviceable riding habits and rarely wore her hair in anything other than a pinned-up braid, for the next three weeks she was expected to dress, eat, and smile like a lady of fashion.

Rose sighed. She didn't have a choice. She'd promised her sisters that she'd take advantage of the duchess's kind invitation and, come what may, she would do just that. *I owe Lily and Dahlia this unexpected opportunity.*

And unexpected it had been. Despite supposedly being Rose's grandmama's bosom confidante during girlhood, her grace hadn't been the most attentive godparent. Over the years the duchess had dutifully sent Rose and her sisters an annual Michaelmas letter and a small gift, and a short, repetitive birthday greeting, but that was all. The duchess's correspondence had been so predictable that it had become something of a joke at Caith Manor, with Lily pretending shock every time a birthday or Michaelmas letter was read aloud over tea, while Dahlia silently mimicked each line before it was even read.

For the hundredth time since the duchess's invitation had arrived by liveried footman last week, Rose wondered what had prompted it. *Not that it matters. I should be grateful for a rare opportunity to re-enter society, something I never thought to do again after That Night.*

It hurt less to think of that time as That Night rather than as "Your Raging Scandal," as Aunt Lettice always referenced it. Thank goodness Rose would be spared her aunt's presence this week, at least. While she was fond of her aunt, one could take only so many sad sighs and long faces before one went stark, raving mad.

She'd rather remember other, better times. Like the half hour before things had gone awry, when she'd been basking in the attention of the handsomest man she'd ever met. If she closed her eyes now, she could see those sherry-colored eyes and that handsome face as he bent to press his firm lips to hers. A shiver went through her. *Stop that! I should be thinking about Lily and Dahlia, not a handsome wastrel.*

Because of her rash actions six years ago and the ensuing scandal, her sisters had been denied all that she'd foolishly squandered for a childish passion: a season in London, balls, scores of invitations, and—more significantly for Lily and Dahlia—the opportunity to meet eligible men.

Her sisters were growing into beautiful women, and they were wasting away in a countryside populated with few eligible male prospects. Lively Dahlia had even begun casting glances at their neighbor, a grumpy, taciturn widower fifteen years older than she was. If Dahlia could only meet younger men with charming manners and handsome grins, then she wouldn't be content with—

"Miss Balfour?" A footman bowed and then gestured toward the wide doors centered beneath the ornate portico.

Rose took a deep breath and smiled. "Yes, of

course. Thank you." She walked toward the large doors.

Two identically liveried footmen opened them and stepped to each side.

Steeling herself, Rose crossed the threshold and stared in wonder. Never had she seen such an entryway. The high ceiling was painted with a beautiful mural that depicted the creation of the earth in delicate blues, golds, and greens. The walls were covered in robin's-egg-blue Chinese silk painted with gilt and green flowers and decorated with gold sconces. The parquet floor sported a playful trompe l'oeil pattern, and the overall effect was breathtakingly beautiful.

A tall, somber-looking man in a black frock coat approached her and bowed. "Miss Balfour, welcome to Floors Castle. I'm MacDougal, the butler. May I assist you with yer pelisse and bonnet?"

"Yes, thank you." She pulled off her gloves and tucked them into her pocket before she unbuttoned her pelisse and handed it with her bonnet to the butler.

"Thank you, miss." He carefully handed her possessions to a waiting footman while she turned to a nearby mirror and attempted to pat her mashed curls into a more attractive fashion.

After a moment, she grimaced and turned from the mirror. "That's the best I can do for now."

"Of course, miss. I trust yer ride here wasn't too uncomfortable?"

"It was very pleasant."

He smiled broadly as if he, and he alone, were responsible for her coach ride. "Och, I'm glad to hear that, miss. The weather is lovely fer a coach ride, is it no'?"

"I don't think I've enjoyed one more," she lied. Though the sumptuous coach had been comfortable, her mind had been much too uneasy to enjoy it properly.

"Excellent, miss. If ye'll come this way, her grace is anxious to greet ye. She's in the sitting room with Lady Charlotte."

"Oh. I thought I might wash up first." And wrestle her unruly hair into something resembling a style.

The butler's smile disappeared. "They are expecting ye." He didn't say the words in a dire fashion, but she sensed his urgency, nonetheless.

She forced a smile. "Then I can't keep them waiting, can I?"

He beamed. "No, miss."

The butler led her across the entryway and to a pair of massive doors. He turned the knob and instantly a cacophony of barking arose.

The butler sent a regretful look at his polished shoes before saying in a long-suffering tone, "Her ladyship's pugs, miss." He opened the door, and out tumbled a herd of yapping pugs.

Chuckling, Rose bent to pet them.

"Miss, I'd be careful if I were you," the butler said

in a warning tone. "They can scratch, though they dinna mean to."

"What are their names?"

"Let's see . . ." He pointed at each one in turn. "This is Meenie. Tha' is Weenie. Teenie's the brown one with the silver-tipped tail. Feenie's the one with part of an ear missing—a horrible brawl with a local barn cat. Her grace won't allow the dogs out of the house without an escort now. And the very fat silver pug is Beenie. He looks a bit like a large silver bean with legs, dinna he, miss?"

"Yes, he does." Rose scratched ears, rubbed furry little chins, and chuckled as the smallest one sniffed her hem so hard that he sneezed. She noticed that one dog stood to the side, an older one with milky eyes. "And who is this one?"

"Och, tha' is Randolph, miss."

"Poor thing! You can't see well, can you?" Rose murmured. She very slowly held out her hand. The fat pug waddled closer and cautiously sniffed her fingers. "Good boy," she crooned.

His short, stubby tail waggled and he joined the group at her knee.

"Such good puppies." She gave them each an extra pat, and then stood and straightened her gown.

The butler held the doors open and stood to one side. The pugs, obviously thinking he held the door for them, trotted back into the room as Rose followed.

The sitting room was even grander than the entryway. The windows were large enough to be barn doors, the ceiling towered so far overhead that the chandeliers were more for show than light, and both fireplaces (there was one on each end of the room) were big enough that two large cows could have easily stood inside them.

The room was decorated in the height of fashion, too. Gold embroidery glittered on the rich striped and tasseled velvets and brocades that covered every chair and settee. Every bit of wood was either gilded or embossed, while the walls were agleam, covered with deep gold satin.

The butler cleared his throat, jerking Rose out of her reverie. She stepped forward as he called out in his soft brogue, "Miss Rose Balfour."

At the very far end of the sitting room, Rose saw two women seated near one of the large fireplaces. The butler bowed and she walked forward.

The pugs scampered along with her, snorting and grunting like the pigs in the barnyard at Caith Manor.

As Rose reached the sitting area, she instantly knew which woman was the duchess. She was small and slender, her nose impossibly hooked, her eyes a vivid blue, while on her head an improbably huge red wig tilted precariously to one side.

The duchess's crystal blue gaze traveled over Rose in such a thorough fashion that Rose wished she'd taken the time to fix her hair.

Her face heated, Rose dipped a hurried curtsy. "Your grace, it's a pleasure to meet you."

The duchess cocked her head to one side, a puzzled look in her eyes. "*You* are Miss Balfour?"

"Yes, your grace."

"Miss *Rose* Balfour."

Rose looked from one lady to the other before she said in a firm voice, "Yes, your grace." There was a flicker in the blue eyes and Rose felt as if she'd disappointed the duchess in some way. Rose smoothed her skirts, the dogs prancing about her feet as if they could sense her unease. "My gown is sadly crushed from my journey, but I was determined to thank you immediately for your gracious invitation."

The duchess managed a smile, though she by no means looked welcoming. "I'm glad you joined us so quickly." She gestured to the lady on the opposite settee, who sat watching Rose as if at a play. "This is Lady Charlotte, my companion."

Rose turned to the other woman and was instantly reassured by the woman's warm smile and twinkling gaze.

"How do you do?" Lady Charlotte's soft voice made Rose think of warm cookies.

Rose curtsied. "I'm well, thank you. I hope you're the same."

"Oh yes." Lady Charlotte set aside her knitting and patted the settee beside her. "Come and sit for a few moments before you retire to your bedchamber."

"Yes, do sit," the duchess agreed. "When we're done here, MacDougal will take you to your room and have a bath brought. I find a nice hot bath so refreshing after travel."

"That would be lovely." Rose sat beside Lady Charlotte and instantly Weenie and Beenie jumped into her lap. She had to hold them in place, since there was barely room for just one, and she laughed at the armful of squirming puppies.

"Oh, you bad dogs," the duchess said. "How rude of them! Weenie! Beenie! Stop bothering our guest."

"Oh, they're fine." Rose chuckled and said to the dogs, "I can see that I'm going to have to pick one of you to claim my lap, and it's too difficult to choose, so you'll both have to get down." She gently placed first one and then the other onto the floor.

The duchess smiled a little, which softened her face considerably. "They've taken to you. They don't normally do that with strangers, do they, Mac-Dougal?"

"No, yer grace. Never, tha' I can remember."

The duchess watched Rose as she petted Beenie's head. The dog grunted blissfully. "Miss Balfour, I'm delighted you decided to visit us."

"Oh, I wouldn't miss it for the world," Rose lied, trying to keep her smile locked upon her lips.

Margaret heard the lie and was surprised. *She's more excited about the dogs than at being at Floors Castle. Interesting. I suppose that means she's not a social climber.* Margaret eyed her guest a bit longer. *I never expected her to be so plain, either.*

Miss Balfour was as far removed from the women Sin usually pursued as one could imagine. The gel's unruly black hair was held in place by a number of pins, half of which were sticking out, while the other half struggled to remain in place and failed miserably. She was brown, too, rather than the milky pale preferred by society, and far too thin for the day's fashion of draped gowns, which were more suited to women with bosoms and hips. *Why, she's no more than a thin, wiry scamp of a gel. She's far from Sin's usual bits of fluff, which makes this even more interesting.*

Charlotte broke the growing silence. "So, Miss Balfour, tell us more about yourself."

"What would you like to know?"

"Everything," Margaret stated baldly.

Miss Balfour blinked, but Lady Charlotte added with a kind smile, "What do you like to do, dear? When you're at home, that is?"

"I ride a lot, and read. My mother is no longer with us, so it's just me, my two sisters, and my father."

"The horticulturalist."

"Why, yes. Father is a bit of a recluse and spends most of his time in the greenhouses, so I fear we don't have many guests." Miss Balfour hesitated. "I do hope you find nothing in my behavior to give you pause. We don't socialize formally at Caith Manor and—"

"You'll be fine, dear." Charlotte smiled reassuringly and picked up her knitting needles and began to knit once again. "If you've any questions, you've but to ask one of us and we'll set you to rights. Won't we, Margaret?"

"Of course," Margaret agreed, liking Miss Balfour's unusual plainspoken ways more and more. "I'm sure we can set you upon the right path of any—"

Weenie jumped into Miss Balfour's now empty lap and she chuckled and patted the dog, seemingly unconcerned about the creases the animal might cause her gown.

"You like dogs, I see," Margaret said, still trying to decide what to make of this decidedly odd girl.

"Indeed I do. MacDougal told me all of their names in the hallway." She looked at the other pugs now lined up at her feet. "Why do all of their names rhyme except Randolph's?" She indicated the older dog that sat some distance away, panting as if he'd just run up a flight of steps. His tail wagged as she said his name.

"I've had him for twelve years, while the others are far more recent acquisitions. I suppose I wasn't in a rhyming mood then."

Miss Balfour nodded, and another loop of her hair fell from a pin.

Margaret and Charlotte exchanged a look. Miss Balfour, unaware she was being measured, hugged the dog in her lap and said absently, "I love animals. Better, in fact, than I like people."

As soon as she said the words, she sent Margaret an embarrassed glance. "Not that I dislike people, for I don't. People are very nice and I think they're—" She gestured, obviously desperately searching for words.

"I daresay we all feel that way at times," Margaret said. "But don't worry about our house party. We are a small group this year. Smaller than ever before."

"Yes," Charlotte said. "Her grace decided to have a very *private* sort of affair this year. Quite *intimate,* even—"

"I wouldn't call it intimate," Margaret said firmly, sending Charlotte a warning glance, which she didn't seem to notice. Margaret turned back to their guest. "When I first wed Roxburghe, we used to invite forty couples or more for the weeks prior to the ball, but over time we've reduced that number, and this year, I invited even fewer as Roxburghe won't be here until the night before the ball."

"The duke's not in residence?"

"I'm afraid not. He's quite entangled in politics, you know, and with the question of the Regency growing in urgency, he doesn't dare return home any sooner." Margaret smiled at her young guest. "Lady Charlotte and I would love to visit with you longer, but I'm sure you would like to rest before dinner."

"I am a bit tired," Rose agreed. "Have the other guests arrived?"

"They're all here except my great-nephew, who should arrive later this afternoon."

Lady Charlotte smiled benignly, her needles clacking along. "You will enjoy your time here. There's so much to do at Floors Castle. There's whist, croquet, billiards, rides by the river—I'm sure you'll be very busy."

"Very," Margaret agreed and turned to Mac-Dougal, who still stood inside the doorway. "Please escort Miss Balfour to the Blue Bedchamber."

MacDougal bowed.

Margaret turned back to her guest. "I look forward to speaking with you more over dinner. Meanwhile, I do hope you'll enjoy your stay with us. We have an excellent stable, and Roxburghe is a great reader and has stuffed the library with mounds of books. You are free to borrow as many as you'd like."

Miss Balfour's face lit up and for a moment, she appeared quite pretty. "Oh, thank you!"

Margaret instantly thought, *So, my dear Sin, is this what you saw that intrigued you so? Or is there more to her even than this?* She smiled. "You're welcome, my child. MacDougal, pray show Miss Balfour the library on your way to her room. She may wish a book to pass the time before dinner."

Miss Balfour set Weenie back on the floor, stood, made her curtsies, and followed the butler to the door.

Margaret watched the girl leave, absently patting Randolph's gray head as he pressed against her hand.

As soon as the door closed, Charlotte said, "Well. That was interesting."

"Very." Margaret leaned back in her chair, pulling Randolph into her lap. "She's very thin and brown."

"From riding, I daresay. Her eyes are well enough, but her hair—" Charlotte shook her head. "She looked a bit like a milkmaid. I quite thought Sin's flirt would be beautiful."

"Well, she's not beautiful," Margaret said. "She's passingly pretty, if that. I've never known Sin to pay attention to the horsing set, either."

"She's not very fashionable, either. That gown—" Charlotte scrunched her nose. "She strides rather than walks, too."

"Yes, as if she didn't give a flip for convention." Margaret tapped her fingers on the arm of her chair and then looked down at Randolph. "What do you think, love?"

Randolph's little tail wagged hard.

"You liked her, didn't you? And so did Meenie." She looked at her foot, where Meenie lay. The dog perked up when she met Margaret's gaze. "You don't normally take to strangers, either."

Meenie sniffed the air, which made her look as if she were nodding.

"Miss Balfour definitely has a way with animals," Charlotte agreed thoughtfully. "Perhaps that's the key."

Margaret laughed. "Perhaps it is. If anyone were close to the animal state, it's Sin. Perhaps this Rose knows how to soothe the savage beast. We won't know until we see them together—and that, my dear, makes me look forward to the next three weeks."

"If he doesn't lead her astray first."

Margaret's glee faded. "Astray?"

"She doesn't strike me as very worldly. And Sin . . . You know what he is."

"I suspect she's far smarter than that, but we will keep an eye on them. I refuse to allow that poor gel to be importuned under my own roof."

"Really?" Charlotte said in mild surprise. "I rather thought you'd hoped Sin would do just that."

"Only to a certain point. I won't have her ruined. I *am* her godmother, you know. Still, we will make certain they spend a fair amount of time together. More, perhaps, than either plans on." Margaret put Randolph onto the rug. "Come, Charlotte, let's walk the dogs in the garden. We can discuss the situation there, where the servants won't overhear."

Three

From the Diary of the Duchess of Roxburghe
When one is charged with assisting a beloved family member with their love life, it is important to know the wishes of that family member. This can be tricky, especially when one is working from a position of Stealth and Greater Knowledge.

I don't yet know exactly what qualities Sin saw in Rose Balfour that sent propriety tumbling to the wayside all those years ago, but I have a sneaking suspicion that I'm about to find out . . .

So close, and yet so far. Rose grasped the ladder railing and leaned forward. She had to stand on her tiptoes, but she was rewarded when she managed to barely—just barely—reach the book she wanted on the shelf.

The small, slim tome was bound in soft red leather and looked like a journal. It had caught her eye when she was on a lower rung looking up in awe at the shelves upon shelves of books. The vibrant color coupled with a lack of a title on the spine had made her itch to peek between the covers, so she'd rolled the ladder over, gathered her skirts, and climbed to the top.

She looped an arm through the ladder to steady herself and opened the small book. Ah, her favorite Shakespeare play, *As You Like It!* Smiling, Rose lifted the book and took a deep sniff of the wonderful scent of leather and old paper. Truly, there was nothing like it.

The book begged for immediate reading and she decided to settle into one of the plump blue velvet chairs in front of the fireplace and enjoy her find. MacDougal had said it would take a half hour before her bath was ready, and it would be wondrous to get lost in a book while she was waiting. She would just slip the small book into her pocket before climbing down so she'd have a free hand to help keep her skirts out of the w—

"There you are."

The low, masculine voice froze Rose in place. She knew that voice. She swallowed hard, hoping her wildly beating heart wasn't visible from across the room as she slowly turned her head to look at the one man she'd never thought to see again.

Lord Alton Sinclair was known to the *ton* as Lord Sin for a number of reasons, none of which should be discussed by a lady. He was still just as tall and broad shouldered, his hair still a dark golden-blond. His thick, dark brown lashes gave his eyes a sleepy, seductive look, but what truly drew the eye were the strong, square line of his jaw and the Roman-emperor cast to his aquiline nose.

He stood in the library doorway, glaring at her as if he wished her to perdition.

Rose's face and neck warmed. His hair was longer now, and his face more marred by dissipation. Only his sherry-brown eyes looked exactly as they had when she'd last seen him: blazing with anger.

Rose forced her stiff lips into a smile. "Lord Sinclair, how pleasant to see you. I didn't know you'd be here."

"Of course I'm here. This is my great-aunt's house. In fact"—his smile was that of a cat who had cornered a mouse—"she invited you at my behest."

Rose stiffened. "Her grace is your *great-aunt? And* my godmother?"

"Apparently so."

Does that explain the unexpected invitation? A flicker of disappointment settled over her. Until hearing that, she'd rather liked the duchess. Had soft-spoken Lady Charlotte been in on the plot, too?

Sin walked forward with an ominous smile. "So, Miss Balfour, we meet again. Aren't we fortunate?"

Politeness bade her to come down from the ladder, but it seemed safer up there, away from the simmering storm of a man crossing the room toward her. She tried for a casual tone. "I hope you're well. It's been a very long time since we last met."

"Six years. Six very *trying* years."

His smoldering anger jangled along her nerves and she had to fight the urge to climb farther up the ladder. "I'm sorry to hear that you've had a trying time."

His brows snapped together. "Don't pretend you thought it would be otherwise."

She blinked. "Why would I know anything about your life after we parted? I haven't seen you since."

His mouth firmed into a straight line, his eyes blazing hotter now. "Don't play the innocent with me. I *know* you."

Good heavens, what is this all about? It was true that she'd caused herself and her family a good deal of embarrassment, but he, like all rakehells, was immune to scandal. Unless a man stepped firmly over the boundaries of society, like Lord Byron in sleeping with his half sister, very little could sully their names. A woman, meanwhile, could be ruined by something as innocent as a kiss.

The whole thing was grossly unfair, and Rose didn't appreciate Lord Sin's obliviousness to that fact. But it wouldn't help to confront him; he was obviously in no mood for calm, reasonable discourse.

Perhaps she should just offer him the apology she'd wished to offer all those years ago. At the least it would make her feel better, for she owed him one.

She cleared her throat. "Lord Sinclair, I'm glad you're here." She began to climb down. "I've been wanting to apologize to you since our last meeting and—"

"Stay." He now stood at the foot of the ladder, one large hand resting on a rung by her ankle. The glint of an emerald ring on his left hand was echoed by his tie pin.

"Stay? Here on the ladder?"

"Yes." He stepped onto the lowest rung.

"Oh no, that's not necessary. I will come down and—"

He took another step up, his shoulder brushing against her calf.

Rose clung tightly in place. "Lord Sinclair, please! We cannot talk here, it's— For heaven's sake, we're on a ladder! We can speak at dinner, perhaps, when we're both—"

"Oh, no. We will not put off this meeting one moment more." He took another step up, his eyes locked with hers, every movement a threat.

Her mouth dry, Rose took a step up the ladder, her chest so tight she could scarcely breathe. "Lord Sinclair, if you'll return to the floor we can sit by the fire, which is much nicer than trying to balance while—"

"*No.*" His expression was unyielding as he climbed another rung, his hands firmly gripping each side of the ladder about her knees and blocking any desperate exit she might wish to make.

"That's ridiculous!" She steeled her crazed heart,

which was beating even harder now. "Lord Sinclair, please. This is most unusual."

He laughed, low and ugly. "Don't put on your missish airs for me. You are a tease of the worst kind, and you made me the laughingstock of London." The words crackled with fury.

She wet her lips nervously. "You're exaggerating." *Who would dare laugh at him?*

"No, I'm not."

She tried to calm her thoughts, which would have been much easier if he weren't leaning against her legs, his blazing gaze far too close for her comfort. She didn't dare look away, for it seemed that looking directly at him gave her some modicum of control.

To discourage him from coming any closer, she slipped an arm through the closest rung and twisted a bit so that—should he dare climb any higher—her shoulder would be at a right angle to his chest. It was a small protection, but it was all she had while on the ladder. "Lord Sinclair, however you feel about what happened all those years ago, I doubt anyone—other than us—remembers it."

He couldn't have looked more incredulous had she told him that she'd just taken a walk with a minotaur. "You cannot believe that."

"Who would bother to remember a few moments at some ball six years ago? I do, of course, since I made a fool of myself. I'm truly sorry that you were a victim of my very youthful and painfully impulsive nature. I cannot tell you how often I've wished to take back my actions of that night."

A flicker of surprise crossed his face. "You're apologizing."

"Yes. Isn't that what you wanted?"

His jaw tightened. "An apology isn't enough."

She met his gaze steadily. "Everything that happened that night was my fault, but there's nothing I can do to change it now. The best thing we can do is to leave it in the past where it belongs, and move on." When he merely continued to stare at her, she frowned. "Lord Sinclair, I wrote you a letter that very night and explained—"

His laugh was full of derision. "Oh yes, your letter. You humiliated me in front of the biggest gossips of the *ton* and then sent me a few scrawled lines as if that made up for it."

"It was over by then, and—"

"*Over?* Miss Balfour, the scandal had just begun—and you just walked away, instead of staying to face the gossips. After you left they were like vultures, tearing my name apart a piece at a time."

"But you didn't do anything wrong."

"That's not what people believed. Everyone thought I was the aggressor in our little encounter and that it had shaken you so badly that you'd run off to the countryside, terrified by the thought of spending another moment in my presence."

"But that's not why I left at all! I didn't wish to

cause you any more trouble, and I thought that was the best way to avoid an unpleasant aftermath."

"It was the worst way. There was *quite* an aftermath, my dear Miss Balfour." He leaned forward, his chest against her legs. *"For me."*

She felt like a butterfly pinned in a display box. "Oh dear."

"People talked about what they had seen, and made up what they hadn't. Within a fortnight the story went from my attempting to kiss you to the full-blown attempted seduction of an innocent. And apparently I was so violent in pressing my unwanted attentions on you that you were forced to go into seclusion."

"That's ludicrous!"

"Oh, it gets worse. Weeks after the event, details emerged that were not evident at the time—your gown was ripped, the pins torn from your hair, one of your shoes lost when you'd tried to flee and I'd held you against your will. Afterward, no gentleman, however desirous of a connection with my family or fortune, dared leave his daughter within talking distance of me, a man so depraved that he had violently attacked an innocent in a nearly public place."

"You *must* be joking. Not a single word of that is true! The people there must have seen that I was perfectly fine and that my gown was never torn nor my shoes missing nor—nor any of that drivel."

"They were there, and they did see. And then, as they repeated the story over and over, they added whatever incriminating details they could think of to make their version of the story more delectable." He eyed her coldly. "Had you been there, you could have set the rumors straight. But you weren't there. You'd fled and left me to deal with a growing assault of scandalous rumors."

"I had no idea! My aunt was insistent that I leave town until the talk died down. My only intent was to minimize the damage I'd done and—"

He climbed to the next rung, his chest now against the side of her thigh.

Rose's heart thudded against her collarbone, a wild tingle racing through her, as intoxicating as champagne. This was the exact feeling that had gotten her into such a mess to begin with. For some reason she still couldn't fathom, being near Lord Sinclair caused her to experience the oddest, most restless urge, and sent her usually calmly ordered senses reeling. It was a feeling she'd both loved and feared, even now.

She'd remembered the feeling well, but not the intensity, nor the fact that his proximity made her entire body burn. That was a new symptom of what was surely some madness.

"For the record," Sin said, "I hold your aunt responsible for the events of that night as well as you."

"My aunt wasn't even in the garden."

"Exactly. Had you been on a leash as you'd deserved, the events of that night would have never happened."

Rose's temper flared. "My aunt had nothing to do with this."

He sneered at her. "Your aunt is as unprincipled as you."

It took all of her strength not to smack his head with her book. *How dare he?* "Do not pin your—nor my own—weakness upon my poor aunt. Your reputation was hardly unsullied to begin with, Lord *Sin*."

"Until you came along, people spoke of me as a Corinthian, but no one thought me a seducer of innocents."

She'd already opened her mouth, but at his words, she paused. There was indeed a difference between the two. And in accepting that fact, Rose saw the tableau from a new perspective, and her heart sank. *Good God, it had looked like a seduction.* There they were, Edinburgh's most elusive bachelor in a fountain and a shaken and red-faced debutante wringing her hands nearby.

And then I just left him to face the whispers. She bit her lip. For the last six years, she'd told herself that she'd left to allow the incident to blow over faster, but if she were honest, she'd admit there was another reason she couldn't wait to leave town—she'd been shocked at her own reaction to Sin's kiss.

It had been the coward's way out and apparently Sin had paid the price.

She took a deep breath. "Though I wish I could, I cannot go back in time and repair the past. But I have apologized and very sincerely, too. As sad as it is to say, there's nothing more to be done about it."

His gaze narrowed. "So little, so late." He climbed another rung, his chest brushing her hip in an alarmingly intimate way.

Rose tightened her grasp about the side rail and held her book to her chest like a shield, her traitorous body tingling alarmingly. Gulping, she took a nervous step up the ladder, away from the six-foot-two temptation.

Undeterred, Sin followed. "The world would be shocked if they only knew what really happened that night, wouldn't they, Miss Balfour?" He climbed up another rung and suddenly his face was level with hers, his chest against her shoulder.

She looked directly into his eyes and any words she might have said in her own defense were lost. His eyes were streaked with gold that gave him a faintly lionlike appearance. And as she looked into his eyes, she was torn by two desires: to run away from him as fast as she could, and to lean against him and absorb the shivery pleasure simply touching him gave her.

She was astounded that being close to him still had that effect on her; she had to fight the impulse to press against him and once more feel his lips on hers—

Stop that, she told herself severely, her face heating at the boldness of her thoughts. If only she could take another step up the ladder—but his arms were now on either side of her.

Trapped, she cleared her throat. "People didn't cut you direct, did they?"

"They didn't shun me completely, since I've a title and a place in society, as well as a fortune."

"Then why do you even care—"

"Because they mocked me, Miss Balfour. For months after, I was called Lord '*Fin*.'"

Rose had an instant memory of him climbing out of the fountain, a lily pad upon his head, water streaming down his face. To her horror, from deep inside her rose a giggle.

She didn't mean to laugh, but being nervous always gave her the giggles, and the thought of this powerful, seductive man being called such a ridiculous name tickled every bone in her body.

As she giggled, Lord "Fin" glared all the more, which made her even more nervous and made her laugh even harder.

"Oh yes, laugh, Miss Balfour," Sin snapped. "Laugh as you did that night. For it is that very laughter that revealed you for the scheming harpy that you are."

His icy tone sobered her laughter back to a faint but persistent giggle. "I'm very sorry to hear about the Lord F—" She waved a hand, not trusting herself to say it out loud for fear it would set her off again. "Truly, I had no idea."

Sin didn't know what offended him more: the fact that after shoving him into a fountain and then laughing in his face, Rose Balfour had blithely left him to face the mess made by her actions, or that—after learning of the indignities he'd been forced to suffer— she had the audacity to stand here now and laugh *again*.

"Just as I thought," he snapped furiously, wishing he could simply throttle her and be done with it. "Your actions were deliberate; you knew what you were doing when you left me to face the scandal. You knew your absence would look damning!"

Her laughter faded, though her eyes twinkled as she said with a bit of exasperation, "I knew no such thing! What on earth could I hope to gain by such a stratagem?"

"Revenge, Miss Balfour. You were angry that I didn't respond to your childish attempts to seduce me."

"Of all the silly— Lord Sinclair, you are being far too dramatic. I didn't plan on embarrassing anyone. All I wanted was to kiss you. That, I'll admit to doing. If it makes you feel any better, I've regretted it ever since."

He stiffened. *She'd* regretted it? Meanwhile, *he* was being dramatic? He was so furious he didn't know what to say. For years he'd been imagining the satisfaction he would feel at hearing her admit her fault, but she'd stolen even that with her unaccommodating attitude.

Bloody hell, she's the most infuriating woman I've ever met. Infuriating and impossible to understand. He wasn't quite sure what to make of her; he never had been. Her constant juxtaposition of flashes of bold sensuality and pragmatic common sense, interspersed as they were with moments of seemingly breathless innocence, confused the hell out of him.

He eyed her critically, wondering how she'd lured him into the garden to begin with. Her eyes were still the only feature one could call "beautiful," as they were a vivid blue surrounded by thick black lashes; the rest of her was merely average. Though she had a heart-shaped face, her mouth was too wide and her too-brown skin was yet marred by a faint dusting of freckles across the bridge of her pert nose. She was thin and had no real figure to speak of, her breasts quite small and her hips lacking the flared shape one expected in a woman. Worst of all was her unruly hair.

She was plain, unremarkable, and unmemorable. Which was why it irritated him that he couldn't be near her without his body reacting as if she were Aphrodite.

Even now, a pure, hot surge of lust made him lean forward so that more of his body touched hers. *Damn it, what is this? She's not the sort of woman I've ever been interested in, not in looks, nor action, nor temperament.* Had he any sense, he would leave right now and return to the safety of his bedchamber. Instead, he was holding her firmly caged within his arms, his body aching for more of her.

As stirred as he was, she didn't seem at all affected by his presence, for she arched an eyebrow at him. "That's close enough, thank you. I would like to point out that you had a horrid nickname *before* our little incident. If you hadn't been called Lord Sin to begin with, no one would have thought to call you Lord Fin."

He opened his mouth to reply, but she continued without heed, "And don't tell me that you were truly distressed by being cut socially, because I know that you rarely attended social events to begin with. I'm surprised to find you here at your aunt's, for this seems like a far tamer amusement than you usually enjoy."

He scowled. "Don't push me, Balfour. That would be most unwise."

"I'm not pushing you; I'm *disagreeing* with you. But perhaps you prefer biddable women who just agree with your every word." She pressed her book to her chest as if it were a prayer book, attempting to look demure as she said in a theatrical falsetto, "Yes, Lord Sinclair. Whatever you say, Lord Sinclair." She tittered in a way that made his teeth ache. "Oh, Lord Sinclair, you're *so* funny! I vow, but you're the smartest peer in all the realm! You're the most—"

"*Stop that.* Before you make more of a fool of yourself than you already have, I should tell you that I had a purpose in bringing you to my aunt's house. A very specific one."

A look of wariness entered her blue eyes. "Oh? And what is that?"

His feet now rested on the rung below hers, his hands to either side of her. He leaned forward and lowered his voice seductively. "I remember that kiss, Miss Balfour. Do you?"

Her heartbeat fluttered in the delicate hollow of her neck, like a bird caught in a cage. "Of course I do."

"I also remember how it affected you."

She flushed. "Affected? I wasn't— That is to say, I thought it a very nice—"

His lips brushed the delicate shell pink of her ear and she shivered. "If I'm to be condemned for seducing you, then I should be granted the pleasures of that seduction, not just the pains."

"Th-the pleasures?" Her voice was breathless.

He smiled then, his first genuine smile of the day. His hips held her soft body captive against the rungs of the ladder, making him instantly aware of how much more he wanted from her. "Oh yes."

She blinked as realization slowly settled on her face. "You're going to *seduce* me?"

"Oh yes, my little Rose. You've owed me that pleasure for six years, and the time has come for you to pay."

Four

From the Diary of the Duchess of Roxburghe
Charlotte and I oversaw the seating for dinner and
are satisfied we've given Sin every advantage possible. I can tell that he believes he has the upper
hand in this little game, but after meeting Miss Balfour, I have to wonder if his confidence might be
misplaced.

There's something about her, a shimmer of independence and stubbornness. Most men would
dislike that, but I believe Sin may find her independence captivating, and her stubbornness more than
a match for his own. Time will tell . . .

Sin had expected a flicker of fear at his threat. Instead,
Miss Balfour arched a delicate eyebrow. "So you've
decided to seduce me merely because people assume
it's already happened?"

"You owe me what you promised with that damned
kiss." He trailed the back of his hand over her cheek
and to the deliciously warm spot behind her ear.

He was pleased when she caught her breath, her lashes fluttering as she gasped. *Ah, so you do feel it, then.* "We have three weeks together, Miss Balfour. During that time, I shall seduce you. And you—" He let his hand drift from her cheek to her neck, to the fascinating hollows that harbored the wild flutter of her heart. "You will make up for the mockery I've had to endure since our last meeting."

"So you feel that you are owed." Her color high, Rose took a steadying breath before she met his gaze evenly. Finally, she gave a short nod. "Very well. You may attempt to seduce me. I can't promise to *succumb*, but it's only fair that you be allowed the attempt."

Sin didn't know whether to laugh or—hell, he didn't know what to do. "Miss Balfour, you seem to be suffering under the illusion that you have a say in the matter. I will not *attempt* to seduce you. I *will* do it."

She smiled kindly. "We will see, won't we? Meanwhile, feel free to seduce away. At the least, it will give you something to do other than moan about the past, which you seem sadly given to."

Her audacity was like the icy strike of hail. Heedless of their precarious perch, he slipped his arm about her waist and pressed against her.

She gasped and clung to the ladder rail, still clutching her small book. Yet her rapid breathing let him know she was instantly affected.

He smirked. "My foolish, foolish Rose. I remember how passionately you reacted to that kiss. If I wish you in my bed, all I have to do is this . . ." He bent to touch her cheek with his lips, feather-soft and gentle, more warm breath than else. A deep shiver wracked her and her eyes slid closed, her breath quickening. He moved his lips to her lashes where they trembled on her cheeks. Lightly, he traced them, and she swayed slightly.

The wild beat of her pulse in her throat sent his own blood thrumming through his veins, and he bent to place his lips on that crazed beat, kissing it and then rubbing the edge of his teeth across it.

"L-Lord Sinclair, that's quite enough—"

"Oh, I haven't even begun, my sweet Rose." He leaned close to whisper in her ear, his breath trailing across her skin as he brushed his fingers over her lips. "Are you certain you can refuse me?"

She took a slow breath and opened her eyes, her gaze far steadier than he'd expected. "Your touch is quite intoxicating." She pushed his hand away. "Does it feel the same for you?"

He'd be damned if he'd put that arrow in her quiver. "I've had more experience than you."

"Yes. Of course." She plastered a smile on her lips, though it trembled the tiniest bit. "Lord Sinclair, I'm no longer the child I was six years ago. My passions are more controlled now."

He laughed softly. "You think you can resist me?"

"You think you can tempt me?" she snapped back, and then flushed at his lifted brows. "Fine, you can tempt me, but I'm a grown woman, one with age, and—and experience. I am not the weakling you seem to think me."

Experience. So the little Balfour isn't an innocent now—if she ever was. He wasn't certain why, but having that tidbit confirmed didn't afford him the satisfaction he'd thought it would. In fact, it set his jaw on edge, and his voice was unexpectedly harsh when he said, "You will succumb; the only question is how quickly."

He captured one of her thick, silken curls and threaded it through his fingers. It curled and clung, as stubborn as she was. As he twisted the curl about his fingers, the back of them grazed her neck and she gasped as if he'd touched her far more intimately.

He released her curl and slid his hand along the rung where her shoulder was pressed and, grasping the rung, anchored them both in place. Then, Sin captured her lips, kissing her deeply, roughly, thoroughly.

God, she tasted of sunshine and heat. Had she tasted this good six years ago? The thought was barely coherent over the thundering of his blood in his ears. He tasted and teased, and she responded instantly, tempting and tormenting him in return. It was exactly as it was all those years ago: he'd touched her and something primal and heated beyond anything he'd ever experienced had roared through his blood.

She moaned against his mouth, sending his senses and thoughts reeling. All he truly knew in this moment was that he had her here, alone, in his arms. He gloried in her submission, in how she opened to him like a bud under a hot sun.

Rose thought she would drown in her own madness: her entire body was aflame as she responded to delicious kiss after delicious kiss. *What is it about this man? No one has ever affected me this way.*

She moved against him restlessly, unwilling to stop. How could something so overwhelming, so incredibly *perfect* be wrong in any way? His touch was exactly as she remembered, passion and instant heat.

She opened her hand to grasp his lapel and as she did so, the book slipped from her fingers. Rose instinctively broke the kiss to grab for the falling book.

Thunk!

Her forehead smacked Sin squarely in the chin just as the book hit the floor.

She slapped a hand over her forehead as bright colors flashed behind her closed eyelids. "Ow, ow, ow!"

Rose cracked open her lids to see Sin pressing a hand to his chin, blood between his fingers. "Oh no!" she said. "I'm so sorry. I dropped my book and— Your chin—"

"It's but a scrape," he said curtly.

Stung by his tone, she frowned. "As I said, it was a bad idea to hold a conversation on a ladder."

Sin lifted his brows. "I wouldn't exactly call what we were having 'a conversation.'"

Her face turned a lovely pink. "It started out as one," she said, suddenly prim. "I tried to convince you to talk in the chairs by the fireplace, but nooooo, you had to talk here." She shook her head. "What were we thinking? Here, I have a kerchief. Let me—" She twisted to reach into her pocket and as she did so, her shoulder mashed Sin's fingers against the ladder.

He instinctively jerked his hand free. The second he let go he knew his mistake, but it was too late—he fell to the floor, landing on his shoulder. Pain lanced through him and he groaned.

"Oh no! Don't move! I'm coming down!"

"No, stay there—" But it was too late. Teeth gritted, he hurried to move away from the bottom of the ladder before she stepped on some other vulnerable part of him.

She reached the floor and dropped to her knees beside him. Large swaths of her hair had fallen from its pins and hung about her shoulders in unruly black curls, making her pale blue eyes look far too large for her heart-shaped face. Her forehead had a faint circle of blue that he suspected ringed a good knot from where she'd hit his chin.

Sin rubbed his shoulder. What in the hell was it about this woman, that she could so easily cause him to lose control? And lose control he did—of his thoughts. Of his circumstances. Of himself. It was infuriating.

Rose reached into her pocket and pulled out her handkerchief. "Here, let me—" She dabbed his chin.

"Ow!" He grabbed her wrist and shoved her hand away. "You've done quite enough, thank you."

She dropped back on her heels, hurt in her eyes. "I didn't mean to hurt you."

"I know," he returned coldly, realizing that even now, with his chin afire and his shoulder thrumming, he was achingly aware that she smelled of lavender and rose. Of the seductive curve where her neck met her shoulder, and of the delicate hollows that called for further exploration. Even pained and bruised, he wanted to kiss her again, over and over, until she begged him to do more. He, who could have any woman he wanted, yearned for this one plain, rather awkward woman with a hunger that was almost painful. It was ridiculous.

Sin frowned, suddenly realizing that this was what had fueled his anger for all these years—not that she'd embarrassed him in public, but that even after such a humiliation, he had still desired her and couldn't stop. For weeks, months, and longer, he'd thought of nothing but her, but she'd disappeared without a trace and her aunt had refused to share her location, saying only that she lived in the Scottish countryside.

He had been left with an empty yearning, unable to forget how she'd felt when he'd kissed her, of her slender body against his, of the scent of her hair and the sound of her laugh—it had been sheer hell. She'd haunted him. He'd thought that by meeting her again, this spell she'd cast would be broken and everything would be set to rights.

But now that he was with her once again, he found himself lusting for her every bit as fervently as he had at that first meeting, an almost instant yearning that began the second they were in a room together, one that wouldn't end until . . . until what? Until he possessed her? Until he'd quenched his thirst for her?

He gave a frustrated growl and climbed to his feet.

"Wait! I was trying to—"

"You are *very* trying, damn you."

Her lips thinned and she stood as well, shaking her skirts into place. "Well, that didn't last long." When he looked confused, she added, "Your attempt to seduce me. Surely you don't toss curse words at women you're trying to get into your bed."

His gaze narrowed. "You knocked me off a ladder."

"Humph. All I can say is that if this is your idea of a seduction, then you have a lot to learn about women."

"I kissed you on the ladder and you didn't protest. Nor did you try to stop me. You participated, and with enthusiasm. Your seduction is well under way and, so far, has been met with nothing but success."

Color flooded her face and she scowled.

Satisfied, he bent to retrieve her book from the floor. She stepped forward to take it, and he realized that the top of her head barely reached his shoulder. Somehow, his memory had made her taller.

Bloody hell, how had this tiny woman with her mob of mad curls and saucy mouth caused so much havoc in his life in only two meetings? He had no idea. All he knew was that he wanted to claim those red lips yet again and bruise them with kisses until she cried out and—

She pushed a stray curl from her cheek with a simple gesture that was somehow sensual. He watched, almost enthralled, as her slender fingers brushed her neck and he instantly wanted to follow her fingers with his lips and—

Their eyes met, locked, and clung. Heat swirled between them, as palpable as the waves that rose over a fire. He almost leaned toward her when she cleared her throat and said in a breathless tone, "Lord Sinclair, since we are to be fellow guests for the next three weeks, we should make peace."

"How do you propose we do that?"

"I'll apologize for accidentally knocking you off the ladder and you can apologize for trapping me there."

He looked at the bruise on her forehead and grimaced. "No. You owe no apologies for today. What happened was—" Good God, was he really going to say it? But yes. It was the truth, damn it. Besides, she was right in suggesting that this seduction was off to a very rocky beginning. He needed to make up some ground, and why not with a truth? Nothing was more disarming, and heavens knew the woman who stood before him could stand to be disarmed. He touched his bruised and cut chin and grimaced again. "This was all my fault."

She blinked in surprise.

"I should have let you climb down before I attempted to kiss you. I will not be so foolish again."

"That's . . . that's very kind of you."

"Don't sound so surprised."

Her lips quirked. "I'm sorry. What I meant to say was 'Thank you.'"

"You're welcome. But do not think this changes anything between us. I will seduce you."

She squared her shoulders, a light in her eyes. "We'll see about that."

"Yes, we will. But for now, I will take my leave of you." He bowed, bringing his eyes down to hers. For a long moment, he held her gaze. "I shall see you later tonight."

"T-tonight?"

He hid a smile at her breathless tone. "At dinner."

"Oh. Yes. Dinner." She managed a smile.

He bowed. "Until then." With a faint smile, he strode into the hallway, closing the door behind him.

Well, that hadn't gone the way he'd expected. But their path was now set. All he had to do was remember his purpose: to sample just enough of her to satisfy his seemingly insatiable craving, and then go on with his life, finally freed from that damned kiss from so long ago.

Sin walked through the foyer toward the stairwell, his senses highly alert, his entire body tense and awake. By God, he was looking forward to the coming weeks. Judging by his first attempt, it wouldn't take much to stir her desire. This time he wouldn't be the only one suffering pangs of unanswered passion.

As he walked past the door to the sitting room, it opened and the Roxburghe pugs came tumbling out, yapping happily at the sight of him. Lady Charlotte followed.

Her gaze widened as she noted his chin. "Oh dear," she said. "What happened?"

"I was on the library ladder and I fell."

"Were you dizzy? There's an ague going about that makes one quite unsteady. I'll send for Doctor Mac-Creedy and—"

"I assure you there's no need. I'm quite healthy."

"Oh." She eyed him narrowly. "Too much port, was it?"

He laughed. "No. *Too much Rose. She makes a man as giddy as a bottle of the best Scotch.* He bent to pat a pug that was mauling his boots and then straightened. "I think I'll retire to my room until dinner. That is, unless you need something?"

"Oh no," she answered, her gaze sharp.

"Good day, then." Sin made his bow and climbed

the stairs, aware that she remained at the bottom, watching him. He couldn't ignore it. *Hmm. It appears that I may be far more closely observed at my great-aunt's than I expected. I will put a stop to that immediately; I'm not here for anyone's amusement but my own.* That decided, he continued to his bedchamber, feeling oddly lighthearted for a man with a bruised and cut chin. The game had begun.

Five

From the Diary of the Duchess of Roxburghe

Charlotte saw Sin with a cut upon his chin today, which he blamed upon a fall from the ladder in the library. Even more odd, while on my way to my chambers to dress for dinner, I saw Miss Balfour sporting a definite bruise upon her brow, which she claimed came from an incident involving the same ladder.

I vow, but I'm dying to know what happened . . .

"Ow! Dunn, stop!"

Sin's valet sighed and dropped a cloth into the washbowl. "My lord, I was merely trying to clean the cut on your chin."

Sin sniffed the air suspiciously. "That doesn't smell like water."

"That's because it's whiskey. It will clean the cut better than water."

"I asked you to shave around the scrape, not force whiskey into it. That stings like hell."

"Then it's working," Dunn said without any visible remorse. "If you get an infection you will not need a shave, but a surgeon."

Sin went to the mirror over his dresser. The scrape on his chin was beginning to turn bluish and was a little swollen. "Damn. I look like a prizefighter."

"Yes, my lord. I don't suppose you'd care to tell me how you gained your injury?"

"I was helping Miss Balfour select a library book."

Dunn waited, but when Sin said no more, the valet merely added a dry "I see." He crossed to the wardrobe, opened it, and stood staring at the contents. "Do you anticipate a further visit to the library this evening? If so, I would suggest the claret waistcoat. It will obscure any bloodstains."

Sin sent his valet a hard look. "I suppose you think you're being humorous."

Dunn's mouth quivered faintly, but he managed to control it. "The claret waistcoat, my lord?"

"It doesn't matter. Just bring me one and be quick about it, or I'll be late for dinner."

"Yes, my lord." The valet brought the waistcoat and assisted Sin into it. "And now your coat, my lord."

Sin nodded and allowed Dunn to assist him into the coat, wincing as he moved his shoulder.

"Your shoulder, too, my lord? Good heavens, that must have been a very heavy book."

"You have no idea." Sin took a final glance in the mirror, made a minute adjustment to his cravat that left Dunn murmuring with approval. "I shall need the emerald cravat pin, please."

Dunn fetched the pin from the pin box. "I take it your wounds are actually from an encounter with Miss Balfour, rather than a mere book selection."

"Perhaps."

"That *is*, after all, why you came to the duchess's house party."

Sin's gaze narrowed. "I don't believe I ever said that."

Dunn gave a superior smile and turned to replace the pin box on the dresser. "I am aware that Miss Balfour is the reason we are here. I hope you won't mind if I voice a concern."

"Would it matter if I did?"

"No, my lord. I'd find a way to work it into a conversation eventually."

"Then out with it, damn it."

"I hope you're not going to do anything rash where Miss Balfour is concerned."

"Rash? Me?" Sin held the pin in front of his cravat and regarded it in the mirror.

"Yes, my lord, you. I remember how you were in the months after your last encounter with Miss Balfour. It is the one area where you are not so controlled."

Sin paused, his hand hovering. "You think I'm controlled?"

"More than most people, my lord. Not that it's a

bad habit, for it gives you great advantage in games of chance. It has not, however, been so propitious for your relationships."

"I don't have relationships."

Dunn raised his brows as if that proved his point.

"I don't have them because I don't *wish* to have them," Sin said impatiently.

Dunn bowed. "Of course, my lord."

Scowling, Sin slipped the pin into place. He might balk at the strictures of society, and refuse to socialize with the bland virgins his grandmother and great-aunt had been pushing his way since the day he'd inherited his title, but he wasn't 'controlled.' He merely knew how he liked his life, and made certain it happened accordingly. Who didn't? He was just fortunate enough to have the means to make it so. As for his relationships, he'd had plenty—more than his fair share, to be honest.

It was silly to even think about Dunn's unfounded charge. Besides, he had better things to do than deal with impertinence, like finding ways to get Miss Balfour alone, and avoiding Aunt Margaret's infernal quizzing.

Miss Balfour had thrown down quite a challenge, almost daring him to seduce her.

She had a lot to learn. He'd already shown his cards, so now it was time to show her how well he could shuffle the deck. "Dunn, there's no need to wait up on me."

"Staying out late, my lord?"

"Not tonight. I plan on being in bed quite early, in fact." He'd pursued Miss Balfour enough for today; it would be wise to give her some time to wonder what he might do next. There was nothing more seductive than anticipation.

He had three entire weeks to show Miss Balfour how wrong she could be. Three luscious weeks, and he planned to enjoy every one of them. First, though, he had to assess the competition offered by his aunt's guests. Smiling, he bid Dunn a good night and left his bedchamber.

Five minutes later, Sin looked about the sitting room. "Good God."

Aunt Margaret sighed. "I know. The new linings for the curtains are atrocious, aren't they? I wondered at the Wellington Blue, for it seems an odd color to me, but Charlotte swore it was all the rage and I buckled. Now I'm stuck with them."

"I hadn't even noticed your blasted curtains. *These* are the other guests?"

"Why, yes." She sniffed. "Sin, you smell of whiskey."

He grimaced. "My valet used it to clean the scrape on my chin."

Her gaze sharpened. "Oh yes. How did you get—"

"It doesn't matter," he said shortly. "You were speaking of your guests?"

She shrugged. "I believe you know most of them

already." She nodded to the small group sitting upon settees at the far end of the room, all dressed in the height of fashion and dripping with jewels. "You know Mr. and Mrs. Stewart, cousins of the Earl of Buchan, and their daughters, Isobel and Muriella."

The Stewarts all resembled one another in their weak chins and gray hair, even their middle-aged daughters. Mr. and Mrs. Stewart were in their eighties, so thin and slight that they looked as if a strong wind might blow them away. Beside them their daughters looked brawny, though one was tall and gaunt and the other short and squat.

Margaret then gestured to two women who sat in a pair of chairs by the fireplace. "And I'm certain you've met Miss Fraser and Lady McFarlane, both excellent whist players."

Neither of the ladies in question looked well enough to sit at a card table. One of them had nodded off to sleep and the other didn't appear to be far behind.

"And over there is Mr. Munro." Margaret gestured toward an older, quite plump man with a balding pate.

"Why is he hovering over the port decanter?"

"He always does. He's an acquaintance of Roxburghe's and is quite well-off, with a large estate near Stirling. Sadly, he's turned into a horrid flirt and I now wish I hadn't invited him."

"And the other elderly man?"

"Lord Cameron is not elderly; he's middle-aged."

Sin lifted his brows.

"He's a neighbor and a frequent whist partner when the vicar can't make it." Margaret regarded Cameron with favor. "You'll enjoy him. He's quite a wag when in his cups." She beamed around the room. "As I said, none of them should be a stranger to you."

"Aunt Margaret, while I'm sure they're all quite nice, these guests aren't in your usual style. They're all so—" He'd been about to say "old," but then realized that most of the guests were near Aunt Margaret's age or younger.

"They're all what?" The martial light in her eyes told him that she'd guessed what he'd been about to say.

"They're not . . . what I expected."

"What, or rather, who, did you expect?"

"Mr. Bailey, Lord MacDonald, Earl Spencer, Miss Sontieth, Lady MacTavish—the ones you usually invite to your amusements."

"Ah, yes. Apparently there's a horrible ague going about."

Something about the way she said that made him turn to regard her more closely. "Your *younger* friends have all fallen ill with the ague while the *older* ones have avoided it?"

"Odd, isn't it?" She didn't meet his gaze, but instead fidgeted with an emerald bracelet clasped about her wrist. "But there's no explaining an ague."

He wondered what bee had gotten into Aunt Margaret's bonnet. "Miss Balfour and I will be oddities by virtue of our ages."

Margaret looked about the room as if surprised. "Oh dear," she said. "I suppose you're right. I never thought of it."

"Aunt Margaret, I don't know what game you're playing, but you're playing deep. You have only ten guests total, and you usually invite twenty couples or more." Now he'd have to work twice as hard to steal Rose away unnoticed. By virtue of not having gray or white hair, he and Rose would be instantly missed.

He eyed his great-aunt with a narrow gaze. "What are you up to?"

"Me?" Twin spots of color showed through the powder on her thin cheeks. "I'm not up to a thing. I'm merely trying to help."

"Help with what?"

"You seemed interested in this Balfour gel, and I didn't think you needed the competition of any other youngsters."

Sin almost choked. "Competition? You thought I couldn't handle— Good God, madam! No one insults me the way you do."

She didn't look the least put out. "That's a pity. You'd be more bearable if people didn't always fawn over you. And don't tell me you're not spoiled from it."

He scowled. "If you feel I'm too spoiled for good company, then I'm surprised you invite me here year after year."

"I do it because you're my great-nephew, of course. In fact, you're my *favorite* great-nephew."

"I'd never have known that by the things you say to me."

"Caring for someone doesn't mean you're always polite. Sometimes it means you tell them the truth, whether they wish to hear it or not. In fact, I've been wanting to discuss this with you for some time; over the years you've grown a little arrogant."

"Nonsense."

"It's not your fault, of course. When your father and mother died, my sister thought thrusting all of the responsibility of the title directly on your shoulders would make you a man. It did, of course, but not necessarily the right sort of man."

"You've said enough, madam," he said frostily. "Plenty of people have inherited larger estates and at younger ages."

"And with equally disastrous results," she replied with asperity.

"The Sinclair estate and house have never been in better repair."

"Oh, you've a knack for the management part of it, but it hasn't been good for you. There's been nothing—and no one—to challenge you and make you think about someone's wishes other than your own. And now that your brothers have all grown and married, you're even more insufferable than ever."

Bloody hell, first Dunn and now Aunt Margaret. "If you feel that way, then perhaps I should leave."

"And miss spending time with Miss Balfour? And after I changed my guest list to give you an advantage?"

"Damn it, I'm not trying to fix my interest with Miss Balfour!"

Aunt Margaret arched a disbelieving brow. "If you're not trying to fix your interest with her, then why did you demand that I invite her?"

"My interest in Miss Balfour isn't romantic in nature."

"My dear, what *other* interest can there be between a man and a woman?"

"She has been a thorn in my side for a long time and I thought the time had come to remove that thorn. That is all."

"You're not planning her some harm, are you?" The pugnacious angle of Aunt Margaret's chin reminded him of his grandmother. "Let me remind you that this gel is a guest of mine, *and* my goddaughter. If she mentions one unacceptable incident, you will deeply regret it."

"Miss Balfour will have no reason to mention any 'unacceptable incidents' to you or anyone else." *I intend her to find every incident to be very acceptable. So acceptable that she'll long for more.*

"I should hope not. The gel is under my protection

while she's under my roof and I won't have her reputation impugned."

If Rose were an innocent, Sin would also be concerned about reputations and protections. But she'd clearly stated that she was a woman of experience. "If anyone is in need of protection, it's not her. But that's neither here nor there. Aunt Margaret, it's time you stopped this infernal tendency to matchmake."

"Me? I didn't even think of inviting Miss Balfour until you mentioned her."

"But you've already started meddling. Just look at the guest list."

"You must admit you could use some help. Miss Balfour is an attractive woman, and other eligible men—most of whom have better address than you—might outshine you."

"No one has better address than I do, when I wish it. As for Miss Balfour, she's brown, freckled, and unfashionable. I doubt any other eligible males would pay her the least heed."

"She's also lively, charming, and has a breathtaking smile." Before Sin could reply, Margaret held up a hand. "Let us agree that Miss Balfour is not your usual sort. She's very independent, and not at all a social climber, nor does she seem to care for fortune."

Sin frowned. "That is not my *usual sort* of woman. That is merely the type of woman my title and fortune attract."

Aunt Margaret's brows lowered. "Sin, there will

always be those who are attracted to us for our name and wealth, but there are also those who will wish to be with us simply because of who we are."

He laughed derisively.

She bit her lip. "Oh dear. You poor boy."

"Nonsense." He grinned. "I've been blessed with wealth and a title and I wouldn't have it any other way, so don't look at me as if I were once again a boy and came to you with a skinned knee."

"But no one should live as if—"

"I'm perfectly happy the way I am, Aunt Margaret."

"Happy? Really? Even though you think that every woman you've met thus far has been interested in you only for your title and wealth?"

"I don't think it; I know it. Several even told me so."

"Oh! Why, those—" Aunt Margaret clamped her lips closed. "I have a name for women like that, but I won't say it here. Sin, you're wrong if you think those horrid few represent the whole. Why, look at Miss Balfour. *She* doesn't seem interested in your title or fortune. In fact, she seems very uninterested in you overall."

Not for long. He patted his aunt's hand on his arm. "You leave Miss Balfour to me, and have a little faith that I can charm a woman when I wish to."

She gave an inelegant snort. "I have plenty of faith in you, but we all have our limits, dear." She patted his hand as if he were a three-year-old and she'd just handed him a tea cracker. "No need to thank me for assisting you, though I'm still not perfectly clear on your motives—"

"Your grace, how are you this evening?" Miss Isobel Stewart stood before them. Tall and gangly, she was known for her bold speaking. Or, as Sin thought of it, "ill-bred blurting out every thought in her empty head." He considered this tendency, and not her iron-gray hair, which had been teased into a rather frightening mound upon her narrow head, to be the reason she was unwed, even thought she was related to half of England's best families and was reported to be quite an heiress.

At her side stood her sister, who was as short and round as her sister was tall and thin. Miss Muriella Stewart stood on her tiptoes as she squinted up at Sin. "Who's this?" she asked.

Her sister turned to her. "Lord Fin—" She tittered behind her glove. "I *mean*, Lord *Sinclair*."

As he always did when faced with such impertinence, Sin raised an eyebrow.

Miss Isobel's grin faded and she turned a deep, unattractive red and quickly became engrossed in adjusting the tassel on her reticule.

Aunt Margaret interjected smoothly, "My dear Misses Stewart, it was so kind of you both to accept my invitation. We are just waiting for one more guest and then we will adjourn to the dining room."

Lord Cameron, who like Mr. Munro was now

gawking through his quizzing glass at the painting of a nude woman reposing on a cushion, turned at this. "I certainly hope so, for I'm famished."

Mr. Munro let his quizzing glass fall, and it landed upon his stomach like a bird perched upon a gravy-stained rock. "It's well after eight. It does no harm to eat a bit late once or twice, but it's bad for the digestion if one does it too often."

"Miss Balfour will be here soon and— Ah! There she is now. Excuse me, please." The duchess hurried across the room.

"Lud!" Mr. Munro said, lifting his quizzing glass to gaze at Rose. "Who's the beauty?"

Sin frowned. Rose, a beauty? He turned and watched her walk toward Aunt Margaret, who must have said something waggish, for Rose broke into a smile that transformed her face. The sound of her soft laughter tickled his ears and made him feel restless. *Damn it. She does have a lovely smile. Perhaps if she didn't always make me so mad, I might have noticed that before.*

Mr. Munro chuckled with pleasure. "A vision!" He immediately began adjusting his neckcloth and, noticing the stain on his waistcoat, scrubbed at it with a thick finger.

Lord Cameron stared at Rose. "I've not met her; I'm sure I'd remember if I had."

Miss Isobel sniffed. "Whoever she is, she's horridly out of fashion."

Her sister squinted across the room. "Lud, she's wearing mauve. Mauve has been out of fashion for the last three years."

Sin found himself wishing them all to the devil. If Aunt Margaret had invited her usual sparkling set, Rose wouldn't have stood out at all. Now she was easily the most attractive woman in their small party, and was garnering all of the benefits and pains that entailed—cattiness from the women and unwanted attention from the men.

"I hope I sit near her at dinner." Munro smoothed his too-tight waistcoat. "If not, I'll speak to her afterward. I just wonder who she is."

Miss Muriella said, "Her name is Rose Balfour. I met her this afternoon coming out of the library, and her grace introduced us. Her father created the Balfour rose." When Munro didn't appear to appreciate this information, she added, "Surely you've heard of it?"

Munro wrinkled his nose. "I don't know one flower from the next. Why would I?"

"It's quite well-known. Sir Balfour is a horticulturalist of some note."

Lord Cameron looked down his large nose at Rose. "So her father is a mere gardener? Odd that her grace would invite a nobody to one of her house parties. She used to be more particular, although . . ." His gaze narrowed on Rose. "For some reason, the name seems familiar."

"Personally, I think the duchess has shown excellent taste," Munro said with ponderous gallantry.

Rose and the duchess reached them, and Aunt Margaret did the introductions. The Misses Stewart fawned while also being barely polite. Lord Cameron was openly curious, and Mr. Munro held Rose's hand far too long.

Finally Aunt Margaret turned his way and said rather blithely, "Miss Balfour, I believe you already know my great-nephew, the Earl of Sinclair."

She briefly inclined her head. She might have said something, but Munro interjected himself and lost no time in bearing her off to the other side of the room, where he could be heard paying her such extravagant compliments that Sin winced. Fortunately, MacDougal then arrived to announce dinner and they all left for the dining room.

Dinner proved to be no more satisfying since Aunt Margaret hadn't seated him near Rose. They were on opposite ends of the table, she surrounded by Mr. Munro and Lord Cameron, while he had Miss Muriella on one side and a dozing Miss Fraser on the other. Miss Muriella was quite content to monopolize the conversation, garbling on and on about the Regent, the state of the Bristol Road, and the lobster soup— she never paused for a second.

Meanwhile, Rose held reign at the other end of the table, their conversation much more lively than at his end. The meal seemed to go on forever, and Sin was relieved when the men finally excused themselves to the library for port. At least there, Sin was certain Munro was behaving himself.

Conversation was desultory as the men waited for the women to join them, and when they finally did, Aunt Margaret came in leaning upon Rose's arm.

Rose felt the gaze of everyone in the room, which made her acutely uncomfortable. When she usually socialized she was escorting her sisters, and as they were prettier and livelier, she rarely received such intense interest. Sin alone seemed indifferent, looking as bored as if he were at an opera performance.

His chin showed a bruise now, and she'd noticed him wince and rub his shoulder when he'd held out Mrs. Stewart's chair at dinner. *Well, it serves him right. How dare he announce that he's going to seduce me, so certain of his success that he had no fear in telling me his intentions?*

His arrogance made her determined to resist him, even as something about him tugged her toward him and made her long for his touch. It was really *her* nature she'd have to fight, not Sin's. The memory of their encounter in the library flashed into her mind and a shiver tingled through her. *Blast it, what is it about him that makes me react so? And why don't I enjoy the company of less threatening men?*

When she'd been in London for her season, the poet Byron had been taking London by storm and men of his stamp were all the rage. Byron was soft-looking and spoke with an assumed affectation that made Rose cringe. Aunt Lettice had been in swoons over him, but Rose had been thoroughly unimpressed.

No, she preferred a far different sort of man. She liked a man who looked like a man, one with broad shoulders and muscled arms. A man who could fill out the knitted breeches that were so fashionable today as they molded to his powerful thighs. Her eyes found Sin across the room, her gaze moving up his legs, and then higher . . . Realizing suddenly that she was staring, she jerked her gaze up and found Sin regarding her with an amused look.

Rose spun away, her face hot. As she did so, she accidentally locked eyes with Mr. Munro, who promptly began making his way toward her.

Oh, no. I had enough of him during dinner. Rose hurried to Miss Isobel's side for shelter. Just as she reached Miss Isobel, MacDougal appeared with a tray that held glasses of sherry for the ladies. Rose gratefully took one.

As soon as the sherry was served, the duchess lifted her own glass. "My dear guests, may I have your attention?"

Everyone turned to the duchess, who beamed at Rose. "Miss Balfour was telling us over dinner how much she enjoys riding."

Everyone now stared at Rose. She placed her empty glass on MacDougal's tray and he promptly handed her a full one.

"And so," the duchess continued, "Lady Charlotte has suggested that we take a lovely ride tomorrow afternoon to the picturesque ruins of old Roxburghe Castle, followed by a picnic. There's a wide, even pathway that wends through the woods and along the banks of the River Tweed. For those of you not inclined to ride, we will have carriages awaiting, as well."

A smattering of "hear, hear" and applause met this announcement, Miss Isobel the loudest of them all. Rose could only suspect that someone had once told Miss Isobel that she looked especially fine in her riding habit.

As the duchess answered questions about the coming amusement, Rose glanced longingly at the door. Could she make her excuses and slip away? If only—

"Politeness dictates that you must stay at least another ten minutes."

The deep voice set her pulse thundering. Sin was standing far closer than she expected, and she had to tilt her head back to see his expression.

His smile reminded her of a cat with cream. "At *least* ten minutes."

"And then I shall retire *alone*."

"Of course." He shrugged. "Who suggested otherwise?"

Oddly, disappointment flickered through her. "You suggested it earlier, when you said—" Her gaze narrowed as his eyes lit with amusement.

"I told you I was going to seduce you, but I didn't

say when. I suggest that you relax until then, and simply enjoy the amusements offered by my aunt."

MacDougal appeared to retrieve her empty glass—when had she finished it?—and she captured a full one from his tray.

"Careful," Sin said. "Aunt Margaret's sherry has more of a punch than most." He stood so close that when she lifted her glass to take a sip, her elbow grazed his chest. She stepped to one side.

He followed.

"What are you doing?"

"Why? Does it make you nervous?" His wicked smile let her know that he was perfectly aware of his effect on her.

Two can play at that game. She very casually leaned forward. "Why do you ask, my lord?" Her breasts brushed his waistcoat.

His smile disappeared.

She peered up at him through her lashes, exhilarated. "Is something wrong? Am I standing too close?"

His gaze darkened. "I'd be careful if I were you, Miss Balfour."

"Why? Are you afraid I might lead you astray? Oh, wait. You are supposed to lead *me* astray. How could I have forgotten?"

He reluctantly smiled. "The last time we were this close, I ended up with a sore chin and shoulder. You seem to bring bad luck with you, Miss Balfour."

The genuine humor in his deep voice dissolved her desire to best him. She'd been prepared for anger, irritation, anything but that devastating lopsided grin.

She never knew what to expect from this man! He was a mystery, one that begged for more exploration. *But that's a very dangerous way to think of him.*

She said lightly, "I'm glad you've recovered from your meeting with the library floor."

He gingerly moved his arm. "I believe 'recovering' is more apt, but thank you." He lifted a brow. "How was dinner? Your end of the table seemed quite lively."

"Yes, your aunt kept us amused with tales about her younger days at court. Meanwhile, the conversation on your end of the table appeared somewhat sleep inducing."

"Sadly, Miss Fraser found the food a bit bland in the opening course and proceeded to sleep through the rest of our meal. At one point I worried she might fall into the turtle soup."

"She seems to sleep a lot," Rose said with a chuckle.

His gaze flickered to her forehead. "You didn't bruise as much as I expected."

"I rarely do. I'm quite hardy." She looked about the room. "Unlike most of the other guests."

"Yes, it's a somewhat creaky party. I fear that if you came to Floors Castle expecting gaiety, you're to be sorely disappointed." His eyes gleamed. "Fortunately, we have our challenge to keep us busy. We can—"

"What fun!" Lady Charlotte's soft voice broke into their tête-à-tête. "I do love a good challenge!"

Rose and Sin turned to find Lady Charlotte at Sin's elbow. She looked expectantly between them. "Pray tell, who has challenged whom, and what are the stakes?"

Sin's smile was gone. "It's nothing."

Rose feigned surprise. "Lord Sinclair, surely you're not reneging *already*?"

His gaze narrowed. "I never renege." He turned to Lady Charlotte and said in a stiff tone, "I merely challenged Miss Balfour to a ride—"

"Actually, he's challenged me to quite a bit more than a mere ride," Rose said, smiling sweetly. "We're just now naming our stakes."

Lady Charlotte looked pleased. She turned and called out, "Your grace, do come and hear! Lord Sinclair and Miss Balfour are engaged in a challenge of some sort and they have a *wager*!"

Instantly every eye turned their way as the duchess came to stand with Lady Charlotte. "Well?" the duchess said impatiently. "What's this challenge?"

Sin made an impatient sound. "It's nothing. A gallop during our ride tomorrow."

"That's all?"

"No," Rose said promptly. "It's a series of challenges. That's the first one we've decided upon."

The duchess looked pleased. "Excellent! That sounds quite amusing."

"I'll keep track of the wagers," Lady Charlotte offered. "MacDougal! Pray fetch the writing desk from the library."

"Put me down for twenty pounds on Miss Balfour," Munro said.

Lord Cameron wasn't far behind. "Pardon me, Miss Balfour, but I must support my own. Twenty on Sin."

Soon the Misses Stewart had chimed in, both of them supporting Sin. Their father surprisingly put two pounds on Rose.

During the clamor, Sin leaned down to Rose. "What did you hope to gain by that little maneuver?"

"Chaperones." She smiled sweetly. "Lots and lots of chaperones."

"Deaf and nearsighted chaperones, who will not be of any use to you." He shook his head. "Even if you had a thousand chaperones, I'd still find a way to you."

"And I'd still find my way free. You will not seduce me, Lord Sin. *Ever.*"

"We will see about that," he said with a grin. She was never at a loss for words, nor was she afraid of showing her earthy side. Just a few moments ago, he'd surprised her regarding him as if she'd like to ravish him right there in the middle of the library. Her heated look had both amused and surprised him. She'd said she was a woman of experience, and only one who was very comfortable with herself would be so bold in such a public setting.

She wanted him as much as he wanted her, which made him wonder . . . why *wasn't* she interested in his fortune and title? On the evening of their first disastrous encounter, Rose could have easily claimed that he'd ruined her and then demanded that he marry her to make things right. But she'd never suggested such a thing.

So it was true; Rose was different from most women he knew. But why was that?

"Miss Balfour, why did you accept my aunt's invitation?"

"Because I was honored to have been invited to Floors Castle, of course. And how could I say no to my own godmother? She's a very determined woman."

"You have no idea how determined she can be. And meddlesome to boot." His gaze flickered past her to where the duchess was standing by Charlotte, overseeing the listing of the wagers. "My aunt seems to think you are a good rider."

Instantly, Rose's eyes lit up. "When I'm at home, I ride every day."

It was almost magical, the way her face changed when she was interested in something. Liveliness and excitement transformed her from mildly pretty to breathtakingly beautiful. It was as if her very spirit was visible in her eyes.

Sin found himself leaning forward, wishing to taste that warmth, which was ridiculous. He drew back. "You will be pleased with the mounts. Roxburghe's stables are without compare, as my uncle personally selected the stock. Except, of course, for the fat, sluggish few that he keeps solely for my aunt's friends."

"I look forward to a morning gallop tomorrow," Miss Balfour said. "It's been a week since I rode."

"You think to gallop with so many delicate bones perched on spiritless slugs? You dream, Miss Balfour."

"I hadn't thought of that. Then how do we meet our first wager?"

"We will ride off once we reach a good stretch of road."

"Alone?"

"Afraid?" He'd said the word mockingly and instantly she stiffened.

"*Never.*"

So Miss Balfour had some pride when it came to being challenged, did she? If that was so, his life had just become infinitely easier. He watched her as he said, "If you fear being alone with me, then you can just hide here within the castle walls, and never leave my aunt's side. It would be a cowardly way to live, but—" He shrugged.

"I'm not a coward, Lord Sinclair, I am more than ready to—"

Mr. Munro was suddenly with them. "Already teasing your opponent, eh?" He beamed at Rose. "I put my money on you, for her grace vows you're a top-notch rider." He flicked a glance Sin's way. "No offense to you, of course."

"None taken."

Munro bowed. "Thank you. I'm not much of a horseman myself, although I plan to ride tomorrow." Munro eyed Rose as if she were his dessert. "I wonder what other amusements her grace has planned?"

Sin said, "There's no telling what my aunt has in store. I daresay there will be dinner every night at the unfashionable hour of eight, whist at the shockingly late hour of nine and perhaps ten if the company gets carried away, with the unalleviated gaiety dispersed by many, many naps."

Rose replied with admirable gravity, "It's fortunate that I enjoy a good nap, myself. In fact, I wish I'd had one today after traveling here."

Sin had a sudden image of her rising from a late-afternoon nap, her eyes heavy with sleep as she stretched, her lithe form clad only in a chemise.

He found his gaze on the neckline of her gown. A faint hint of lace showed above the material. *So, you have a softer side. I wonder if I—*

"My dear boy!" Aunt Margaret hurried up. "Charlotte needs your help in assigning mounts to our guests. Normally Roxburghe would deal with that, but he's not here."

Apparently his chance to speak with Rose had passed. Forcing his disappointment away, he bowed to his aunt. "Of course. I will be there in a moment as soon as I finish speaking to—" He realized that Rose had moved away and was now talking to Mr. Stewart, much to that ancient codger's delight, while Munro hovered behind her.

Aunt Margaret looked on with approval. "Ah, yes, Munro. I wish I could take credit for that, but I must say I didn't invite him with any such intention. But now that he's showing such interest, I must say it wouldn't be a bad match for the gel."

"Munro and *Rose*? Surely you jest."

"Why not? He's quite wealthy and has a large stable, which she would enjoy. And she's still young enough to give him an heir. It would be a very good match for them both."

"He's two score years older than her."

"I've seen happy unions with more years between them."

"And I've seen unhappy ones with fewer."

"So the number of years must not matter," she returned. "Besides, I cannot see how you, who've never been married, can profess to know what makes a good match. I, on the other hand, am an expert."

"I can promise you that Rose Balfour is not interested in Mr. Munro. He's far too tame for a woman like that."

"Ah." Aunt Margaret smiled serenely as she turned to watch Mr. Munro practice his heavy-handed wiles on Rose. "I predict that Miss Balfour won't escape Floors Castle without an offer."

Sin frowned.

"Mr. Munro seems quite taken already, and they've just met. And then there's Lord Cameron—"

"No."

She gave him a surprised look. "What do you mean 'no'?"

"They're both too old for her. Besides, Cameron was sneering at her before dinner."

"That's because he mistakenly thought her father a gardener. I have since explained things. Either man would make a good match for Miss Balfour."

"Blast it, you said you wouldn't matchmake."

"I said I wouldn't matchmake for *you*. Miss Balfour, however, is obviously in clear need of my help. She has no dowry to speak of, no inheritance waiting, and while she's fair enough and is from good stock, she doesn't possess the beauty necessary to make the first two conditions unimportant. Still, she might be just what Munro and Cameron are looking for."

"Neither of them is looking to settle down."

"Nonsense. They both want a gel of good birth and who possesses passing good looks, who is young, healthy, and virginal—" Margaret sent him a surprised look. "I'm sorry, did you say something?"

"I just coughed. Pardon me. Since you seem to know what benefits your gentlemen friends would receive from a connection with Miss Balfour, what would she get out of such a mismatch?"

"Financial standing, a social position beyond what

she has now, and a husband to dote upon her every wish. What more could she ask for?"

"Maybe youth. Vigor. *Teeth.*"

"Lord Cameron has his own teeth." Margaret narrowed her eyes at the other candidate. "I'm not so certain about Munro. They seemed somewhat clacky at dinner, so I'm suspicious. Still, he's hardly stopped staring at her all evening. Just look at him now."

Sin followed Aunt Margaret's gaze to where Munro was talking eagerly to Rose. The thought of Munro's liver-spotted hands on Rose's sun-kissed skin made Sin's stomach tighten.

Aunt Margaret smiled benignly. "They would make a handsome couple, wouldn't they?"

"Good God. It would be like seeing a caterpillar chomping on a young, tender leaf."

"Sin!" Margaret said with exasperation. "What's gotten you into such a mood?"

"I'm not in a mood."

Aunt Margaret snorted. Just then the Misses Stewart joined Rose and Munro, breaking up their unsettling tête-à-tête. Good. Munro wouldn't get a word in edgewise now.

Still, Sin couldn't help but glower as he headed toward Lady Charlotte. His plans for Miss Balfour were not progressing as they should, and now she'd managed to add a layer of protection in the form of antiquated chaperones. Not one damn thing had gone right.

He firmed his jaw. Perhaps he'd been unrealistic in expecting to easily seduce Rose. Something needed to change. Because one way or another, he was going to get Rose Balfour alone tomorrow, and when he did, woe betide her.

Feeling more hopeful, he sat with Lady Charlotte and gave her his full attention. Tomorrow would come soon enough.

Six

From the Diary of the Duchess of Roxburghe
I believe I've discovered the source of Sin's taste for
disreputable women. If one does not ask for much,
one won't be disappointed at not receiving much.
I now hope more than ever that Miss Balfour will
manage to reach my great-nephew on some new
level and, in the process, disabuse him of some of
his misconceptions about women.

Meanwhile, I asked MacLure, one of our best
grooms and a former major in the army, to chaperone Miss Balfour, as I believe Sin will attempt to
get her alone.

Men are, if nothing else, predictable. Fortunately
for us all, women are not.

The day broke gray and overcast. Rose awoke at dawn
from a fitful slumber, her dreams filled with heated
kisses from a man with sherry-colored eyes and a
smug smile. Not wanting to wake the servants, she

rose, pulled on her robe, added wood to the fire, and settled in with a good book.

She usually enjoyed a nice, quiet morning read, but her mind kept drifting to Sin. Unable to focus, she set the book aside and went to stand at one of the large windows overlooking the front lawn.

She was still astounded by her reaction to him. This time, when he'd kissed her and those incredible sensations had flooded over her, she hadn't panicked, but had enjoyed them. Immensely. But . . . was that really better?

Rose, Rose, what are you doing? She sighed and leaned her head against the window frame, watching as a puff of wind rippled across the lawn. The scent of dampness came with the wind and she shivered and pulled away just as a soft knock sounded on her door.

"Come in!" she called.

The door opened and a maid came in carrying a laden breakfast tray. "Och, ye're awake. I dinna know ye was already up or I'd have come sooner." Annie carried the tray to a small table beside the fireplace. "Ye've already stoked the fire, too. I suppose if I'd been a wee bit later, ye'd have dressed wit'out me, as well."

Rose smiled at the censure in the maid's voice. Upon discovering that Rose had arrived without a maid of her own, the housekeeper, Mrs. Cairness, had assigned Annie to attend Rose. Annie was a large, strapping girl with wispy blond hair and a freckled, round face. She was much given to gossip, and Rose liked her very much.

"I would never dress without you," Rose assured her. "Besides, my riding habit has far too many buttons for me to try to dress alone."

"Guid. I've no wish t' be tol' I'm not doin' me dooty." Annie uncovered a plate and then poured tea into a china cup, steam rising into a delicate curl. "Come and ha' yer breakfast, miss. Ye'll be needin' it if ye're to ride in this weather."

Rose crossed to her seat and began to butter a piece of toast while Annie went to the large wardrobe and opened it.

"I had all o' yer clothes pressed yesterday by the laundry maid, and she was in raptures aboot yer riding habit. Said 'twas lovely, e'en more so than the ones worn by Princess Charlotte when she stayed here. I've been itchin' t' see it, though—" Annie stuck her head around the edge of the wardrobe. "Do ye think ye'll go, as 'tis so cloudy?"

"I don't know about the others, but I will go even if it rains. I love a brisk ride under a gray sky, and a little rain never hurt anyone. It'll just be more atmospheric."

"So it will, miss, unless it comes a downpour."

"If it does, I'll take shelter until it's done. We're to be in a forest, I think."

"Tha' ye are. Ye've an answer fer everythin' this morning, haven't ye, miss?" Annie grinned and then disappeared behind the wardrobe door. She removed the riding habit and carried it out to the bed. "'Tis a bonny habit, miss."

"Thank you."

Annie ran an expert hand over the soft skirt. "'Tis guid 'tis wool, fer wit'out the sun, it could get a mite chilled today."

Rose finished her toast and dusted her fingers on her napkin. After a quick sip of tea, she came to watch Annie shake out the habit's full skirts. Last night, the second Rose had seen the two Misses Stewart and their Paris-designed gowns, Rose had known that her clothing—most of it borrowed from Lily—was sadly out of fashion. Not that she cared much; to her, a gown was a gown. But a riding habit was another matter altogether.

A riding habit isn't a gown. It's armor. She smiled. "I shall wash up." She went to the water closet situated off her dressing room, and returned clean and clad in her chemise. "Running water in every water closet. I shall be spoiled when I go home."

"The duke redid the entire castle when he knew he was to marry her grace. Only the best fer his duchess, he said." Annie helped Rose into a full petticoat, tying it at her waist. "There. Now let's ha' a seat at the dressing table so I can pin up yer hair."

Rose said with a warning smile, "I fear my hair won't stay pinned."

"Aye, 'tis thick, but soft as can be, which is why it

willna' hold the pins." Annie picked up a brush and began to pull it through the long strands. "But 'tis no' tangly, miss. Tha' is a blessin'."

"Yes, it is." Rose waited until Annie finished brushing her hair and started to put it up, before she said, "The duke must love the duchess very much to put in such luxuries for her."

"He thinks she walks upon water, miss. We all do."

"That's quite a compliment."

"She's a guid duchess, she is. We all thought the duke was a confirmed bachelor and had no hopes o' his ever marrying, but one day, he ups and tells us all tha' he was bringin' home his duchess. We was all surprised, even his lordship's valet, fer he'd ne'er said a word aboot her afore then." Annie leaned in and said in a low voice, "MacDougal says the duke knew his lady fer years afore, but she was married to someone else. Once't her husband died, he waited until she'd put off her mourning afore he spoke to her. He's a very proper man, is the duke."

"The duchess was married before?"

"Aye, this is her fifth marriage. She's outlived four husbands, she has."

"Goodness!"

"'Tis no' that unusual. Me own mam was ninety-seven when she died and she'd been married five times. Women live longer than men, miss. 'Tis a simple fact." Annie finished pinning Rose's hair and went to fetch the riding habit from the bed. "I think the duchess lived all o' her husbands into the ground. She's a strong woman and hard to keep up wit'. But the duke is her match in tha'. He's a vigorous man, he is, full of vinegar and always movin'. He used to travel a guid bit, too, and was always in London when the weather turned. We hardly ever saw him here at Floors 'til he married."

"And now?"

"Now he dinna like to be away from home. He says her grace gets into scrapes when she's bored, and he must be here to rescue her from her schemes."

Rose chuckled and stood as Annie brought her the riding habit. "And does she need rescuing?"

"Not often, though she is a schemer, miss. Mac-Dougal—he's been her butler since she was first wed at seventeen—says she's no' one to take life sittin' down."

"That's a good way to live." Rose decided she should get to know her godmother better.

"So 'tis."

Rose stepped into the full skirts with Annie's help and settled the habit into place.

Annie attacked the long double row of buttons that fastened up her back and at each elbow. She helped Rose put on her boots, and then fetched the coat that went with the habit, and buttoned it on, as well. "'Tis a mighty lot of buttons to be sure, though they're pretty as can be once they're all fastened."

And those buttons served two purposes today—

they offered an intriguing fashion detail, and they provided protection. No one could seduce a woman who was riding a horse *and* protected by rows and rows and rows of buttons.

As soon as she had the thought, though, she doubted there were enough buttons on earth to deter the light she'd seen in Sin's eyes last night. Her heart fluttered at the thought.

Annie bent to give the skirts a final shake. "There ye are, miss."

"Thank you." Rose looked at herself in the mirror and gave a satisfied nod. Annie had pinned Rose's hair very simply, holding her determined curls in place with a mound of pins. Rose knew it wouldn't last, but she liked the way it looked.

But it was the habit itself that made Rose truly smile. The severity of the cut did wonders for her boyish figure, giving her a more defined waist, while the full skirts gave the impression of hips where she had very little. It was a pity to be so dependent on fashion to form one's figure, but there it was.

But perhaps the best thing about the habit was the color. Of a deep blue, with a touch of lighter blue in the ribboning, it made her skin look golden and her eyes even bluer. "Annie, can you find the white woollen wrap for my neck? It's chilly this morning."

"Very guid, miss." The maid brought the white scarf and a pair of riding gloves and placed them on the bed, along with the high crowned hat. She then turned back and regarded Rose with admiration. "It's beautiful, miss. I've never seen one like it."

"I saw a habit in *La Belle Assemblée* and drew a pattern from it. My sister Lily sewed it."

"Ne'er say so, miss. Why, it looks like something the duchess might have ordered from Paris."

"I shall tell Lily you said so; she will be overjoyed. No one loves fashion more than her. It was she who thought adding these would offset the severity of the habit." She pointed to the light blue ribboning that decorated her cuffs, and the matching double line that traced the bottom of her skirts. Those two simple additions made the tailored habit exquisitely feminine.

Annie shook her head in admiration. "Och, miss, 'tis beautiful and jus' the thing fer a slight miss like ye."

"Thank you." She wondered what Sin would think of the habit. For once, she didn't look like a skinny rail with a gown hanging on her. What she'd give for curvy hips or a noticeable bosom, something to give her a more hourglass-like figure.

Annie reached out and tugged a long curl that had fallen from its pin. "Och, no. 'Tis already fallin' down. Come an' sit down at the dresser once't again, miss. I'll pin up yer hair so it won't fall when ye take a fence."

"If you think you can. My hair's not so tame." Rose followed Annie to the dressing table and sat in front of the mirror. "How long have you worked here, Annie?"

"Fer four years, miss," Annie said as she placed the pins in a small tray on the table and began to carefully add them. "'Tis hard to get a position here, fer the duchess is known fer her guid nature. That's no' to say tha' she dinna expect things to be right, fer she do. But as Mr. MacDougal points out, as the duchess is usually in the right o' it, tha' is no' a difficult thing to take."

Rose smoothed the ribbon at her wrist before saying casually, "I suppose, working at Floors, you also know Lord Sinclair."

"Ye mean Lord Sin?" At Rose's surprised look, the maid blushed. "Dinna mind me, miss. Her grace calls him tha' and I forgot 'tis no' polite to use it in public. I'll do better aboot tha', I will."

"Oh, I don't mind." Rose picked up a comb and absently ran her finger along the ivory teeth. "He's quite a handsome man, isn't he?"

"Indeed he is. I've heard her grace says there's no handsomer man in all o' the kingdom. She laments tha' 'tis unfortunate he knows it."

"He is very aware of himself, though I wouldn't call him vain."

"Nay, miss, fer he dinna value tha' as some would. But he's no' blind to it, neither, and he's willin' to use it when it suits him. I suppose all men are tha' way, though, when ye think on it."

"He's different, though. I'm not sure how, but . . ." She shrugged.

Annie paused, her gaze finding Rose's in the mirror. "Och, miss, ye dinna fancy 'im, do ye?"

"No, no. Of course not!"

"Guid, fer I've heard some worryin' things aboot the man, I have. Aboot how many women he's chased and all sorts o' things."

Rose replaced the comb on the dresser. "I was just curious about him."

"I dinna blame ye fer tha'. Do yerself a favor, miss, and stay away from him. He's a known bounder, he is. Too handsome fer his own guid. I once't heard the duchess say he'd been running his own life since he was a lad of seventeen and tha' it ruined him. And he's far too many women runnin' after 'im to settle on jus' one."

"Oh? There none that he's more fond of than the others? No one special?" Rose found herself holding her breath as she asked the question.

"There is one I've heard aboot, a Lady Ross. But she is no' only older than he, but she's wed as well. They've been seein' each other on the side fer well o'er two years."

"Goodness. And Lord Ross doesn't mind?"

"He's a diplomat and is oot of the country a guid bit."

"Ah. Lord Sinclair must be deeply in love to continue with the relationship for so long." Rose's stomach felt odd, as if her toast wasn't sitting well. "Two years . . . that's something."

Annie laughed. "Lord, no. No' according to Lord Sin's—pardon me, miss, Lord Sinclair's valet, Mr. Dunn, who is as flash a cove as ever walked the earth. 'Tis naught but a flirtation."

"For two years?"

"I daresay her ladyship has been convenient, miss. Me mam, bless her soul, tol' me tha' was the worst thing ye could be to a man—convenient."

"I daresay that's true."

"Aye, I've heard the duchess say time an' again tha' no woman will e'er tell him no, which has ruined him fer the rest of the world."

Well, I'm not joining those hordes. She would be the one to say no, and she'd say it as many times as she had to, no matter how he made her feel whenever he was close.

"Of course, Lord Sin has no problem sayin' no t' others. The duchess is always invitin' him to visit, but he rarely comes. 'Tis odd he's here now." Annie shrugged. "But again, there's nothin' aboot this house party as is normal. Mr. MacDougal says in all his years workin' fer her grace, she has ne'er invited so many ancients to her house. We dinna know why—" Annie caught Rose's gaze in the mirror and gave an apologetic laugh. "Och, how I do go on. I was fergettin' me station."

"No. I was quite interested. I've sisters at home and it's nice to have a coze with a woman my own age."

Annie chuckled. "Ye willna find tha' among the other guests, will ye?"

"No, I won't." *Why did the duchess invite these guests, then? Did Sin have anything to do with that?*

Annie finished pinning Rose's hair and then plopped her hands on her hips and regarded it from several angles. "I think that'll keep yer hair in place, miss. Shake it once, though, t' be certain."

Rose shook her head vigorously, surprised when no strands fell free. "It stayed perfectly!"

Annie beamed as she returned the unused pins to the small waxed paper that had held them. "I've ne'er seen such thick hair. 'Tis lovely when 'tis down, but when ye try to pin it up, 'tis a tragedy awaitin' a stage."

Rose laughed and stood up, tied her scarf about her neck, and then tucked it in. "Annie, thank you. I don't know what I'd have done without you."

"There, miss. 'Tis me dooty." Annie opened the door. "Have a delightful ride."

"I shall," Rose said as she left.

Sin found his great-aunt standing under the portico, looking far younger than her seventy-plus years. Her pugs were romping across the smooth lawn, watched by two harried footmen.

He frowned at her morning gown. "You're not riding?"

"Not today, no. I've too much to do, getting things ready for the picnic."

"Let Charlotte do that for you. You love to ride."

"Perhaps next time. Besides, both Misses Stewart

are riding and their mother has charged me with seeing to their safety."

"Ah, you'd be stuck with the slowpokes, then."

"Sadly, yes." She glanced up at the sky. "Do you
think it's going to rain? Perhaps I should send some
umbrellas with one of the servants."

"If it rains, we'll just return here."

A groom came around the corner leading two very
sturdy-looking ponies.

The dogs barked and the footmen began to herd
them inside.

Staring at the ponies, Aunt Margaret didn't seem
to hear the commotion. "Good God. Who will be riding those? We normally only allow children on the
ponies."

"The Misses Stewart, I believe. I assure you the
ponies are well up to carrying the weight of their riders."

Another groom came around the corner of the
house, leading two horses notable for the amount of
gray about their noses. "And those are for Mr. Munro
and Lord Cameron?" she asked.

"The bay is Camelot and the black is called Chagrin. They're very well behaved."

"And almost old enough to be let out to pasture."

"Oh, they've a few good, slow rides left in them."

Aunt Margaret plopped her fists on her hips. "Sin,
have you been drinking?"

"Not yet. If you dislike my choices of mounts,
talk to Lady Charlotte. She was in total agreement

with me when we discussed it last night. I wished to ensure none of your guests would be injured, and with so many older and inexperienced riders, this made sense."

Another groom came around the corner, this time leading two prancing horses. One was a large, powerful-looking gelding, the other a smaller, sweet-stepping mare.

"And those are for you and Miss Balfour, I take it?" Aunt Margaret said drily.

"Both you and she seem to think she is quite the horsewoman."

"For her sake, I hope our assessment is correct."

The two Misses Stewart appeared in the doorway, Miss Isobel resplendent in blue, Miss Muriella in green. They preened a bit, so he supposed they were proud of the riding habits that were cut in a style more suited to younger women. The cut of their habits didn't concern him, but the fact that their necks and wrists dripped with heavy layers of lace that flapped in the wind did.

Sin saw his great-aunt staring at the lace and he said in a low voice, "Aren't you glad I didn't give them more restive mounts?"

"Lud, yes. Such silliness. If you can get them to agree to ride those demmed ponies, I'll be eternally grateful. Both Misses Stewart think they can ride, but they cannot." She turned and waved. "My dears!" she called. "Why don't you join us over here?"

The two women began to pick their way across the lawn toward them.

"Bloody hell, how tall are the heels on those boots?" Sin asked.

Aunt Margaret merely grimaced.

As the sisters arrived, Aunt Margaret smiled. "I was just telling Sin that I think the ponies might be better for this weather. Aren't they adorable?"

Miss Muriella beamed. "Ponies? I love ponies!"

But Miss Isobel was made of sterner stuff. "Won't they be shorter than the other horses? And slower, too?"

"They are shorter," Sin agreed, "but not necessarily slower. It's sometimes nice to ride at a pace that allows for discussion." He looked directly at Miss Isobel and said in a meaningful tone, "A nice, slow, steady pace."

An eager look crossed her face and she simpered. "Oh yes! A slow ride can be most enjoyable." She said in a lower, more meaningful voice, "I do love a *cozy* conversation."

Oblivious, Miss Muriella turned to Aunt Margaret. "Mama and Papa are in the sitting room. Mama said to tell you that as MacDougal has brought them some tea, they are quite comfortable there until the carriage is brought around."

"Excellent. It will be a little while, for I want to get you all off on your adventure first. One of the footmen will bring hot tea to you here, too, so make certain you avail yourselves of it. Oh, there he is." As the footman hurried over, balancing a tray with several steaming mugs, Aunt Margaret said, "There's Lord Cameron and Mr. Munro. Pray excuse me as I introduce them to their mounts."

Sin smiled as Aunt Margaret went to greet the two men who had just exited the castle via the terrace doors. Miss Isobel continued to chatter on about various rides she'd taken and sights she'd seen, her sister often chiming in.

They were all ready except for Rose. Should they send someone to her room to remind her of the time? Perhaps she'd overslept—

The front doors opened and Rose walked onto the portico, the tail of her skirt thrown over one arm, her hat perched at an audacious angle upon her head. She paused and drew on her gloves.

Sin wasn't prepared for the way his chest instantly tightened, his body awakening as if she'd touched him.

Her riding habit fit her perfectly, tight about her narrow waist and smooth over her small, rounded bosom, the skirts frothing over her hips to the ground. She wore a plain white scarf about her neck, neatly tucked into her riding coat. Her hair, pulled back from her face in a style as severe as her habit, emphasized her blue eyes and thick black lashes. With her hair confined, Sin noticed that Rose's eyebrows were delicate slashes that tilted up a bit at the ends, giving her a devilish look.

Miss Muriella giggled over her mug. "What sort of a riding habit is *that*?"

"I'm sure I don't know," Miss Isobel said, fingering the expensive lace at her wrists. "It's a bit plain, don't you think?"

"Very plain and rather boring." Miss Muriella's gaze darted to Sin. "Don't *you* think so, Lord Sinclair?"

"Actually, no, I don't. But what do I know of fashion?"

Miss Isobel eyed him up and down and said in a voice heavy with approval, "More than most men, I'd say."

Miss Muriella pursed her lips. "I wonder who will win today's challenge, you or Miss Rose? Of course *we* wagered on *you*, Lord Sinclair."

Miss Isobel nodded. "When will this race be held?"

"After we reach our picnic area," he lied.

Both of the women looked disappointed. "We'll have to wait that long?"

"I'm afraid so. We'll need to mark the course and set a judge at the finish." He turned to them. "I hate to leave you, but I promised Aunt Margaret that I'd see that Miss Balfour knows which is her horse."

Miss Isobel fluttered her lashes. "I'll see you on the trail."

"Of course." He bowed to them and left, crossing the lawn. His intentions today were simple: to get Rose away from prying eyes and tempt her with more kisses. There was no need to rush into this seduction;

everything pointed to his success. It would be foolish to ruin it with haste.

He reached Rose's side to find her staring at the ponies in surprise.

"Those are for the Misses Stewart," he told her.

"Ah. And those slugs?" She pointed to the older horses.

"For Mr. Munro and Lord Cameron."

She smiled. "So I get one of those, then." She nodded to the gelding and mare that were being walked by two grooms.

"The mare is yours," Sin said. "Lady Charlotte said she is one of Roxburghe's favorites."

"Roxburghe has excellent taste." She eyed the horses as if they were on an auction block. "Excellent shoulders. Nice hocks, too. I'd wager she's quick."

"Not as quick as my mount." He nodded toward the brute he'd chosen.

Rose looked at the horse critically. "He's a beauty, but don't be so certain he's faster. Size doesn't always guarantee performance."

His lips twitched. "If you say so. My aunt is gesturing that it's time we mounted. Come, I'll help you up." He walked her to her horse and, with a groom holding the bridle, Sin placed his hands about her waist and lifted her.

She was so small that he almost lifted her too high, throwing her into the saddle with a bit of a bump. "I'm sorry. Are you hurt?"

"From that? Heavens, no." She laughed down at him, her eyes sparkling. "However, your masterful performance was duly noted by the Misses Stewart. I believe they're waiting for you to assist them onto their horses, as well."

He turned and sure enough, both Misses Stewart had waved off the footmen and were standing by their ponies, looking at him expectantly.

Sin glanced about for the other gentlemen, but both Mr. Munro and Lord Cameron were already mounted.

He scowled up at Rose. "The least you can do is not look so pleased."

She gurgled with laughter, took the reins from the groom, and guided her horse to where the other riders were.

Sin had no choice but to assist both Misses Stewart onto their ponies, then he mounted his own steed.

"I believe you're all ready now," Aunt Margaret said from the front steps.

"Except that we don't know where we're going," Mr. Munro said, sitting upon his horse in a very uncomfortable manner. He looked a bit like a sack of flour stuffed into a too-tight riding coat.

"You're taking the river trail," Aunt Margaret said. "Simply follow the road to the river and go north about a mile, and then cross the bridge. The road will take you through a forest and then along the river. It's a very pretty ride and will lead you to the old castle ruin, where we'll meet you with a cold luncheon." She gestured toward the groom. "MacLure knows the way and he will ride with you."

Sin hadn't noticed the groom until then. The man was his height—about six foot two—but broader and built like a bear. His bent and broken nose proclaimed him to be a prizefighter.

The groom looked first at Rose, and then directly at Sin before he touched his hat as if in a salute. Sin cut a glance at his aunt just in time to see her gesturing at MacLure. On seeing Sin, she froze with such a hare-caught-by-a-hound look that he instantly understood. MacLure was their chaperone.

Damn it! *Aunt Margaret, what are you up to?* Sin sent her a look so she would know that he was aware of her machinations, which only made her smile.

Fuming, he turned his horse down the drive and set it to a smart trot. No groom would keep him away from Rose.

Seven

From the Diary of the Duchess of Roxburghe

If this were a chess game, I'd say "check."

Sin looked positively thunderous as he rode off this morning. He didn't like the idea of having a chaperone, which proves how much one was needed.

I do hope he doesn't forget his manners. But if he does, I'm certain MacLure will remind him of them.

Rose didn't enjoy the first hour of her ride, as the slow pace tried her patience. *I will gallop later*, she told herself over and over.

Her horse felt her impatience, too, and several times Rose had to rein the animal in when it tried to burst into a canter.

The ride was pleasant, the wind not too chilly, the views beautiful and peaceful, but the wide, smooth trail begged to be galloped upon. Rose wished she could distract herself by talking to her fellow guests, but unfortunately, Mr. Munro had attached himself to her side. For the next half hour, he kept up a nonstop soliloquy whereby he expounded upon his views on nature, nature's value, the overemphasis of nature in the education of the youth of today, and how dangerous nature could be if one didn't respect it.

The more he talked, the more the smooth path called to her. But there was no escape. The group rode two by two, so there was no chance of slipping past those in front of her.

She leaned a bit to one side so that she could see Sin at the head of their little retinue, riding a little in front of Miss Isobel Stewart's pony so as to make conversation impossible. As he had the tallest horse and she the smallest, they made a ridiculous pair. Behind them, Lord Cameron held forth on the importance of good port to a wide-eyed Miss Muriella, who looked up at the older man as if he were as wise as Solomon.

And behind them all rode the groom. Rose glanced back at him from time to time, but he merely smiled and touched his hat. *I wonder why he's with us. He's not leading us, carrying supplies, or offering assistance.* It was odd, to say the least.

As if realizing her interest had waned, Mr. Munro changed his topic to the taxation of properties, managing to hint at his annual worth and how many houses he owned without sounding too conceited. Rose thought that anyone who considered taxation a better topic than nature deserved to be shot.

After a while the sun managed to find a spot to peek from, and a gorgeous golden light shone down through the trees, dappling the green with its refreshing gleam.

It was torture. Rose had just decided that she would rather offend the entire party and go galloping wildly into the woods than listen to another hour of Mr. Munro, when Sin held up a hand.

The movement brought them all to a stop.

Sin looked over his shoulder, his expression serious. "Did you hear that?"

The group became silent.

"I think . . ." He tilted his head to one side as if to listen closer. "It sounded like a fox's cry. I hope it's not rabid. They can be very dangerous."

The Misses Stewart exchanged nervous glances, while Rose tugged off her gloves so that she could adjust her scarf where it had come loose.

"'Ere now, me lord," the groom said from where he'd pulled up behind the group. "Dinna be makin' the ladies nervous."

Sin looked surprised. "I don't want to alarm anyone, but I'm sure I heard the cry." He moved his horse to the side of the path and looked at the groom. "Come and see if you can hear it."

MacLure clucked his horse and threaded his way past Rose and on to the front of the group. He pulled even with Sin and drew up his horse.

They were silent as they sat, the horses occasionally puffing out a deep breath, or a bird tweeting overhead. Rose could hear the river faintly now.

Mr. Munro broke the silence with a nervous laugh. "Lord Sinclair, perhaps you only *think* you heard a fox cry."

"No, I'm sure I heard it." Sin turned his horse until it faced the others. "If we'll be quiet a bit more, I know you will all hear it, too."

They all sat silently, the Misses Stewart looking more and more put out as the horses shuffled. Even the groom began to look irritated.

Finally, Sin shrugged. "Perhaps it was just wounded and is now in its den."

Miss Isobel said with relief, "I daresay that's what happened."

The groom shot Sin a sullen look, but didn't say anything.

Sin's gaze moved past the group to Rose. "One moment more."

He rode his horse to where she sat, and then pulled his mount between her and the rest of the group. "Miss Balfour, you've dropped your glove."

Both of her gloves were still in her hand. *What is he do—*

"Allow me to get it for you," he said loudly. As he bent down, he said in a low tone, "Hold tight!"

She tightened her grip on the reins and frowned. What—

He slapped her horse on the rump. *"Hie!"*

The mare, all too ready for a run, bolted.

Rose's hat went tumbling, but she didn't care. *This* was riding! She bent low, the mare's mane whipping against her hands as the horse gathered herself into a full-out joyous gallop. She caught a flicker of something at the corner of her eye just before Sin pulled into view. Bent low over the neck of his horse, he flashed a grin.

Rose laughed as they thundered down the path, galloping neck and neck.

Sin's eyes were alight under the brim of his hat, which was firmly pressed onto his head. He grinned at her and gestured to their right, indicating a barely noticeable path that led off the main trail. Rose followed without hesitation.

This path was far narrower, with low-hanging branches and rocks protruding at unexpected places, making them slow to a trot. They turned a corner, and suddenly the river was beside them. The path widened a bit, the branches not so low.

The mare shook her head and blew through her nose, overjoyed at the ride. Rose felt the same exhilaration.

Sin must have also felt it, for when he glanced her way, his eyes were so bright they seemed golden. The entire moment was golden. Rose couldn't think of anywhere she'd rather be than here, riding down a forest path with Sin.

Then she caught herself. *He plans on seducing you,*

but first he must disarm you. His kindness in planning this escape is a mere ploy.

Instantly, the fun of the day seemed to fade. As if depressed at her thoughts, the sun slid once again behind a cloud.

She shouldn't be disappointed. Where Sin was concerned, she had no expectations. All she wanted was to get through her three weeks at her godmother's, secure her goodwill for her sisters, and then return to her home and horses. That was all she'd ever wanted.

Wasn't it?

Before she could examine her feelings more closely, Sin slowed his horse to a walk. She automatically did the same.

"We should walk the horses for a while. I don't want to tire them too much."

She nodded, trying not to get caught in her own thoughts. "I don't hear the others. I think we gave them the slip."

"I hope so. When we return, we'll tell them you allowed your reins to go slack and when I bent to retrieve your glove, your mount ran away with you." His smile was sardonic. "It should garner you a lot of sympathy."

"I beg your pardon, but I *never* let my reins go slack. Perhaps we should tell them that *you* couldn't control *your* mount."

His eyes narrowed, his smile fading. "I'm the one who came up with our escape plan."

"For which I'm thankful. If I'd had to listen to Munro

tell me how much he's hidden from the Crown in taxes for the last thirty years, I'd have burst into tears—"

"I knew you were bored."

"—*however*, at no time did I ask to be rescued. I would have thought of something myself, and it wouldn't have included me having to pretend to be a poor rider."

His jaw tightened. "And would your plan have included eluding our gaoler?"

They'd stopped riding and were now sitting in the middle of the trail. "Our gaoler? You mean MacLure, the groom?"

"Who else? My beloved great-aunt apparently decided we needed a chaperone, one on a fast enough mount that he could catch us should we flee."

"I wonder why she did that?" Rose said, surprised.

"Because she somehow knew I was planning on doing *this*." Sin bunched his hand in her scarf, tugged her close, and kissed her, his mouth insistent and demanding. Her heart pounded as he deepened the kiss, sending spirals of yearning through her.

She moaned and she could hear his ragged breath in the silence of the woods. She wanted this. Wanted him.

She leaned toward him, using her free hand to hold his arm to keep their horses even. *It's just a kiss, just a—*

His hand cupped her breast, warm and firm, his thumb finding her nipple through the layers of material.

Instantly, every thought incinerated and turned to ash.

All she could think about was the feel of his hand on her breast, of his hot mouth on hers, of the taste of him as he thrust his tongue between her lips, possessing her with a thoroughness that awoke her entire body. God, she wanted him to—

She opened her eyes. *What am I doing? This is exactly what he wants.* She pulled away, her breath harsh in the silence as she stared at him. Yet even as she pulled away, her heart pounded with a yearning so powerful that her chest ached from it. With every breath she took, she wanted to lean back toward him, to feel his hands on her once more, to— *No!*

She didn't realize she'd said the word aloud until she heard it ringing in the air.

Sin was staring at her, his breathing as ragged as her own, his hand still cupped about her breast. "Rose . . ." His voice was harsh, heated. He dropped his hand from her breast to her hip.

For a long moment they just stared at each other.

Rose collected herself first. "That was . . . You are an excellent kisser."

He let out a ragged breath. "Rose, I wasn't—"

"I know what you want." She gave him a tight smile. "You warned me."

He frowned and rubbed a hand over his face. As he did so, his horse shifted and they moved apart. "I planned to kiss you, but I didn't expect—"

"Please, you were quite clear about your intentions. And, although I enjoy kissing you, my answer is still no."

His jaw tightened and his brows lowered. "Perhaps I was overly hasty. You can't deny this—" He captured her elbow and leaned close to rub his cheek against hers, a faint sheen of stubble sending a tingle through her. "Come. One more kiss, and I won't ask for another all day. I promise."

She closed her eyes and gripped the reins until her fingers ached. The temptation to kiss him again was so strong that it was like an actual thing, a cherry tart or a thick slice of cake. All she had to do was turn her head and it would be hers.

It's only one more kiss. That's nothing.

But that wasn't true. He was taking her down a path where each kiss led her to more and more indiscretions.

Suddenly, she understood true temptation: how it could look so beguiling that you believed you had to have it or you'd be lost.

But there was one thing that was more important than getting another kiss, and that was to beat this man at his own game before he beat her. *Blast him for ruining this.*

Rose opened her eyes.

Sin felt the change in her before he saw it. What was so frustrating was that he'd allowed his eagerness to ruin his own plans. He'd had no intentions of kissing her while they were on horseback. He'd wanted a soft bed of grass by the river, or a mossy spot beneath a leafy tree. But she'd been practically glowing from their gallop, her eyes sparkling, her lips parted—and he'd forgotten everything but his desire to taste her.

And now Rose was no longer pliant and deliciously aroused in his arms. Instead she was looking at him as if she'd like to shove him off his horse and ride her mare back and forth over his dead body.

She gathered her reins and directed her horse a few paces farther down the path. The river bubbled to one side while a thick screen of trees lined the other. "We should rejoin the others." She sent him a hard look. "But I refuse to say I lost control of my horse."

Sin didn't know what to say. His body still thrummed from her kiss, his cock was rock hard and beginning to ache, and she sat on her mare looking at him so disdainfully that his ire rose in response. "I'm not going to tell them that it was *my* fault. We'll just have to let them guess what occurred."

Anger flashed in her fine eyes and her lips tightened. But just as quickly, she shrugged. "Perhaps we should see who can reach the others first? Let *that* person tell the tale."

"Are you challenging me to a race? A real one?"

"Yes." She laughed then, a soft, mocking laugh that held both a tantalizing sensual promise and the memory of instant humiliation. "Afraid, Lord Fin?"

His face burned. How *dare* she? "Done. We race until we reach the main trail."

She glanced at the path ahead. "It narrows where it turns. We can't ride abreast after that."

"Then the person who reaches the turn first will be the one to reach the trail. What do you say?"

She turned her gaze back to his. "Done."

The words were hardly past her lips when he whipped his horse around with a *"Hie!"*

She cried out in return and he immediately heard the thunder of her mare's hooves. Suddenly they were flying, racing without thought for safety or care, both overwhelmed by a desperate need to win.

Sin bent low over Croesus's head and guided the horse to the stream edge, where the firm, damp dirt would give the horse's hooves better purchase.

He let the big brute have his head. The horse loved to run: Sin could feel it in every stride as the corner came closer. Soon he'd turn onto the narrow path and block Rose's—

The mare's head suddenly appeared in his side vision. He glanced over and saw the horse running for all it was worth. Rose's mare was small but full of heart, and she was rapidly gaining.

Rose was bent close, her hat long gone, her hair free of pins and flying about her, the wild blue-black curls frothing like a mermaid's.

His horse stumbled a bit, and he turned back to guide it around the rocks that lined the side of the river. Rose pulled closer and they were soon neck and neck.

Rose shot him a furious glance, then bent lower to talk into her horse's ear. To Sin's astonishment, the little horse suddenly strained ahead and began to pull away, as if her hooves had been magically blessed.

Sin gritted his teeth. B'God, he'd show Rose that she wasn't the only one who could talk to a horse.

Sin bent over Croesus's shiny neck and said sternly, "Move yourself, man! We're about to be made fools by a pair of rambunctious females. If you lose this, you won't be able to lift your head in the stables without some mare snickering at you."

Croesus lowered his ears and strained forward, his hooves biting into the earth and churning up small hunks of mud and rock that flew wildly.

They were so close that Sin could almost lean to the side, slip an arm about Rose's waist, and lift her onto his own horse and hold her there while he—

Croesus stumbled, regained his footing . . . and then, with a loud whinny, tumbled head over heels into the river with his rider.

Icy water raced over Sin and he sputtered madly, fighting until his feet touched the river bottom. Coughing wildly, he stood, water cascading down his face. He wiped his hands over his eyes and saw Croesus standing to one side, shaking the water from his thick coat.

Yet it wasn't the humiliation of taking a tumble that pumped much-needed hot blood back into his brain, but the mocking laughter that filled the air.

Eight

From the Diary of the Duchess of Roxburghe
Men think they like to be challenged. The truth is,
they only like to be challenged if they win.

Growling, Sin headed for the riverbank. Croesus
followed his lead, tossing his head as if trying to shake
water from his ears.

Rose was still astride as she and that hell-horse
of hers laughed, bobbing its head up and down as if
in glee. Sin ground his teeth as he struggled to walk
onshore, his soaked clothing weighing him down, his
boots full with water. Thank God they were close to
the house; he'd freeze if he had to ride very far.

He grabbed his horse's reins and checked Croesus
for injuries, glad to see that the horse was fine. Assured
of this, he continued to where Rose sat on her mount.

Her curls fell about her face; her nose and cheeks
were rosy with the cold. It spurred his ire even more
that she could look so damn pretty while he was
soaked and furious.

She gulped back her laughter, trying to regain her composure. "That was quite a fall you took."

"I would advise you not to say another word."

She bit her lips but a giggle slipped through. "I'm fairly sure you made two somersaults before that spectacular splash. Were you ever in a traveling circus?"

"Not. Another. Word."

Rose now heard the voices of the other members of their party. "Oh dear. It looks as if they found our path and are coming to meet us." Her gaze swept over him. "Well, Sin, whose horse do you think they'll believe wasn't under control now?"

"You wouldn't dare." He sat and tugged off his boots, emptied the water, then stood and stomped them back on. He grimaced down at the squishy wetness, then his gaze locked on the damp earth by the river.

He frowned and stepped closer.

Rose watched him, still smiling. "What is it?" He looked so serious that some of her humor disappeared.

He didn't answer, but followed some sort of trail that she couldn't see from where she sat. He took a few steps down the river, and then a few more.

Finally, he lifted his head. "You and that hell-horse drove us into the river."

Rose shoved back a thick curl that was tickling her neck. "I might have edged you toward it." She'd thought that a rather clever ploy, until he went down. "But only close enough for the water to slow you down."

"That's cheating."

"No, it's not, it was strategy. You'd have done the same if you'd thought of it."

His jaw remained firm.

"Come, Sinclair. I didn't cause your horse to stumble."

He merely brushed his wet hair back from his face.

She sighed. "You're being dramatic again."

His mouth became a harsh line.

Perhaps she shouldn't have said that. "I didn't mean to cause you or Croesus any harm. But it was a fair race. You must admit that."

He crossed his arms over his chest.

Blast it, he's going to pout. "Look, I'm sorry." She guided her mare to Sin's side and then leaned over and held out her hand. "Truce? If we're fighting when the others arrive we'll have to explain things, and I don't think you want that, do you?"

He scowled up at her, his hair plastered back from his face. Just as she was about to withdraw her hand, he reached out and took it, his fingers cool against hers.

She gave him a huge grin. "A truce, then."

He didn't answer, staring at her hand, his thumb pressed against her wrist where it peeked from the sleeve of her riding coat. She swallowed against the waves of heat his touch caused.

A distant sound arose and she lifted her head. "The others are coming."

His gaze bored into hers. "I warned you what would happen if you laughed at my misfortune again."

With a quick, smooth yank, he jerked her from the horse and straight into his arms. Then he walked toward the river.

"Sin! What are you—"

He lifted her up, and with a great swing, tossed her in.

The icy water stole her breath. She gasped once, and then she was sinking. She held her breath as she fought to rise, but her floating skirts obscured her view and for a full second, the world was black. As her skirts finally began to sink, she could see the blue sky through the water above her, but her skirts were now sinking down, down, pulling her with them.

Strong arms encircled her and lifted her clear of the water. Sin's deep voice murmured, "Thus am I avenged. This time."

"Oh! Y-y-you blackguard!" she stuttered, shivering, trying to shove her tangled wet hair out of her face. "Y-y-you th-th-threw me—"

"Good God!" Mr. Munro's voice shrilled. "What happened to Miss Balfour?"

Sin grinned at her with intolerable smugness. "I believe the others have arrived. Shall I pretend to stumble and drop you again? Or will you explain to them how it was, indeed, you who lost control of your mount and landed us both in this wet place?"

"You w-w-wouldn't d-dare."

He lifted her up a few inches, his muscles bunching against her shoulder. She clawed desperately for purchase. "B-b-blast you, Sinclair, don't you d-d-dare d-d-dunk me again!"

"So you agree?"

"N-no." When his eyes narrowed, she hastily added in a low voice, her teeth chattering noisily, "B-but I w-won't tell them it was y-y-your fault, either. We'll j-just tell them the t-t-truth, that we were r-racing and we b-both ended up in the w-w-water."

Sin's gaze narrowed. "You're freezing. I think MacLure has a blanket rolled up behind his saddle." Sin turned and waded back to the riverbank.

She gave a sigh of relief. Finally, Sin was being reasonable. She glanced toward the riverbank, where their party was now assembled. MacLure, looking grim, had already dismounted and was headed their way, his boots splashing in the water.

"Good God," Miss Isobel said in a shocked tone. "What happened?"

Sin answered before Rose could. "Poor Miss Balfour's horse stumbled and she took a fall into the river."

She sent Sin a dagger glare. That wasn't what they'd agreed to say at all!

He ignored her and added, "Fortunately, I was close by and managed to rescue her from the icy waters."

Ignoring MacLure, who'd arrived at their side, Sin

carried her onto the shore, her skirts pouring water. Once there, with a great show of false solicitation, Sin set her on her feet, water sloshing from her boots. Had her skirts not been so waterlogged, she would have happily kicked him.

The others watched with varying degrees of sympathy, except the groom, who immediately began to help Rose wring the water from her skirts.

"Poor Miss Balfour," Miss Muriella said, who didn't look the least upset. "You are wet through and through. I fear both you and Lord Sinclair will freeze before we reach the house."

"How horrid!" Lord Cameron climbed carefully down from his mount. "Miss Balfour, please make use of my coat." He began to undo the many buttons on his long coat.

"Th-th-thank y-y-you." Rose shoved her hair to one side and wrung it out. Her clothing was so heavy that she could barely stand, parts of it dragging her down while other parts clung like a second skin. She couldn't think of a time when she'd been more uncomfortable.

"No, no, there's no need for you to take Cameron's coat." Mr. Munro now climbed down as well. "Miss Balfour, please take *my* coat instead. Cameron here has a weak heart and needs his wool or he'll catch the ague."

"Nonsense," Cameron returned, looking displeased and trying to unbutton his coat more quickly and merely fumbling more. "I'm as healthy as a horse. I will be fine without a coat while we return to the house and—"

Munro put his coat about Rose's shoulders, and Lord Cameron uttered an impolite curse.

Rose was instantly warmer, though she didn't want the weight he'd just added to her shoulders. "Th-thank you."

Miss Isobel glared from the back of her pony and said in a petty voice, "Well, I'm certainly glad that *I* didn't fall into the river. But then, *I* would never ride a horse in such a manner."

Rose could think of no reply that was polite enough to be uttered.

Cameron, meanwhile, eyed Munro with a sullen look. "I can see that I will have to call you out before this weekend is through."

"Name your seconds," Munro returned without pause. He reached out and grasped the lapels of his coat where they rested against Rose and tugged them together. "There, Miss Rose. All better now, I daresay. My, but you are a slight thing, aren't you? I'm not surprised you fell off your horse, for a puff of wind would send you toppling and—"

"Release her."

Sin's voice held such an edge that everyone turned to stare. His gaze was locked on Mr. Munro's hands, which were tightly clasped about the lapels of his own coat, his thumbs resting against Rose's wet chest.

Munro's face turned bright red, and he let go of Rose as if he'd burned his fingers. "Sin, for the love of— Good God, I didn't mean to—" He gulped and turned to her. "Miss Balfour, I'm most sorry for—"

"Mr. Munro, please," Rose said, weary and miserable. "You did me a very great favor by lending me your coat. No one thought you were being anything other than kind—did they, Lord Sinclair?"

Sin merely glowered.

Lord Cameron laughed uncertainly. "Munro, I'm certain you meant no harm."

"That's right," Miss Isobel spoke out, surprising everyone. "He was merely assisting Miss Balfour."

Mr. Munro shot her a thankful glance.

The groom brought Rose's mare. "Come, miss. We need to get ye home. Shall I help ye up? Those wet skirts will be difficult to manage."

"Yes, please," she said gratefully. It took several moments, but with MacLure's help, she got back on her horse, her skirts still dripping. Her mare wasn't happy about the added weight and showed it by attempting to buck, which frightened Miss Muriella into a little scream.

With a firm hand, Rose set her horse to rights, and then managed a smile for the small company. "I must get back to the house. Perhaps the rest of you should continue ahead to meet the duchess and carriages for the picnic?"

MacLure spoke up. "Pardon me, miss, but the

carriages willna have left the hoose yet. Her grace dinna wish fer Mr. and Mrs. Stewart to be oot in the elements in case it rained, and I heard her tell Mac-Dougal that they'd leave a wee bit later than planned. Ye'll ha' plenty of time to change into dry clothin', if ye're worried aboot missin' the picnic."

All Rose wanted was to soak in a tub of hot water until the steam and sweet-scented soap untangled her feelings. "Thank you. I believe that will be our best option."

Mr. Munro, who seemed suddenly to have realized how cold it was and was rubbing his arms, added his enthusiastic endorsement.

So with Munro leading the way and the groom hovering close to Rose, they turned back down the narrow path and returned to the castle.

Nine

From the Diary of the Duchess of Roxburghe
I have concluded that neither my nephew nor Miss Balfour is able to refuse any challenge made by the other, regardless of how reckless it may be.

I am beginning to worry that neither will survive what is either the oddest courtship known to man, or the most serious game of one-upmanship I've yet to witness.

Either way, the outcome is sure to be vastly entertaining.

From the sitting room windows, Margaret and Charlotte watched as their guests appeared on the road leading to the castle.

Charlotte's eyes widened. "Good God, is that— Oh dear! *Both* Lord Sinclair and Miss Balfour are soaked to the bone!"

"So I see."

"What has happened? The path goes near the river, but not that close."

Margaret pursed her lips. "If I had to venture a guess, I'd say it was the same circumstances as gave them both bruises in the library."

"You don't think he's *hurting* her, do you?"

"Lud, no! If I thought that, I would never allow him in my presence again. Besides, *both* of them seem bedraggled after their meetings. I suspect they are challenging each other and neither has the good sense to know when to back down."

Charlotte turned wide eyes on her friend. "That sounds dangerous."

"And I think it sounds very promising. Sin needs a woman who won't back down when he grows foolish."

"But someone could get hurt."

"Nonsense. We can rely upon them to also rescue each other."

"I hope so." Charlotte was silent a moment. "Who do you think won the race?"

"Judging from their expressions, neither."

"Blast!" Charlotte pulled a small piece of paper from her pocket, looked at it, and sighed. "I had five pounds on Miss Balfour. Do you think they might race again? Perhaps if we ask them—"

"Charlotte, look at them; they're both miserable. I forbid you, or anyone else, to ask them to restage that demmed race."

"Very well. I suppose you're right. Mr. Stewart was holding the wagers. I'll explain everything and have him return the funds." With a wistful sigh, she tucked the paper away. "Perhaps we need to find a way to get Sin and Miss Balfour to spend some time together, but not competing?"

"I don't care if they compete, but they must stop arguing and start *talking*. Oh, look! The party has reached the portico." She and Charlotte watched as several groomsmen rushed to meet the returning guests.

"Margaret, do you think Sin is truly interested in Miss Balfour?"

Margaret hesitated. "I don't know. I'm still not completely certain, but he was far too angry at not being able to find her after The Incident for there not to be something there. Not love, for they'd barely met. But whatever it was—or is—no woman has ever affected him so much."

"He was quite determined to find her."

"He was like a madman. So I suspected he would jump at the chance to finally confront her here; there's too much unfinished business between them."

Margaret watched as Sin stalked from his horse and glared at MacLure, who was reaching up to assist Rose from her horse. Though Margaret couldn't hear what was said, it was obvious that Sin won the encounter, for the groom stepped away and allowed Sin to assist Rose. The second her boots touched the flagstones, Rose grabbed her wet skirts, heaved them over one arm, and made her way to the door as fast as her weighted skirts would allow.

Sin watched her go, then spun on his heel and marched in the opposite direction.

Charlotte sighed. "Oh dear. It looks as if they're not even speaking. They really haven't talked much, have they? Just argued." She shook her head sadly. "It doesn't sound like love to me."

"I don't think it is—yet. They must get to know each other, and that is where they're failing. If only there was some way to get them on the same side instead of opposite sides . . ." Margaret's gaze was unfocused, her voice distant.

Charlotte waited.

After a few moments, the duchess smiled. "I have it! Charlotte, I've been thinking about this all wrong."

"How so?"

"They need a common enemy, someone they must overcome together." She caught Charlotte's confused expression. "Never mind. Give me the list of wagers."

"The list . . . but why?"

"Just give them to me and I'll explain later."

Charlotte removed the small paper and handed it to Margaret, who tucked it into her own pocket. The odd smile on her face gave Charlotte hope. "I know exactly what to do to keep our troublesome couple together," the duchess said. "What's the one thing Sin won't do?"

Charlotte pursed her lips. "The one thing you want him to?"

"Exactly. Now come." Margaret slipped her arm

through Charlotte's and they strolled toward the door. "We should see to our guests. Two of them have stomped off, but the others will be cold, tired, and ready for lunch."

The next afternoon, Sin came downstairs to find Rose standing in the foyer pulling off her gloves. Her back was to him, and she was humming a tune he didn't recognize.

It was the first time he'd seen her since their disastrous ride. Last night he'd eschewed dinner and had gone for a wild gallop through the chilly evening air, staying out until all of his aunt's guests had retired for the evening. The punishing ride had been good for him: his frustrations and soreness had disappeared with the exertion. The clarity of thought also served to remind him that he had a limited amount of time to seduce Rose, and he had to stop allowing his pride to get in the way.

This morning he'd awoken much refreshed and able to view his fight with Rose from a more honest perspective. He'd even managed to chuckle when he thought of how the two of them must have looked, slogging into the house soaked from head to toe.

As he'd dressed, he'd wondered if Rose was also seeing the humor in the situation, or if she was still angry. The urge to talk to her had made him hurry through his dressing and, leaving behind an astonished Dunn, Sin had made his way to the breakfast room.

The room had been empty except for Mr. and Mrs. Stewart, who had been eating dry toast and sipping tepid tea. Pushing aside a surprisingly sharp feeling of disappointment, Sin had decided to wait in case Rose joined them. He had asked MacDougal for a cup of coffee and *The Morning Post*. When they arrived, he'd taken the seat farthest from the Stewarts and had tried to read, but to no avail. The elderly couple had filled the silence by discussing the many foods they could no longer eat. They also expounded on their various health issues in graphic detail.

Sin had learned far more about the Stewarts than he'd wished to and he'd finally bestirred himself to ask a footman if Miss Balfour had already eaten. Upon being informed that she'd been the first one to breakfast hours ago, he'd made his excuses and escaped, cursing the waste of a good thirty minutes.

For the next hour, Sin had wandered through the house, and then out onto the grounds. He'd given up all hope of finding Rose and was climbing the stairs in search of MacDougal to enlist the butler's superior knowledge of the castle when the front door had opened and Rose had walked in.

She was wearing a dark green pelisse over a walking dress of pale yellow that made her look even younger than usual. She undid the ribbons on her straw bonnet and tugged it off, and then tried to smooth her riotous curls. The step he was standing on creaked, and she turned, her blue eyes wide. For a moment she stared at him, then her lashes dropped and she gave him a small, colorless smile. "Lord Sinclair. Good morning."

It was the exact greeting she would have given a stranger. His chest tightened. "Good morning." He came the rest of the way down the stairs. "I was looking for you."

Her gaze grew wary. "Oh?"

He smiled. "Have you thought about how we must have looked yesterday, trudging through the house in our dripping clothes?"

Her lips quirked, and the sparkle he liked returned to her eyes. "We must have looked ridiculous."

"Utterly." He leaned against the newel post at the bottom of the stairs as a footman approached to take her pelisse and bonnet.

They waited for him to leave before Sin asked, "I see you've been marching about the grounds."

"Ah, the mud on my boots gives me away."

"Not as much as the mud on your cheek."

Her hand flew to her cheek, but at his soft chuckle, she dropped her hand back to her side and gave him a curious look. "You are in a much better mood this morning."

"Yes. Enough so that I realize that I owe you an apology. I shouldn't have tossed you into the river."

"No, you shouldn't have. However . . . I did run your horse into the water—a little. So perhaps I deserved it."

"Perhaps we deserve each other." He realized that he wanted nothing more than to swing her into his arms and bury his face in her ruffled curls. "Where are the others this morning? I can find no one except Mr. and Mrs. Stewart."

"The gentlemen were walking up from the stable when I came past; I think they were looking at a horse Mr. Munro wishes to purchase from Roxburghe. Most of the women are gathering on the terrace for the archery contest."

He thought of how Miss Muriella could barely see across a room to identify her own sister, and how Lady Charlotte squinted whenever she looked across the dining room table. "That sounds dangerous."

"Only if you're a target."

"Are you skilled at archery?"

Her eyes sparkled. "Oh yes. Caith Manor is secluded, so we often shoot to while away the hours. I daresay I've drawn far more bows than you."

"So you think you can beat me?"

"Oh yes," she purred. "And with this hand." She held up her left hand.

The cheeky wench! Sin left his station by the post and captured her tormenting hand. "Rose, when will you accept that I will always win?" He pressed her fingers to his lips, his gaze locked with hers. *"Always."*

"Pah!" Her color high, she tugged her hand free. "I bested you yesterday."

"You *cheated.*"

"I had a *strategy*. A successful one, too," she said with a playful smile.

She looked at him through her lashes and his irritation faded away. "Stop trying to bamboozle me," he said, exasperated with himself. "You're not going to change my mind by trying to look innocent. I'm immune."

A gleam appeared in her eyes. "You didn't feel immune when you kissed me yesterday."

"Neither did you," he pointed out.

Her gaze narrowed. "In a direct contest, I wonder which of us could withstand the temptation of the other the longest?"

"That would be quite a contest." The idea of teasing her in such a way made his cock stir. He'd tease her until she panted for more, until she begged him to take her, and then he'd—

"You're breathing hard." She said it in the same tone that she might use to mention the weather or discuss a book she'd just read.

He found himself imagining how enjoyable it would be to shake her from her pragmatic self and awaken the bold, adventurous part of her that kept slipping through. "I'm doing far more than breathing hard. I'm imagining all of the things I'd like to do to you."

Her eyes widened. "Now? *Here?*" She gestured to the foyer around them. "But someone could come at any moment!"

"Which is half the fun, don't you think?"

Her mouth opened, and then closed, and then opened again. Her gaze flickered past him, to the steps and front door, and then back, but there was no fear in her gaze, only excitement. "Fun?" she asked. "Or is it madness?"

"Is there a difference?"

She started to answer, but then frowned. "Yes. There is a difference."

She looked sad, as if that thought were forced from her.

He slipped a finger under her chin and lifted her face so the morning sun shone directly on her. "It's hell being bound by propriety, isn't it?"

She managed a smile. "No. I'm just being silly. Sin, we can't do this—"

He took her hand and walked to the back hallway until they were tucked out of sight of the bright foyer. Once there, he turned to her. "Is this better?"

An odd light entered her eyes and he could almost feel the excitement building in her. She was coming alive, blooming before his very eyes. *She likes the excitement of the unknown as well as I do. We are alike in that, we two.*

"Shall we?" he asked. Without awaiting an answer, he stepped forward until he was almost toe-to-toe with her, then he captured her hand and placed her fingertips on his chest. "Can you feel that?"

Beneath his embroidered waistcoat was his cambric shirt, barely muffling the rapid beat of his heart. "Can you feel that?" he whispered. "Feel my blood thundering?"

Her eyes widened and she nodded.

"You do that to me." He lifted her hand and pressed his lips to her own tumultuous pulse, her skin warm beneath his lips. Their eyes locked as the air about them grew thick, and he slid his lips from her wrist to her palm, blowing gently as he did so.

She shivered and swayed toward him.

He dropped her hand and moved away.

Disappointment flickered over her face and he grinned. "Now we know who is less able to resist the other."

Rose's jaw firmed. "Do we?" To his surprise, she grabbed his hand and placed it at her throat. Her skin was warm and slightly damp from her recent exertions, her pulse fluttering wildly.

Her boldness held him in place. At the touch of her warm skin under his fingertips, he decided to show her how unaffected he was, and gently slid his hand over her shoulder to the back of her neck to draw a shiver.

She gasped and, with a shaky breath, pressed herself to him, which made his cock harden instantly. He slipped his hands about her waist and—

The sound of approaching footsteps made them part just as Miss Isobel appeared at the top of the stairs. She leaned over the banister.

Sin quickly stepped away from Rose and leaned against the opposite wall so that it appeared as if they were engaged in a desultory conversation, a proper amount of distance between them.

"Ah, Miss Balfour and Lord Sinclair!" She waved and then came down the steps to join them. "Good morning," she said, looking toward the drawing room doors. "Have either of you seen her grace this morning?"

"No . . ." Rose and Sin said at the same time.

Rose cleared her throat. "I haven't seen her grace since yesterday. She wasn't at breakfast this morning."

Miss Isobel frowned. "I wonder where she is? She graciously offered to bank—"

"Miss Isobel, there you are!" Aunt Margaret came out of the small salon just to Rose's left.

Sin belatedly realized that the doors, which were usually closed, had been wide open. *Damn it, had she been listening?* He wouldn't put it past her.

"Good morning, Miss Isobel," Aunt Margaret said.

Miss Isobel made a quick curtsy and then looked around the foyer. "Where are the pugs, your grace?"

"Charlotte made the error of putting large bows about their necks this morning, which looked lovely, but sent Weenie on a rampage. She hates ribbons and started quite a fuss. MacDougal removed what was left of the bows and took them all for a walk to settle them."

"Oh dear."

"Yes, Charlotte is very sorry for her behavior. By the way, after adding the wagers I received this morning, I must say that you seem heavily favored to win."

Miss Isobel beamed. "What a pleasant surprise."

"You are taking wagers?" Sin asked Aunt Margaret.

"Yes, on the archery contest we've planned for this afternoon."

"I'd heard about that." He turned to Rose. "I've half a mind to challenge you to an archery duel, Miss Balfour. I believe I could best you at that, too."

"Too?" Miss Isobel's gaze flickered between Rose and Sin. "In what other things have you bested Miss Balfour?"

"Getting soaked, for one." Aunt Margaret took Miss Isobel's arm and led her toward the small salon. "Sin, your tomfoolery will have to wait another day; the archery contest is for women only."

Sin frowned. "But I wish to shoot, too."

"The men are playing billiards," she said airily. "I believe the vicar is coming and has some special cigars. Mr. Stewart was quite ecstatic about them."

Sin tried not to glower, and failed. "And if I wish to participate anyway?"

"You can't. The rules and contestants have already been set, and people are placing their wagers. You and Miss Balfour already caused enough of a jangle when you didn't hold a proper race yesterday.

It took us an hour to return the funds for the wagers Mr. Stewart had collected, though we're still short ten pounds. I don't know what he could have done with it, but poor Mr. Munro accepted the loss with very good grace."

Miss Isobel nodded. "Her grace is now our banker."

"Yes, and I'm recording each wager, and keeping the money in a tin for safekeeping. Come, Miss Isobel!" The duchess tugged Miss Isobel into the salon and closed the doors firmly behind them.

"My," Rose said, "that was a bit odd."

"Yes, it was, even for Aunt Margaret." He looked at the closed doors. "I wonder what she's trying to do now. Or rather, what she's trying to get *me* to do."

Rose sent him a surprised look. "You think your aunt is attempting to manipulate you?"

"She never stops. The problem is more in deciphering her purpose, so I can thwart her."

Rose chuckled. "You and your aunt have a very interesting relationship."

"She tries to interfere, and I try to stop her. We've been having this dance since I first stepped into my father's shoes at seventeen."

The smile on Rose's face fled. "That's very young. What hap— I'm sorry, I shouldn't even ask."

He shrugged. "It happened a long time ago. My parents were killed in a carriage accident." He wasn't certain why he'd told her that; he could count on one hand the number of people he'd spoken to about his parents' deaths.

"I'm sorry. That must have been devastating. It's difficult to lose a parent."

There was something about the way she said it that gave him pause. His gaze narrowed on her and he noted the faint downward turn of her soft lips. It was only there for a second before she smiled politely, but it was enough. "You've lost a parent, too," he said.

"My mother died when I was eleven. Father threw himself into working on his greenhouses, which left me with most of her household duties and the care of my two younger sisters."

Just as I assumed the care of my two younger brothers when I was seventeen. He knew the weight of that simple sentence and he found himself regarding her in a new light. "That's a heavy burden for one so young."

"I suppose so, but it's never felt like it."

He eyed her for a long moment. "That explains quite a bit."

"Such as?"

"Such as why you're always ordering me around." It also explained why she flared to life when challenged. He'd been forced to grow up too quickly as well, thrust into a world filled with heavy responsibilities and cares. It had left him with an almost unquenchable thirst for excitement, one he recognized in Rose.

Sin suddenly realized that however he felt, Rose must feel it twice as strongly, as her childhood had been taken from her at an even younger age. At least he'd had a few years of joyful freedom before he'd been called back from school to step into his father's shoes. A pang of sympathy hit him, but he frowned and quickly shoved it away. Rose deserved a lot of things, but not pity. Never that. No, she deserved fun, excitement, and the freedom to enjoy it without feeling the pull of responsibility—all of the things she'd been denied in her childhood.

He could arrange for some of those things now. Those things wouldn't change the true circumstances of her life, but they could add a little spice to the thin gruel life had served her.

He grinned at her. "For the record, Balfour, not only do you attempt to order me around, but you're damned high-handed in the way you do it, too."

She bristled. "Well, you give quite as good as you get, so that sword cuts two ways."

"I'm sure it does," he agreed. "Now I know why you were in London with your aunt, and not a closer relative."

"Aunt Lettice is my father's oldest sister." Rose made a face. "She didn't relish bringing me out and only did so grudgingly. After our disaster at Lady MacAllister's, she's flatly refused to bring out either of my sisters, though she'd promised to do so."

"That's unfortunate."

"Yes. I feel very guilty about it and worry that they'll be stuck in the countryside, with no options for their futures."

She feels responsible for her sisters, much like I felt for my brothers. Until this moment, he'd never considered what made Rose who she was. Now he'd been given a glimpse and he found that he wanted to know more. "It's a pity you can't get my great-aunt to take your sisters under her wing. She likes nothing more than finding wives and husbands for unsuspecting unmarried people."

Her lips quirked. "I assume that you're speaking from experience."

"After I inherited my title, both my grandmother and Aunt Margaret made certain that neither I, nor my two brothers, had another day of peace."

Rose grinned and then gave the closed door an arch look. "If the duchess is as scheming as you say, then we should see what she's doing."

"Yes, there's no reason to let her weave her webs in peace." Sin opened the door and then bowed. "After you."

"Thank you." Rose entered the parlor and Sin followed.

Ten

From the Diary of the Duchess of Roxburghe
There are times when I'm struck by my own bril-
liance. Today was one of those times.

The small parlor was beautiful. The walls were covered
with colorful Chinese paper depicting a fanciful garden
scene of flowers. Thick rose and gold rugs covered the
floor, while a grouping of gold, feather-stuffed settees
flanked a marble fireplace. Chairs and small tables
were artfully placed to encourage conversation.

Lady Charlotte was seated at a small desk before
a broad set of windows. Aunt Margaret, Miss Isobel,
and Lady McFarlane were all clustered there, holding
various amounts of money, eager expressions on their
faces. They briefly looked up as Rose and Sin entered,
and Aunt Margaret's gaze narrowed before she turned
back to Lady Charlotte.

"Two shillings for making a bull's-eye," Miss Isobel said.

"Which contestant?" Lady Charlotte asked.

"Myself."

Lady Charlotte had started to hold out her hand for the coins, but stopped and looked up at Aunt Margaret. "Can she set a wager on herself?"

"I can bet *for* myself, but not against," Miss Isobel said impatiently. "Isn't that right, your grace?"

Margaret nodded with authority as if she'd been banker in numerous other gambling enterprises. "Of course."

"Very well." Lady Charlotte took Miss Isobel's coins, counted them, stored them in a small tin box at her elbow, and then dipped her pin into an inkwell and made a mark in a large ledger. "There. You're in the book."

"What book?" Sin asked.

Aunt Margaret frowned. "The Roxburghe Betting Book."

"I've never heard of it."

"If you visited more often, there would be fewer surprises."

Charlotte patted the book with visible enthusiasm. "It's leather, just like the one at White's gentlemen's club." At Sin's astonished look she added, "Or so I've heard."

"Hmm." *What is Aunt Margaret into now?*

Lady McFarlane leaned on her cane to place a dirty shilling and a bent penny on the desk beside the book. "I'll put all of my money on dear Miss Muriella."

Lady Charlotte made a show of counting the money, and then stored it in the tin box.

She started to enter the bet in the book, but Miss Isobel held up a hand. "Lady Charlotte, wait a moment. Lady McFarlane, I hate to see you lose your money."

"I'm not going to lose it; I'm going to double it. The odds are two-to-one."

"They're that high because my sister isn't very good. We often have tournaments at our home and the poor dear isn't at fault, of course, but she can't see very well and her aim is—"

"Ha! Trying to talk me out of my wager, are you?" Lady McFarlane waved a bony finger at Miss Isobel. "It won't work. I'm rather good at wagers. I won two pounds just last month from Lord Poole. Lady Charlotte, please record my wager." She gripped her cane and started hobbling toward the door. "I have my own reasons for wagering on Miss Muriella."

Looking injured, Miss Isobel said, "Fine. I just thought you should know that she can barely see across a room, much less a target set at a distance."

"I know what she can and can't do, blast it." Lady McFarlane paused in the doorway. "Now, if you'll excuse me, I wish to claim a seat in the pavilion before the festivities begin." With that, she hobbled out.

"I should get ready, too," Miss Isobel said. "Thank you both for keeping track of our wagers."

"It's my pleasure," Aunt Margaret said, and Sin was certain it was. No one loved being the center of attention more than his aunt.

Miss Isobel bobbed a curtsy and started to leave, though she paused before Rose. "Miss Balfour, of all those in the contest, your skills are the least known. Do you often shoot?"

"When time permits," Rose said in a demure voice that anyone who knew her would realize was a complete sham.

Miss Isobel nodded. "We'll see, then."

"Oh yes," Rose agreed.

Miss Isobel smiled, her expression one of polite disbelief, though she continued to question Rose about her experience, while Rose easily sidestepped each question with a vague answer.

Charlotte closed the book and stood.

"Hold," Sin said, coming to the desk. "I wish to place a wager."

Aunt Margaret frowned. "On whom?"

"Rose."

Aunt Margaret hesitated. "Do you think that's wise? You and Miss Balfour have drawn enough attention as it is. People will notice that you've placed a wager on her."

Lady Charlotte nodded. "They might talk." She looked around the room and then leaned forward to say in a loud whisper, "Some might think you'd bribed the gel to toss the match."

"I've never heard anything so ridiculous in my life," Sin said.

"It happens," Lady Charlotte said.

"Frequently," Aunt Margaret agreed.

"You two are incorrigible," Sin muttered.

"And then there was that little scene you and Miss Balfour played out in the hallway off the foyer, my dear," Aunt Margaret said. "You must be more circumspect."

He stiffened. She'd overheard that, had she? Damn it! He should have been more cautious. Though he wished to seduce Rose, he had no desire to entrap either of them into anything more than an enjoyable seduction. And all of the joy and unfettered amusement of it would be forever marred if he and Rose were caught in flagrante delicto and then weighted down with yet more responsibilities than life had already given them.

"And," Aunt Margaret continued, "you can start keeping the gossips at bay by not placing wagers on her, which will only set people's tongues to wagging."

Lady Charlotte nodded. "People will talk even more."

"What if I only put a *very* small wager on her?" He pulled out some folded bills and placed them beside the closed book. "Ten pounds on Rose—"

"*Ten pounds?*" Lady Charlotte's eyes couldn't get any wider.

"After the debacle with Mr. Stewart, we're only accepting shilling wagers." Aunt Margaret shot a look toward Rose and Miss Isobel, then she leaned forward and said, "And please think this through."

"If it helps make things seem less obvious, then I'll

place a wager on every woman in the contest. Then no one will think anything of the one I place on Miss Balfour."

Lord Cameron stuck his head in the room. "Lady Charlotte, did you record my wager on Miss Isobel?"

Charlotte picked up the tin and rattled it. "It's already recorded in the book."

He beamed. "Thank you." He caught sight of Miss Isobel and Rose standing off to the side and he flushed. "Sorry, Miss Balfour. I didn't see you or Miss Stewart." He bowed. "I wish you *both* good luck in the contest, of course."

"Of course." Miss Isobel smiled smugly. "Thank you for the wager. I'll do my utmost to see that you get a handsome return."

"I'm certain you will, Miss Stewart." He offered a gallant bow and then left.

Before Sin could press his case, Aunt Margaret said, "Lady Charlotte and I must get ready for the contest now." She looked at Rose and Miss Isobel and called out, "As should the two of you."

"It is getting late, isn't it?" Miss Isobel bade Rose good-bye and hurried out the door.

Charlotte gathered the huge leather book and the tin box and walked to the door with the duchess, who paused to look back at Rose.

"Miss Balfour, aren't you coming?"

"Yes, but I need to put on some walking shoes before the contest. I also wish to have a word with

Lord Sinclair. We will leave the doors open for propriety's sake."

Aunt Margaret sighed. "Fine." She glanced at her nephew. "Don't keep Miss Balfour long." With a hard glance at them both, she left, Lady Charlotte trailing behind.

Sin leaned against the desk and crossed his arms over his broad chest. "So, Miss Balfour, what did you wish to speak to me about?"

Rose's mouth thinned. "The duchess is being very unfair in not allowing you to wager, as it appears that everyone else can."

"That surprised me, too. She's trying to accomplish something with it, I just don't know what."

"Then let us make our own wager. We will have our private archery contest once the women have finished."

He smiled. "You really believe you can best me?"

"Absolutely."

His brows lifted. "That's a rather bold statement."

"Perhaps I am a bold woman." He looked surprised, and she didn't blame him. Until she'd come to Floors Castle, she'd never before realized how bold she could be. When she was home, she was in charge of so many things—dinners and the household, managing their meager finances, and trying to purchase the right horses to breed for income once their current jointure ran out. But at Floors, her only responsibility was to take care of herself, and she found the freedom exhilarating.

She was here for only a few short weeks and then she'd return home, back to her old life and cares. If she didn't take advantage of this time, savor the freedom she did have, would she ever have the chance again?

Suddenly energized, she marched to the desk Aunt Charlotte had just vacated. "We'll write it down, too, so that there are no misunderstandings." She pulled a scrap of foolscap from a drawer and opened the ink-well. "Her grace had the contest prepared with three rings and a bull's-eye. If you hit outside the rings, you get no points. Inside the first ring you get five points. Then ten for the second ring, fifteen for the inner ring, and twenty-five for the bull's-eye."

"Simple. I like that. So whoever has the most points wins?"

That seemed fair. She wrote it down and then looked at her paper. "And what will our wager be? Ten shillings? Twenty?"

"Oh no, my lovely Rose." His voice had lowered to a purr. "We will wager something more . . . personal."

She put the pen down, her pulse racing. "That sounds intriguing." And oh, how she longed to accept. But did she dare? She'd come to Floors Castle for her sisters' sake, yet she kept getting distracted by Sin's presence. She thought of the duchess's stern expression before leaving the room and sighed. "No. I would like to make a more exciting wager, but I can't."

"Why not?"

"I came to Floors with the hope that your godmother might invite my sisters to her amusements, so that they could meet a better quality of suitor. I'd be selfish to ruin that for them. I've already ruined so much for them with my rash conduct before; I cannot be rash again." She fidgeted with the pen, tapping it against the inkwell. "For the record, living with such a trussed-up sense of propriety is a true pain."

"It chafes your fair skin, does it?"

"Worse than wool. But it's how society works. No one said it was fair."

"No, it's not." He regarded her through half-closed eyes as if he were seeing past her.

She dipped her pen into the inkwell. "About our wager, then. Since we're boring old proper sorts, shall we say a shilling per point?"

"No. I'll not accept such a tame wager from you."

"Then you'll not bet." Her commonsense voice was back in place.

Disappointed, he frowned. "It's not fair that you have to follow propriety when it's never done a damn thing for you."

A faint smile touched Rose's lips. "If propriety will give my sisters successful marriages, I'll forever bow in its direction."

"You and I are too much alike to take such a tame road."

She gave a little laugh. "I wish that were true, but I have to do what's best for my sisters." She tilted her head to one side, a thoughtful look on her face. "I wonder why her grace invited me. I'm enjoying myself, of course, but I rarely hear from her and . . ." Rose shrugged. "Whatever the reason, it was very kind of her."

Kindness? Or something more? There was no telling what schemes were floating in Aunt Margaret's head. But then, he'd been the one to insist on inviting Rose. He frowned, thinking back to the letter he'd received from his aunt. He hadn't thought of it before, but why had she bothered to list her so-called "favorite goddaughters" unless she wanted him to know those names, too? She'd known he'd searched for Rose all of those years ago—he'd made no secret of it. Could it be that she'd read something into that search?

He frowned. *Bloody hell, she's done it again.*

"If you don't wish to wager, just say so," Rose said, and he realized he'd been scowling.

"I'm sorry. I was thinking of something else." *Like ways to murder my meddling great-aunt.* "If you're so concerned about your reputation, then we'll put that in the wager as well. That it is to be paid in private, and only if it's completely and utterly safe."

"I suppose we could do that . . ."

He could tell by her husky voice that she was tempted. "Maybe you'd rather wager on something easier than archery?"

"Archery is fine. I'm also very good at bocce ball, pall-mall, and, if I must and it's raining, marbles."

He placed his hands flat on the desk and leaned

forward. "Then make a wager, Rose. A real one. Live a little."

Her eyes lit with excitement. "We'd be very cautious?"

"Very."

"And no one would know?"

"Never. I've no more wish to get caught doing something improper than you, for I've no wish to marry."

She looked horrified. "Lud, *no*."

Torn between insult and amusement, he said, "Good. I feel the same. Shall we wager?"

"Very well. What do you suggest?"

"A touch. One for every point I win by."

"What kind of a touch?"

"Any kind I wish. Any place I wish."

Her startled gaze locked with his and he wondered if she'd refuse. Instead, she said in a challenging voice, "I may win."

"Then you may touch *me*."

"Any place?"

"And for however long you wish."

She looked at the foolscap and bit her lip.

His groin tightened at the sight of her white, even teeth worrying her plump lip. Never had he wanted a woman like he wanted her.

She let her breath out in a whoosh. "That sounds fair." She picked up the pen. "In private. Where no one could see or catch us."

"Of course."

She toyed with the pen. "Then there will be *no* risks."

"None."

A smile slipped over her face. "Very well." She dipped the pen into the inkwell and wrote out their wager. When she finished, she signed it, and then slid it across the desk to him.

Sin signed it as well, his body quickening at the thought of winning . . . or losing. After he handed the note back to her, she sanded it, folded it in half, and then stood, tucking the note into her pocket. "Done. I must go and shoot in the first match. Will you be joining the others to watch the other matches afterward?"

He bowed. "Of course."

"Then I shall change." She headed for the door, calling over her shoulder, "I hope you don't mind losing, Sin. For you will."

But she was wrong. He'd already won, and at the end of this contest was the most intriguing prize of all—Rose.

Grinning, he waited until he could no longer hear her footsteps and then he left, whistling.

Eleven

From the Diary of the Duchess of Roxburghe
Goodness, what a fracas! There were arrows and
fire and blood and, lud, I don't know what else.
I don't know when I was ever more entertained.
I shall have to plan more archery events for my
parties.

Sin stood on the terrace and watched an array of
footmen place bow stands hung with colorful quivers
at the shooting area twenty paces from the targets,
which gleamed with fresh red paint. Each bow stand
held arrows painted a different color—either gold,
silver, or bronze—all of them twinkling brightly in the
afternoon sun. *Aunt Margaret is certainly making this
dramatic.*

As if in answer to his thought, two footmen
appeared carrying large rolls of brightly colored ribbon, which they tied to the corners of the viewing
pavilion. The wind instantly caught them and made
them dance about, adding a festive air, and mir-

roring the colorful cushions placed upon the white lounging chaises that sat in a line beneath the white tent. Aunt Margaret, Lady McFarlane, Miss Fraser, and Mrs. Stewart were already reclining on chaises while a footman served them iced lemonade and grapes. "Like bloody Romans ready to watch the Christians get eaten by lions," Sin murmured, shaking his head.

"Ah, Sinclair!" Mr. Munro came up to him, huffing from his stroll across the lawn. "Lady Charlotte just decided to join the contest, which should be quite amusing."

"So there will be four participants, then."

"Just enough for a proper match. I'm about to join the other men in the billiards room. Care to join us?"

"Perhaps."

Noting that Sin was watching the activity at the archery area, Munro added, "There's a good view of the women from the billiards room, if you're interested in seeing their little competition."

Sin doubted that there would be anything "little" about a competition that included both Rose and Miss Isobel, who were out on the archery course eyeing each other with hostility. *I might as well pass the time waiting for the tournament between Rose and me by drinking a glass of port. That's far better than waiting here in the sun.* Sin turned to Munro. "The billiards room it will be."

"Excellent!"

"I'll join you in a few moments. I just thought of something I should tell Miss Balfour."

"Ah. Giving her a hint or two, are you? Lord Cameron was doing the same for Miss Isobel earlier, so it's only fair that someone give some assistance to the other contestants."

Munro turned a thoughtful gaze toward Rose, who was now regarding her arrows, which had been painted a garish bronze, with distaste. "Perhaps I should give her a hint or two, as well. I haven't shot an arrow in years, but I used to be quite good at it."

Sin doubted that. "You are welcome to advise Miss Balfour in my place. I was only doing so in order to appease my aunt, even though I expressly told her I'd rather be shot in the foot with a blunderbuss."

Munro looked amazed. "You don't wish to advise Miss Balfour? Why not? I'd jump at the chance, myself."

"Because I know exactly what will happen if she doesn't listen to what I tell her—which she won't—and instead does what she wishes."

"Ah. You think that if she loses, she'll blame whoever gives her advice beforehand."

"I *know* that's how it will be and she'll be damned angry about it, too. And so I told my aunt, but she could care less whether Miss Balfour speaks to me for the rest of our visit."

Munro smacked Sin on the shoulder. "You're on your own then, lad. Just don't be too late or the port will be gone." Munro hurried on his way, obviously happy to have escaped a potential pitfall.

Sin crossed the lawn toward Rose. Off to one side stood Lady Charlotte and the two Misses Stewart, all of them drawing their bows, though with varying degrees of proficiency.

As Sin approached Rose, she touched the tip of an arrow and then winced and sucked on her pricked finger. The wind ruffled the bow on her small capote and tugged at the dark curls that fell beneath it.

He came to a complete standstill, noting how her plump lips curved around her finger. *Damn. I'd like to see her try that on my—*

He shook off the image that flew through his head. He was as randy as a stallion, and it was all the fault of the winsome woman standing before him.

Sin had always been attracted to voluptuous women, the sort who never allowed one to forget they were just that—women. And yet, for all of Rose's slenderness and lack of curves, he'd never been more aware of any woman. *How does she appear so feminine without employing womanly wiles? She doesn't flirt, hasn't once given a silly giggle or pretended to drop her handkerchief in an effort to lean her breasts against my arm . . . and yet I cannot stop thinking of her. Perhaps she's just naturally sensual? A woman who's had the blessing of experience and yet manages to exude an innocent-seeming sensuality. Whatever it is, it works.*

At that moment, Rose turned to return the arrow to

the quiver. As she did so, she looked up and their eyes met. Surprise flickered through her gaze, followed swiftly by a smile. She pointed to the quiver and called out, "What do you think?"

He closed the distance between them and eyed the painted arrows. "Her grace has made a spectacle of your contest, I see."

"On her grace's orders, the footmen tried to affix ribbons on our bows. No one could have made a decent shot with those ribbons flapping about, yet it still took Miss Isobel ten minutes to convince her grace that it was a bad idea."

On hearing her name, Miss Isobel left Lady Charlotte and Miss Muriella and came forward, a superior smile on her angular face. "Despite its decorative appearance, I'm quite happy with the tension on my bow. Are you satisfied, Miss Balfour?"

Rose nodded. "The bow is fine. I'm not so certain about the arrows. The tips are sharp, but the paint . . ." She curled her nose.

Miss Muriella and Lady Charlotte joined them. "I like the silver arrows," Lady Charlotte said.

"Me, too." Miss Muriella drew her bow and struck a pose much like those seen in thousands of fountains and gardens across Scotland, the wind ruffling her gown about her plump ankles as she said with genuine enthusiasm, "Behold! I am Diana, goddess of the hunt!"

Then her fingers slipped and she accidentally let go of the wrong side of the bow. The entire thing seemed to pounce on her, tangling over her head as she screeched.

A footman hurried forward to help Miss Muriella free and Rose sent a laughing look Sin's way, which made him smile in return. *God, she is lovely.*

The thought caught him by surprise. She *was* lovely when she smiled and when she talked about how much she loved to ride and when—

"Och, Lord Sinclair, there ye be." MacDougal bowed as Sin turned to face him. "'Tis a lovely day for some billiards, is it not, me lord?" There was no missing the note of censure in the old man's voice.

Sin gifted the butler with a cynical smile. "I take it that her grace sent you."

MacDougal sent a quick glance at the pavilion and then leaned forward to say in a low voice, "Her grace is in a mite o' a taking tha' ye're here. She thinks ye'll be a distraction to the competition."

He'd have his time with Rose later. *And oh, how well I'll use it, too.*

He turned to MacDougal. "Certainly." He walked beside the butler to the terrace doors. "I hope you're prepared for the tournament."

MacDougal's expression turned gloomy and he said in a voice tinged with long suffering, "As best we can, me lord. We've locked the shutters on the lower floor to protect the windows, and have the poor pugs safely tucked awa' in the stable. There's no' more to be done except hide."

Sin chuckled. "Perhaps it's not a bad thing to be in the billiards room, after all."

"If I thought her grace wouldna notice, tha' is where I'd be, too," the butler said fervently.

Laughing, Sin left. In the billiards room he was met by a cloud of cigar smoke and the convivial greetings of his well-satisfied fellow guests. In no time at all, he was afforded the amusement of watching the three elderly men halfheartedly hitting billiards while telling lies about their sporting abilities.

Sin took his glass of Scotch to an alcove of windows directly across from the archery contest. He pushed the curtain back and leaned against the window frame. Below, a footman seemed to be explaining the complexities of archery to Miss Muriella, who looked confused and kept interrupting him to ask questions. Off to the side, Miss Isobel was practice-aiming to decide which fit her better, a tall green- and gold-striped bow or a smaller blue one.

Lady Charlotte was there, too, looking like a demonic cherub with her plump cheeks and her quiver of glittering arrows adorned with a knitted gold cover.

But it was Rose who caught Sin's eye and kept it. While the other three women wore bonnets to keep the sun off their faces, Rose's small lace-trimmed capote did little to keep her nose from freckling. However, the shell-like hat framed her face and held back her curls, and the small brim wouldn't get in her way when she drew her bow. *Well done, Rose.*

Sin watched as Rose lifted her face toward the wind that rustled across the grass, teasing the hems of the ladies' skirts and trying to lift hats from heads. Was she wondering how it would affect her shots? A footman paused beside Rose and asked a question. She answered and he bowed and moved on.

Sin unlatched the window and raised it a few inches, and found that he could hear quite clearly. He pulled a chair over to the window and sat down.

"Dear me," Lady Charlotte said as she squinted across the lawn. "Where's the target?"

Rose looked at the large wooden target sporting a painted red square over a purple background. "It's in the center. Can't you see it?"

The older woman bent forward at the waist, her eyes squinted almost shut. "I think I . . . ah! There it is." She pointed to the large fountain close to the house.

Miss Muriella tittered. "That's the fountain." She took Lady Charlotte's arm, and repositioned her a quarter turn away from the fountain. "That's the target."

Sin heard Rose mutter, "Oh dear."

Miss Muriella had turned Lady Charlotte toward the vicar's buggy, which was tied up by the door, waiting for a groom to drive it around to the stable.

A footman gave a startled exclamation and hurried to show the target to Lady Charlotte.

Sin stifled a laugh.

Aunt Margaret clapped her hands. "Ladies! It's time to begin! Lady Charlotte will shoot first."

And so it began. As the shooting commenced, arrows rained into the nearby woods. Some hit the ground. One or two went almost straight in the air. Another plunged into a closed shutter. One hit the fountain, and one embedded itself in Aunt Margaret's tent.

Sin didn't know when he'd ever been so entertained. His laughter drew the other men to the windows, and soon they were watching the contest, too, port and cigars forgotten.

By the end of the third round, only five arrows had made it to the target, and three of them were Rose's.

Lady Charlotte stepped forward to take her turn, but just then there was a loud bang, followed by a shout, and then a flurry of fur bounded across the lawn.

The Roxburghe pugs were on the loose.

A footman holding a tray of strawberries tripped over a small brown pug. His tray flew into the air and landed on a large bowl of jam, splattering those sitting under the tent, while the strawberries rained upon Mrs. Stewart, who futilely batted at them with her fan. Another footman, distracted by the fall of the first footman, tripped over the end of Lady McFarlane's chaise, hit the corner of the serving table, and knocked over a small burner used to heat the teapot. The resultant flames caused additional mayhem, until her grace had the presence of mind to throw her wool shawl over the burning tablecloth and put out the fire.

Meanwhile, two pugs had found the ribbons that wafted from one of the tent poles and had begun a no-holds-barred tug-of-war. Yet another pug, growling as if ready to kill, chased a screeching housemaid around the fountain.

"Good God," Lord Cameron said, laughing as he pulled a chair next to Sin. "It's madness!"

The pugs tugging on the ribbons suddenly began to pull in the same direction and, with a spectacular whoosh, the entire tent collapsed.

Startled, Lady Charlotte released her arrow up into the air, and it landed in a small thicket near the lake.

Munro, holding his sides, wiped his eyes with the back of one hand. "That was the best entertainment I've had in some time!" He chuckled for some more moments, regaining control enough to say, with a quiver in his voice, "I hope no one was hurt."

Mr. Stewart, whose wife was still struggling to free herself from the tent, puffed his cigar. "None of the poles are even close to where they were sitting."

"Should we go down and help?" Lord Cameron asked, leaning forward to better see the commotion.

"No," Mr. Stewart said flatly. "MacDougal is already helping the ladies out and they seem fine."

MacDougal and his legion of footmen had indeed

raced to assist her grace and her guests from the collapsed tent. The duchess was the first to appear and, except for her temper, she seemed none the worse for wear. She'd miraculously kept her wig upon her head, too, a feat that impressed Mr. Stewart so much that he mentioned it more than once as the duchess and her newly rescued pets gathered on the lawn.

Soon everyone was freed from the tent and Mac-Dougal escorted them all to the terrace, where a hurried tea had just been placed for their delectation.

"I suppose now Miss Balfour will be glad of the advice you gave her before the contest," Munro told Sin. "I wish I'd taken the time to offer my advice, too."

"I doubt it," Sin returned. "They didn't get to play an entire round, so no one won."

Mr. Munro nodded but didn't look convinced. Indeed, his expression bordered on gloomy as he watched the scene outside slowly return to rights, his gaze following Rose as she sat next to Mrs. Stewart on the terrace.

MacDougal set the legion of staff to collect the pugs, carry the chaises back into the house, and find missing arrows. Two footmen folded up the tent with its colorful ribbons, while two more removed the target and bow stands. The archery tournament was over.

As the equipment disappeared, so did Sin's amusement. Damn it, now he'd have to ask MacDougal to set the archery course back up. He looked around at the group of men who were gossiping around him, and then his gaze flickered to the gathering on the terrace. Perhaps now wasn't the best time for their contest, anyway.

With a tight smile, he made his excuses to the other gentlemen and left.

Twelve

From the Diary of the Duchess of Roxburghe
Lord Munro has been very useful. All it took was
a small hint—Charlotte is to be commended for
orchestrating it—and he began his pursuit of Miss
Balfour in earnest.

I expected Sin to take this in very bad part, but
he seems more upset over the weather than over
Munro's constant presence.

I vow, should I live to be a hundred, I'll never
completely understand that man.

"Miss Balfour?"

The voice seemed to come from a very distant
place, which she rather liked. She snuggled deeper
into her pillow.

"Miss Balfour?" The voice was more insistent now.
She scowled. Couldn't they see she was asleep?

"Miss Balfour!"

She jolted upright and found herself staring into

Mr. Munro's beaming face. She threw her hands over her eyes and rubbed them.

"Sorry to wake you," he said, "but you fell asleep."

Blast, this isn't a dream. She dropped her hands to her lap and looked around, trying to regain her bearings. She was slumped in the corner of the settee in the small salon, while a light rain tapped upon the windows.

Lady Charlotte sat in the chair nearby, her knitting needles clacking a steady rhythm, three of the Roxburghe pugs at her feet. She smiled encouragingly at Rose. "Did you have a pleasant nap, dear? I daresay you were still tired from the archery tournament."

"That was two days ago. It's more than likely just the weather." *And the company.*

She'd been disappointed when their archery range had been removed so quickly. After a difficult dinner where Rose felt every glance Sin threw her way while the paper on which they'd recorded their wager seemed to burn a hole in her pocket, she'd pleaded a headache and escaped to her room early. There she spent the night tossing and turning, wondering if she were making a fool of herself over Sin. When she'd finally fallen asleep, her dreams had been filled with him, and she'd relived their kisses over and over. Each time it threatened to become more, she'd awakened, panting and hot.

The next morning, despite barely sleeping half the

night, she'd risen with a sense of pleasant urgency, ready to meet the day and finish their wager, only to discover that the rain had come to destroy her plans. Dispirited, she'd gone in search of Sin when she'd run into Mr. Munro, who'd attached himself to her side as firmly as a barnacle upon a ship. He'd managed to remain there for the last day and a half.

Sin seethed at the circumstances, as did Rose, though not as visibly. Sin had been in a raging mood since the archery tournament, snapping at everyone. Twice now he and his aunt had engaged in an argument that in other households would have been described as a "huge row," but here it didn't even cause Lady Charlotte to stop buttering her bread.

"Perhaps I should read some more?" Mr. Munro said. She longed to just grab the book from his hand and throw it across the room. "I fancy that I can pronounce some of the Shakespearean terms better than most."

"Another time, perhaps. I've a few things I must see to this afternoon. In fact, if you'll pardon me, I should excuse myself now." She stood and tried not to yawn again as the pugs all leapt to their feet and came to stand beside her, staring up at her as if she were their queen.

"Where are you going?" Munro asked, a definite point in his voice.

She patted each pug. "I wish to speak to Miss Isobel about a reticule she has a pattern for."

"I'll come with you." Munro was on his feet, the book discarded, before she could frame a suitable rejection. He proffered his arm. "Shall we? I believe Miss Isobel is in the library with her sister and Lord Cameron."

Rose sighed and started to agree, but a sudden awareness of the quiet made her turn toward the windows. "It stopped raining!"

Lady Charlotte looked out the window. "So it has."

The heavens cracked open and a ray of sunshine slanted over the lawn, directly where the target had been set up the day before.

"It's a sign," Rose breathed. "Lady Charlotte, do you know where Lord Sinclair might be?"

Lady Charlotte's brows lowered. "I believe he's in the library, too, but I don't think you should—"

Rose was already headed toward the door, Munro following.

He tried to engage her in banter as she hurried down the hallway to the library. Rose smiled politely, though inwardly she screamed. She'd never been so tired of one person in her life, mainly because his line of conversation revolved around himself and no one else.

They reached the library and she walked through the open door. Miss Muriella, apparently lulled by the rain, too, was sound asleep on a corner of the settee, a book open on her knee, while Miss Isobel and Lord Cameron stood by the terrace doors.

"I don't see Sinclair," Munro said rather unnecessarily.

"I haven't seen him today," Cameron said with a shrug.

"Nor have I," Miss Isobel agreed. "Perhaps he is indisposed? He did drink a great deal of port last night."

Rose frowned. "He didn't have any more than Lord Cameron."

Lord Cameron smirked. "Yes, but I hold mine better."

Miss Isobel tittered.

Rose pressed her lips into a firm line. "I'll look for Lord Sinclair elsewhere." She dipped a scant curtsy, spun on her heel, and left, Munro puffing beside her.

"Where are you going now?" he asked as she took the stairs at a brisk pace.

"To the billiards room. Perhaps he's there."

"That's a capital idea. I love to play billiards, myself. Do you play, Miss Balfour?" Before she could answer, he was off again. "I once played with the Duke of Richmond, you know. He's a fine chap. His table is—" On and on he went, recalling each game he'd ever had. When they reached the landing, she realized that she wouldn't be able to outpace him, so she purposefully began to walk slower.

Caught up in his own self-engrossing tale, Munro never noticed and led her down the hallway to the billiards room, talking over his shoulder as he went.

They were almost there when she heard the sound of a door opening, and then a firm hand was placed about her arm. Before she could make a sound, she was yanked to one side and enfolded in velvety blackness, her back pressed to something firm as Sin's arms closed about her.

She blinked into the darkness, the black slowly softening to a gray, and she could make out shelves of what appeared to be linens. The faint scent of starch confirmed this. *Good God, we're in a closet.*

She opened her mouth, but Sin placed a finger over her lips. "Shhhh," he whispered.

They were hiding in a *closet*, for heaven's sake. *A closet!* A giggle rose in her chest and she bit her lip to quell it. What a scoundrel! Rose knew she should be outraged, yet all she felt was a deep tickle of amusement and the rare thrill of being naughty.

Munro, meanwhile, was oblivious to her absence. She could still hear him droning on and on as he strutted on down the hallway.

Suddenly, the voice stopped and there was silence. "Miss Balfour?"

She bit her lip harder to keep her giggle subdued. Sin's arms tightened around her, his chin coming to rest on the top of her head.

It was amazingly intimate to stand with one's back pressed to a man's broad chest, his arms warmly wrapped about her. Her desire to giggle softened into a smile as a sense of deep peace spread through her.

Soon, the only urge she had to fight was that of turning in the circle of Sin's arms and burrowing against him.

A loud sigh echoed in the hallway as Munro mumbled something about "looking in the music room" before heavy footsteps came back down the hallway and continued past the closet. Rose watched, her breath held, as Munro's shadow crossed through the light that shone under the door.

As the shadow and then footsteps faded away, Sin chuckled. She felt each reverberation where her back was pressed to his chest and she sighed. It was heavenly.

"He's gone," Sin said in a low voice.

"Thank goodness," Rose said. "I was never so close to screaming in my life. He's horrible!"

"In this closet, you can do anything you wish." Sin's lips were beside her ear, his warm breath making her skin prickle. "Though I hope you won't scream."

She started to turn, but Sin held her tight. "Stay there a moment."

He gently nipped her ear and she gasped as shivers flew through her. "Sin, that's—"

He did it again and, without thought, she tilted her head to give him more access. He nipped and kissed her ear and neck, creating a cacophony of sensations and wiping all thoughts from her mind.

Sin moved with a slow, almost leisurely intent, his mouth never still, his breath warm against her skin.

He nuzzled her neck. "At dinner last night, I heard

you tell Miss Muriella about Caith Manor. Tell me about your home."

She frowned, trying to collect her thoughts. "My . . . home? Why?"

His hands slid to her waist. "Because you intrigue me."

She intrigued *him*?

"Are you happy there?" he asked between laying breeze-soft kisses on her cheek. "What do you do when you are home?" He rubbed his cheek against hers, and she shivered at the feel of his stubbled skin.

"I oversee the house and my sisters and——" She caught her breath as he blew on her ear. "Sin, what are you doing?" she managed.

"Testing your limits." He nipped her ear, his breath warm on the delicate skin.

It was so hard to think. Her entire body was aflame, her heart thudding hard in her throat, her skin tight and tingling.

What did he ask? Oh . . . yes. Caith Manor. "If I tell you about my home, will you tell me about yours?"

"Which one?"

She opened her eyes and turned her head to look at him. "There's more than one?"

His teeth flashed in the dim light. "There are twelve." He slid his hands up from her hips until they crossed over her stomach as he buried his face in her neck. "Tell me about your home."

She took a breath and tried to focus. "Caith Manor

is quite old, and we haven't the money to keep it as it should be. There are plenty of loose—" She caught her breath as he began to kiss her neck. *What was I saying?*

Rose cleared her throat. "Plenty of loose floorboards, chimneys that smoke, and windows that let in cold air."

His hands slid to beneath her breasts.

Her nipples instantly tightened. God, but she *yearned* for him to touch her breasts. She pressed back against him, her hands on each side of his thighs as she grasped the soft wool of his coat.

With her hands to each side, her entire front was available to his touch. And oh, how she wanted him to touch her.

His thumbs pressed against the bottom of her breasts and she breathed deeply, reveling in the moment. All of her life, she'd been the person who'd taken care of things, who'd gone without so that her sisters and father might have more. And though she didn't regret those decisions, she realized she'd missed parts of her own life because of them.

But right now, at this very second, she could do something for herself. Something she would never forget. Something that set her soul afire.

"Go on," he urged, his voice muffled against her neck. "Your home?"

She cleared her throat, her voice husky as she said, "Though Caith Manor is creaky and old, I miss it still."

He kissed her ear. "Have you always lived there?"

"Yes." *Yes, yes, yes.* She matched each with one of his kisses.

He rubbed his stubbled chin over her ear. "What do you do for amusement at Caith Manor?"

"We—" She gulped. She couldn't think of a single thing right now. *Think, Rose,* she ordered herself. "We play chess and whist, we have a boat that we row about the lake near Father's greenhouses, and—" The words disappeared as his lips slid to the corner of hers.

"Yes?" he whispered against her. "What else?"

"W-we sometimes play pall-mall, or shoot arrows at targets we'd hang from the trees in Father's orchard."

It was odd having such a mundane conversation while engaging in such sensual activities. Her mind tried so hard to converse, but her body was aching with distraction. "Caith is on a knoll set in a small wood. There's a tree on the property that some say is over eight hundred years old."

"Lovely," he murmured as he nipped a line along her jaw.

"Oh yes. So lovely," she said with a sigh, her entire body quivering at his touch. "I-I wish you could visit. You would enjoy— *Oh!*"

He slid his hands to her breasts and rested there, gently cupping them. Warmth spread through her.

She gripped his coat tighter and shivered. His thumbs found her nipples through the thin layers of muslin of her gown and chemise.

She moaned softly and turned her face to the side, toward his.

He captured her lips with an instant, deep kiss, and she was swept away on a tide of mad passion. Every bit of her ached for him. Her breasts seemed to swell at his touch, her hips sliding restlessly as his thumbs encircled her hardened nipples. She'd never felt such agonizing sweetness as she yearned for him with an ache she'd never before felt.

She shifted restlessly and he gasped against her mouth. She could feel the hard line of his cock pressed against his breeches. He was as aroused as she. The thought made her swell with pride.

She released his coat and slipped a hand to his turgid cock, amazed at her own boldness.

He caught his breath as her hand cupped him.

Rose was excited at her fearlessness. He wasn't the only one who could destroy a person's ability to think. Unless she was mistaken about the pained pleasure on Sin's face, she, too, had that power. She could make a man like Sin gasp for air as if he were drowning.

She reveled in the heady moment, rubbing his cock through the thick cover of his breeches.

Sin groaned and tugged her hand away, his breathing harsh in the silence of the closet. He rested his cheek against her forehead and said in a husky voice, "Easy, sweet."

"You didn't like that?"

He laughed, low and deep, the sound rumbling

in his broad chest. "I loved it. Almost too much." He turned her in his arms until she faced him and then he swooped her up, lifting her from her feet and burying his face in her neck. She slipped her arms about his neck and held him as his breathing slowly returned to normal.

After a moment, he sighed and slowly slid her to her feet. "I think we'd best leave our closet paradise."

Her heart sank. "But why?" She toyed with his cravat pin.

"Because Munro will come looking for you, and we can't risk him setting up a hue and cry."

"No one knows where I am."

"No one knows where I am, either," he returned. "And that, my dear, could be our undoing."

She sighed. He was right, of course. And she knew she needed to have a care about propriety. But it was becoming more and more difficult to do so. Didn't she deserve a little bit of paradise? At least a moment or two?

She slid her hands down his chest, trying to soak in as much of this time as she could. In a few moments, she'd be out of this closet and back to being polite Miss Balfour. Worse, in a few weeks she'd be back at Caith Manor, where she'd return to her normal life, one she'd always thought she'd been happy with, but now . . . She looked up into Sin's face. She was changing. Was that a good thing?

She wasn't certain. All she knew was that she wouldn't stop. Not now.

He captured her hand and pressed a warm kiss to the palm. "We should make our escape while we can." He stepped past her and cracked the door open very carefully, looking both ways before he pushed it wide.

He grinned down at Rose, noting the downward turn of her lips. "After you, my lady."

She cast a last, wistful look at the closet before she stepped out into the hallway, where he joined her, shutting the door behind them.

She looked so forlorn that he wished they hadn't interrupted their interlude at all. "We'll have to remember that closet if Munro continues to monopolize you."

Her eyes sparkled. "He's been driving me mad."

"He'd talk the ears off a goat."

She laughed. "I already fell asleep during one of his stories."

"How unfortunate. Did he notice?"

"Yes, but only after Lady Charlotte pointed it out to him."

"He's a numbskull. Were you escorting him to the billiards room to knock him unconscious with a stick, perchance?"

"No." She hesitated, a faint flush on her cheeks. "I was on my way to find you."

An odd warmth spread through his chest. "Oh?"

"The sun came out." She lifted her brows. "You, sir, owe me an archery contest."

She looked all of seventeen, standing in the hallway, her hair slightly mussed, her lips swollen from his kisses as she beamed at him.

The warmth in his chest grew. "Then an archery contest there shall be."

"I'll tell MacDougal to set it up." She turned away.

"Wait. Ask him to have it ready in an hour and a half."

She paused and looked back, her brows lowered. "Not now?"

"I have something I need to do first." *Like ride across the chilled moors for at least an hour.* He had to do something to burn the ache from his blood before he was seen with her in public.

Confusion filled her gaze, but she shrugged. "Fine. In an hour and a half."

He bowed, slanting her a look through his lashes that made her cheeks pinken. "Until then, Miss Balfour."

She curtsied back. "Until then."

And with a flutter of skirts, she left.

MacDougal placed his heel against the front of the target and then paced out twenty steps. When he stopped, a footman hurried forward to place a string across the range, which another footman instantly pegged into place.

He stepped back to regard their work. "Will this work fer ye, Miss Balfour?"

The target sat nearly where it had several days ago, and the lawn was a fresh jewel-green, the scent of wet grass permeating the air. The clouds had broken and were being pushed out of the sky by a gusty breeze. She smiled at the butler. "It's perfect."

"'Tis no' as pretty as the blue paint her grace used fer the tourny the other day, but 'tis the best we can do, considerin' how wet the grass is." He watched as she tested the bows. "Are ye certain ye dinna need more than two? I can have more brought fro' the barn, should ye wish it."

"No, two is all we'll need." Rose saw Sin striding across the lawn toward her, and her heart took an unexpected leap.

He'd apparently been riding, for he still wore his riding clothes, his overcoat open and flowing behind him. His dark blond hair was windswept and his rakish smile made her grin in return as she remembered their encounter in the closet.

When he reached the course, he looked it over and nodded. "Well done, Miss Balfour. Now we may settle our wager."

The warmth of his voice was like a physical touch and she shivered, then tugged her pelisse closer about her.

"MacDougal, where are the arrows?"

"They're bein' brought out, my lord." He gestured toward a footman approaching from across the wide lawn, a collapsed bow stand under each arm. "Tha' will be the last o' it, and ye and Miss Balfour can ha' yer tourney."

"It's about time," Sin told Rose with a wolfish smile.

"Lord Cameron, you were right," came Miss Isobel's voice. "The archery course is being reset. We can play another game!"

His jaw set, Sin glanced back over his shoulder to find Lord Cameron and both Misses Stewart approaching. He gave a disgusted sigh. "Next, we'll have—"

"Miss Balfour!" Mr. Munro called as he hurried across the lawn from the other direction. "There you are. Are we shooting arrows again?"

"I could shoot him," Sin offered in a low voice.

Rose sighed. "There are too many of them. Here comes Lady Charlotte, too."

Sure enough, the older lady was scurrying toward them, holding her skirts above the wet grass. Sin shook his head. "Bloody hell. How is it that in a castle this size, with so few people, it is *impossible* to get a few moments alone without the use of a good linen closet?"

"I've wondered the same thing," Rose said.

Then Miss Isobel, Miss Muriella, and Lord Cameron were upon them, joined in short order by Munro, and the group chattered loudly about what a capital idea it was to have another archery contest. MacDougal sent a footman to fetch more bows and arrows, while Munro paced off the target as if he were an expert on setting up a range.

Sin scowled. These past two days, it had felt like fate was conspiring to keep him from Rose. All he could do was sit back and watch her, which had driven him to distraction until he'd taken matters into his own hands and had commandeered the linen closet. That was one of the benefits of staying in one's great-aunt's house—one knew all of the hiding places.

He watched as Rose pretended to listen to Munro's self-aggrandizing about his archery skills, her face a mask of politeness. This was the Rose others knew. The Rose *he* knew moaned when her breasts were touched and loved to have kisses placed upon her ears. Those were secrets that only he knew.

So the rainy days hadn't been a total waste. Not only had he managed to abscond with her to the linen closet for a few delicious moments designed to prime her for more, but he had also, by listening to her conversations with others, discovered some interesting tidbits about her. She didn't care for turtle soup; though she loved Shakespeare, she preferred to read it herself rather than have a pedantic bore read it to her; and she was very close to her sisters. He'd discovered the last fact when Aunt Margaret had inquired after them at dinner last night. Sin didn't think he'd ever seen a more pleased smile upon Rose's face.

There definitely wasn't a smile there now.

Though she was being polite, he could feel her irritation. Just knowing she felt the same way he did helped a little.

A footman spoke with MacDougal, who turned to the group. "I fear we're short some arrows. I should have counted them, but I forgot."

"I know where they are," Rose said. "Several went into that copse by the lake."

"Very good, miss. I'll send a footman to find them."

"It would be faster if I did it myself. I saw exactly where they went in."

The butler looked uncertain. "But miss, it will be wet—"

"When I'm at home, I tromp about in the rain all the time." She turned to the others. "Why don't you begin? I can just go last."

Munro stepped forward. "I'll help you, Miss Balfour."

"No, you won't," Lady Charlotte said. "I'll go with Miss Balfour. I'll not have her wandering about the woods alone with a man."

Rose shook her head. "Lady Charlotte, I don't need anyone to—"

"Come, dear, we're wasting time discussing it." Lady Charlotte headed down the hill, saying over her shoulder, "Miss Isobel is readying for her turn, so we must hurry."

Sin watched the two head toward the copse. Once there, Rose exchanged some words with Lady Charlotte and then disappeared into the woods, leaving the older lady standing guard at the edge of the copse.

Sin smiled. Under the pretext of finding a footman to fetch port and hot tea, he walked toward the house until he was certain no one was watching. Then he slipped into the shrubbery and stealthily made his way down to the copse.

Rose peered into the bushes.

"Do you see them?" Lady Charlotte called from the edge of the thicket.

"No," Rose called back, pushing through a large shrub and hoping there were no spiders. Sunshine dappled the tops of the thick bushes as the scent of damp leaves tickled her nose.

"Thank you for looking, dear. Are you certain you don't wish me to help? We could cover twice as much ground."

"No, thank you," Rose said quickly, pushing farther into the thicket. She would never allow the older, fragile lady to tromp over such rough ground.

"Oh, good!" Lady Charlotte said, her voice fainter now. "Munro is showing Miss Muriella how to aim her bow and arrow properly. She needs a good lesson or two. And I think— Oh, it appears as if Miss Isobel and Lord Cameron are beginning the contest right now."

"Good. I won't be long."

"I think they— Oh, they are gesturing and—I can't

see well, but I believe they mean that we have plenty of time to fetch the arrows."

"*Lovely,*" Rose muttered under her breath. "Those arrows must be here somewhere. Please keep an eye on the contest so we'll know when it's our turn. I'm going in a bit deeper."

A particularly thick shrub looked like the perfect place for nature to hide an arrow, so Rose peered through the limbs, but saw nothing.

Lady Charlotte called, "Lord Cameron is getting ready for his shot now."

"Very good." Perhaps the arrows had been caught by the tree canopy? Rose looked up, turning in a slow circle.

As she turned, she suddenly saw Sin standing in the small clearing. She grinned, unable to stop herself.

He returned her grin, looking wicked and pleased, which was exactly how she felt. "Sin, what are you doing here?"

Lady Charlotte answered, "What's that, dear?"

Sin crossed the small clearing and held up his hand. In it were three arrows. "That's three of them," he said in a low voice. "I found them in the shrubbery over there." He nodded from the direction he'd come. "How many are missing?" he whispered.

"I don't know."

He bent and planted the arrows in the middle of the clearing and then came to her side. He slipped an arm about her waist and drew her to him.

"We're not going to find any arrows like this," she protested halfheartedly.

He lifted her from her feet. "How do you know?" he whispered back.

She laughed softly as she slipped her arms about his neck. "Because I can't look for arrows when your head is directly in front of mine."

"You are a demanding woman."

"And you are an incorrigible man. Please put me down."

His gaze seemed fixed upon her lips. "And if I don't?"

"I could call for help, you know," she whispered.

"You could," he whispered back, a wolfish smile on his face. "But then I wouldn't help you find this." He turned her toward the tree beside them. Embedded in the trunk was a silver arrow.

"Rose?" Lady Charlotte called, concern in her voice.

"I believe I'm close to more arrows! I see some signs that they came this way."

"Very good, dear," Lady Charlotte called out. "Miss Muriella didn't learn a thing from Munro's lesson, for her arrow almost hit a footman. Fortunately he was carrying coats out to the party and was able to catch it in those. He is a very quick young man, I must say."

Rose giggled and Sin's arms tightened about her.

"Oh, now it's Mr. Munro's turn," Lady Charlotte said. "Have you found any arrows yet?"

"One moment more!" Rose answered. "I think I see some in the shrubs."

Sin slid his hands down her back to her hips, holding her gently against him. Instantly she melted to him. "You came all of the way out here for a mere kiss?" she whispered.

"Yes. Are you impressed?" He traced his lips along her cheek.

Shivers ran through her. "Very," she whispered back.

He nipped at her ear, then placed slow, heated kisses down her neck. "You taste so good. I couldn't keep away." His voice was muffled against her neck.

Her knees weak, she clung to him. "You . . . you are very good at—"

"Oh!" Lady Charlotte said, "Miss Isobel is about to take another shot. She hit the outer ring, too. I must say, she's very good. Not as good as you, of course, but she has potential."

Rose had to clear her throat to speak. "I'll be right out."

"Very good, dear. It will be our turns soon."

Rose's heart was pounding so loudly that she could barely hear Lady Charlotte. Sin kissed her deeply as his hands roamed everywhere, touching and teasing. Rose knew she had to stop this, but her body begged for just one more moment, one more kiss, one more—

"Look out!" Lady Charlotte cried.

There was a low whistling sound and Sin jerked

Rose around so hard that she felt like a rag doll. With a solid thunk, an arrow embedded itself in a tree right beside her hip, directly where she'd been standing a moment ago.

For a second, neither spoke.

"Miss Balfour!" Lady Charlotte called. "I tried to warn you, but it happened so fast. Are you injured?"

"No, I'm fine!"

"Thank goodness!"

Rose smoothed her skirt, pausing when her fingers brushed her hip where a thin, perfect cut in her skirt indicated how very close the arrow had been. Her mind cloudy with shock, she touched the place with curiosity. "That was too close for—" She blinked and looked more closely at the tear. "Sin," she said, her voice sounding odd, "there's blood on this. I wasn't hit, but someone had to be—" She suddenly realized he hadn't said a word since the arrow had hit.

She looked at him. He was standing with his eyes closed, his hand pressed to his thigh as blood soaked his buff trousers.

"Damn you, Dunn!"

Sin's valet peered over his spectacles. "My lord, there is no way to clean your wound without causing pain."

Sin scowled. "You said it would hurt—not that it would be agony."

"I'm sorry, my lord. I promise that the next time I

treat an arrow wound upon your person, I'll use the word 'agony.'"

Sin scowled. "Just clean the damn— *Ow!*"

Dunn placed the cloth beside the pan of water and unrolled a bandage. "If you'll stand, my lord, I'll attempt to bandage your thigh."

Sin stood, gritting his teeth at the pain. "I don't know what was worse, getting shot like a damned deer or having to explain to my aunt what I was doing in the woods with Miss Balfour."

"You're fortunate it wasn't a deep cut. Any more so and I'd suggest stitches."

"Yes, I'm *so* fortunate. Now come and help me dress."

"But my lord, it's still two hours until—"

"I have an appointment before dinner."

"Oh?" The valet waited, but when Sin didn't offer any more information, he sniffed and began to set out Sin's evening clothes.

With a bit of difficulty, Sin was soon dressed.

The valet began to straighten the room. "On the surface of things, one could say that it seems you are not doing very well in your contest with Miss Balfour."

"If one didn't enjoy one's position as the valet of an earl, yes, one could say that," Sin returned. As he turned, he caught sight of himself in the mirror and saw the healing cut and faint bruise on his jaw. Combined with the arrow wound, he felt like he'd been in a war.

Still, it would all be worth it in the end. God, she was a tasty armful. When he'd kissed her in the trees, she'd reacted just as he'd wished. *She is weakening. It won't be long until she's—*

"My lord, you are smiling. I fail to see the humor in your situation."

"That's because you don't know what's at stake."

Dunn's gaze narrowed. "My lord, are you *certain* you're keeping your gaze firmly locked upon the real prize—to best Miss Balfour in this contest? It seems to me that you have your eyes locked upon Miss Balfour herself."

"My attention is focused exactly where it needs to be. When you're finished giving me useless advice, can you find my sapphire cravat pin? I will wear it tonight."

The valet fetched the pin and watched as Sin deftly affixed it. "Shall I wait up for you to return after dinner?"

"There's no need. I can put myself to bed." It was possible that he was rushing things, but by God, he and Rose had unfinished business and he refused to allow another moment to pass without seeing it finished.

At one time, he'd thought three weeks a luxurious stretch of time in which to conduct a seduction. Now it seemed far too little. In a few days, one whole week would be gone and he was determined to make the most of what time he had. "Dunn, if you'll just put out my robe before you leave, I'll be fine."

"Very good, my lord. If you change your mind, ring for me. I shall be in my room, rolling bandages and making poultices for your future encounters with Miss Balfour."

"Thank you, Dunn. I appreciate your confidence." Sin limped to the door, his blood quickening. *The time has come for a reckoning, my little Rose.*

Thirteen

From the Diary of the Duchess of Roxburghe
Sin somehow lured Rose Balfour into a copse of woods and then proceeded to rescue her from an errant arrow. I'm glad he wasn't injured badly, but I could have killed the two of them for being alone. Had it not been for Lady Charlotte's quick wit— she vowed up and down that she could see them the entire time and even came up with a fascinating description of the arrow strike—I don't know what we'd have done. As it was, she has prevented any ugly rumors and all is safe.

For now.

Sin owes me for this. I do not like to tell tales unless, of course, it is in pursuit of a goal of my own. Those ends justify the means. His pursuit, however, is far less noble.

Leaving her bedchamber, Rose took out the note Sin had sent through a maid. Her heart thundered, and she hoped her elegant gown made her look calm and self-possessed. Made of celestial blue Spitalfields silk over a white sarcenet slip, ornamented around the bottom and on the sleeves with a band of tulle, it was lovely, one of Lily's favorites.

Pausing in the hallway outside of her room, Rose read the note one more time.

> *Meet me in the small salon at seven—if you dare. We've unfinished business. Don't be late.*

He'd signed it with a flourish that she would have known was his even if she had to pick it out of a hundred signatures.

If she dared? Ha! She'd show him who dared!

She made her way through the hallways, pausing here and there to make certain no one lingered around a corner. Finally, she reached the staircase. The foyer proved more difficult, for two footmen stood by the front door, arguing over which of them was to serve at dinner. After a few moments, MacDougal walked through and sent them scurrying off to their duties.

She listened to their footsteps fade away, and waited a bit longer to make certain no one else was nearby, then lightly ran down the stairs. The door to the small salon was open and, with a final look around, she slipped inside and closed it behind her.

The room was unlit except for the rapidly fading sunset that spilled in from the windows. "Sin?" she asked softly.

No answer met her.

She must be early. She crossed to the window and watched the wind ripple over the lake and up the lawn.

A moment later, Sin entered and locked the door. Her heart, which was already thudding madly, beat even harder.

He was dressed for dinner in a dark blue coat, a maroon waistcoat, and breeches, and he walked with a faint limp. Her gaze flickered to his thigh and her heart sank when she saw the bandage outlined by his trousers. "Does your leg hurt dreadfully?"

"It hurts like the devil." He came forward and there was something determined about his jaw.

"I'm so sorry. I didn't get the chance to thank you for saving me. Had you not pulled me out of the way—" She shook her head.

His eyes gleamed. "Oh yes, I saved you. For this."

She half expected a kiss, but he walked past her to the window. He threw open the sash, then he climbed through.

Rose blinked. "What are you doing?"

"Finishing our wager." He leaned in and held out his hand. "Are you coming?"

She looked at his hand. The whole thing was highly improper. Yet when he smiled at her that way, his eyes alight with mischief, she found that she not only couldn't say no, but she couldn't say yes fast enough.

She put her hand in his, gathered her skirts, and

looked at the sill. "I hope this doesn't mar my gown. It's my sister's favorite and—"

He bent through the window, scooped her up, and had deposited her on the ground outside before she could even guess what he was about. "Blast it, Sin! You just injured yourself! You shouldn't be—"

He kissed her hard and fast, silencing her. Sending her a satisfied look, he tucked her hand into the crook of his arm and led her across the lawn to the archery course.

Once there, he selected two bows and handed her one, then he selected three arrows. "Choose your arrows."

The smell of damp grass, the cooling night air, and the mischief in his eyes made the evening feel like a childhood escapade. Though the castle stared down at them and anyone who looked out of a window could see them, she felt deliciously alone with him.

She grinned and selected her arrows, looking down the shafts to make certain they were straight. "I'll take these."

"You first."

She strung her bow with her first arrow, took careful aim, and then let it fly. It hit the inner circle beside the bull's-eye.

She frowned. "There's a little wind."

"I'll remember that."

She strung the second arrow and took aim. The feather fletching tickled her cheek as she released the arrow, which flew straight to the bull's-eye.

"Impressive."

She had one more arrow. She straightened her shoulders, took a deep breath, drew the bow, took slow and deliberate aim, and—*thunk*—the arrow buried itself in the bull's-eye again.

She laughed. "Well, Sinclair? Can you beat that?"

He picked up his arrow, aimed, and shot. He did the other two in equally quick succession, and every one hit the bull's-eye. One arrow was so close to another that it actually splintered it.

Rose could only stare. "You've won." She could barely believe it, even seeing the arrow split herself. She thought of their wager and her heart stuttered. Things were moving so quickly . . . too quickly? She should slow things down, ask Sin for some time to answer the promise of their challenge.

And yet, some wild part of her wished to push forward. She wanted more of this, more of him. In a few short weeks, when things were back to normal and she was once again dealing with the mundane life at Caith Manor, she'd have these memories of her and Sin to make her smile. It wasn't a lot, but it was far more than she'd ever had before.

Sin replaced their bows on the stand. Then he tucked her hand in the crook of his arm and led her back to their window. After he climbed through, he reached out for her.

"Oh, no. I don't want your leg harmed anymore. Step back and I'll climb through myself."

Rose collected her skirts, lifted them, and stepped

over the windowsill into the salon. It was much darker now, the room cast in shade.

Sin took her hand and led her to the settee before the fireplace. "So I have won. Now it's time to collect my winnings."

Her mouth went dry, but she nodded. He sat down and pulled her into his lap. His warm eyes were ablaze with promise.

Rose suddenly found it difficult to swallow. Oh, how she wanted this man. She knew it was a bad idea, but when he looked at her like that, she couldn't help but yearn for the excitement of his touch.

She was twenty-two years old, and upon the shelf by society standards. Why couldn't she enjoy this pleasure? It couldn't hurt, could it?

Though right now, she didn't even care.

Sin looked into Rose's eyes and wondered if she felt the same yearning ache that he did.

Six years ago, had anyone told Sin that he and Rose had far more in common than anyone else he'd ever met, he would have mocked the idea. But the more time he spent with her, the more he recognized her independent spirit and appreciated her strength. Neither of them enjoyed being told what to do, and neither liked to lose.

She was so different from what he'd assumed all those years ago. He'd expected a hothouse bloom. Instead, he found a much more ragged, and far more interesting, wild Scottish rose.

She shifted against him, nervously biting her lip. The sight of her even white teeth pressing into her full, bottom lip made his cock harden even more. He bent and captured her lips with his. His gentleness disappeared in the onslaught of passion that poured through him, and he kissed her over and over, hot and possessive, his hands resting on her hips.

He didn't just kiss, he demanded, took . . . and everything he asked for, she gave with a willingness that delighted him. She wrapped her fingers around his lapel and pulled him closer.

Sin's arms tightened and he pulled her forward, his tongue slipping through her lips to touch hers. She jerked at the unexpected touch and her breasts, already peaking against her gown, ached for his touch.

He moaned her name softly, and moved his kisses from her lips to her jaw and then to feather down her neck.

The weight of his warm hand on her ankle sent a shiver through her. He slowly slid it beneath her skirts, from her ankle . . . to her calf . . . and then to her knee.

She caught her breath when his warm fingers slid under her chemise to her thigh. She felt so vulnerable being in his arms while he was free to explore her as he wished. It also excited her, though, and she found herself parting her knees for him.

He gently stroked her inner thigh, never breaking the demanding kiss, and she strained toward him, yearning for him.

His fingers slipped up farther, just brushing her most secret spot. She jerked, gasping, and broke their kiss.

He cupped her warmly, his palm moving against her. She closed her eyes and rocked against him, completely captive to the amazing sensations. God, whatever he was doing, she didn't want him to stop. If he tried, she'd grab his wrist and hold him there.

He slid his hand up and drew his fingers feathersoft over her. She arched against him, agonizingly aware of his every move, of the buttons of his waistcoat pressing against her side, of his tongue as he teased her and tempted her lips yet again, of his overwhelmingly masculine scent—but more than anything, of the magic he was performing with his hand.

She couldn't stop moving against him, feeling the urgent new sensations grow stronger and stronger. It was like a fire building even higher, and she didn't know what to—

Suddenly a flicker of fire captured her in its grip and she arched against him as mad waves of passion convulsed through her. He never stopped moving his hand, holding her tightly until she collapsed against him. It took several long moments before she could even think.

Good God, what was that? She wanted it to happen again and again. *Is this why so many people throw their lives away on love?*

The thought captured her attention as her breathing slowed to normal. *Love? Not with Sin.* He was exciting, handsome, and amusing, but he wasn't the sort of man a woman could give her heart to. He would be the first one to admit that, too. She'd already been down that path and she wasn't about to let it happen again.

Her heart sank. What was she doing, playing with the same fire that had burned her years ago? It was madness.

Outside the salon, footsteps could be heard coming and going as the dining room was readied for dinner. Rose pushed herself upright, out of Sin's embrace.

Sin let her go. "That, my little wild Rose, was quite a wager."

"And it was—" She couldn't think of a word big enough to describe her feelings as she turned from him so that he couldn't see her trembling lips. "Quite worthwhile."

He laughed softly. "You are an intriguing woman, Miss Rose Balfour. I never know what you're going to say or—"

"Where is she, then?" It sounded like the duchess was right outside the salon door. "Someone should fetch her. If she's not in the dining room, then look in the library. Like Roxburghe, she can't go without a book in her hand."

Rose stood, moved past him, and glanced at her hair in the mirror. "Oh no!" She moved pins from here and there to reaffix several strands that had come loose. "I'll need Annie to redo this, but at least I can walk to my room now."

She shook out her gown and adjusted the sash at her waist, each moment making her feel more and more ill at ease. Even as she prepared to leave him, she yearned for him, wished with all of her heart that she could return to the circle of his arms. A wave of loneliness washed over her. It was oddly painful, to be lonely for someone who was standing right there with her. She swallowed a sudden lump that had grown in her throat.

Sin seemed wholly unaffected. He leaned against the mantel and watched her with a faint smile. "I'll take you to your maid. But first, we should set another wager. One with even more . . . worthwhile consequences."

And then what? she wondered. *There will be another one? And another one? And each one will draw me closer to you, and yet further away from—* From what? What did she have to lose?

She wasn't certain. Her thoughts were in too much of a jumble for her to figure anything out right now. "We'll discuss that another time," she said quickly. "How do I get back to my room unseen?"

"Out the window, then walk down to the terrace. The library doors are always open. If you see anyone inside, tell them you were admiring the sunset. I'll wait twenty minutes or so and then come in the front door."

She nodded and went to the window, Sin following. She stepped outside, her heart so low that she had to bite her lip to keep it from betraying her. He climbed out after her, then pulled her back into his arms for a hard, quick kiss.

She turned from him and hurried to the terrace doors, her eyes filled with tears.

Fourteen

From the Diary of the Duchess of Roxburghe
Desperate times call for desperate measures.

Thus far, I have been assisting Sin by orchestrating less competition, making certain that he and Miss Balfour can catch a moment or two together (though I always protest it, as a good chaperone should), keeping the other guests busy so they do not intrude . . . All of this so that they might grow interested in each other.

But Sin has not utilized his time wisely.

Therefore, from now on I shall move my efforts to assisting Miss Balfour. Rather than working to bring the two of them together, I shall do what I can to assist her in eluding him.

Being contrary creatures, nothing spurs men more than feminine disinterest. And God knows, Sin needs a good spur.

Several days later, Sin stalked into the library. "There you are."

Aunt Margaret turned from the open doorway leading to the terrace. She was holding one of her pugs, the others panting in various positions at her feet. "Where else would I be? We're planning a luncheon on the terrace. Will you be joining us?"

"No," he said shortly.

"What a pity. You'll be greatly missed." She patted the pug she held, an older one who was almost blind. "Poor Randolph is not feeling well this morning, but I cannot convince Lord Cameron to stop feeding the dogs bits of bacon at breakfast. It's lethal to poor Randolph's delicate constitution." She looked out over the terrace, the warm breeze teasing her blue morning gown. "I've never seen such a warm fall. My Winter Ball won't be a bit wintry."

"I've always wondered why you didn't have it at a colder time of year."

"Because it costs a fortune to keep the rooms warm, and Roxburghe will not hold with having every fireplace blazing for days on end. By having it this early, when people are thinking of winter, I can decorate to suggest the chill. Or I could if it were at least cool."

"I'm sure you'll make it seem wintry."

"If the ices don't melt. I had planned on having over forty ice statues. I may have to come up with an alternative plan." She sighed and then smiled at him. "But I'm certain you didn't come to speak about poor Randolph's digestive issues or my ball."

"No, but I'm glad to find you alone."

Her smile never changed but he detected a wary look in her eyes. "Of course, dear. It's always pleasant to chat with my favorite nephew."

"I would have spoken with you earlier this morning, but you were gone before I came down to breakfast."

"Yes, a few of the guests wished to see the sunrise over the river, so we took a carriage and some hot tea and made an excursion of it." She gave a light laugh. "It has been an exhausting few days! I don't think I've had five minutes to myself, what with the picnics, the ride to the standing stones, visiting the gardens at the church, a lovely game of pall-mall on the front lawn, and whist every night . . ." Her smile faded. "Lud, but Munro is a vicious opponent. I thought he and the vicar would come to blows last night, when he played that ridiculous hand and the vicar called him a——"

"They were fortunate I didn't toss them both out into the garden," Sin said. "Had they continued their bickering another minute, I'd have done it."

His aunt's brows rose. "In a temper, are we?"

Bloody hell, yes, he was in a temper. He couldn't think of a time when he'd been in a worse one.

She tilted her head to one side. "I must admit I was surprised to see you playing whist last night. I thought you detested it."

Sin had been shocked to find himself playing whist, too. He loathed the game, had been bored with the company, and hated the incessant banter people seemed to feel was necessary while playing, but he'd had no choice. After his passionate encounter with Rose five endless days ago, she'd been avoiding him.

For the first day or so, he hadn't minded. After all, it made sense that they should retreat to their corners before the next round.

But as the days passed and Rose made no effort to engage him in conversation, his annoyance grew. Worse, she began to actively avoid him. No matter how he tried, suddenly she was never alone.

Ever.

That had edged his annoyance into sheer irritation and, as the days passed, out-and-out ill temper.

He scowled. *Blast that woman.* He'd thought it impossible to avoid someone when there were so few houseguests present, but Rose was either riding with Munro and a groom, or walking in the garden with Lord Cameron, or playing pall-mall with the Misses Stewart . . . There seemed to be no end to the activities she found to keep her engaged, and all with the other members of their small party.

Sin had reached his limit yesterday morning when he'd come down for breakfast. He saw Rose alone in the foyer at the bottom of the stairs, stooped beside one of Aunt Margaret's infernal pugs, and murmuring silly endearments to it as it lay blissfully at her feet.

He'd watched her for several moments, pleased to have even a silent moment with her even if she were unaware of it. But he must have made a noise, for she'd looked up, and for one glorious, splendid moment, Rose forgot she was avoiding him, and she smiled.

In that second, they were back to where they'd been before their encounter in the salon. Relieved, he'd returned her smile and continued down the stairs toward her. As he did, Rose's smile faded. Before his foot hit the final step, she'd jumped to her feet and whisked herself into the sitting room.

Fuming, Sin had followed her, ready to demand an accounting. But when he arrived, Rose stood with Miss Muriella, who was discussing the latest fashions, while Miss Isobel and Lady Charlotte sat upon a settee, talking about knitting projects.

Refusing to yield, Sin had tried to catch Rose's eye. Though her high color told him she knew of his presence, she kept her gaze fixed on Miss Muriella as if thoroughly engrossed. Not about to rudely thrust himself into their conversation, he'd turned on his heel and stalked off.

Unable to vent his frustration, and unwilling to make a fool of himself in public, he was stuck. But then, last night an opportunity had presented itself when the vicar, who'd been playing whist at Rose's table, excused himself to stand on the terrace and smoke a cigar. Sin had pounced on the opportunity to sit at Rose's table, but he'd no more than announced his intention than Aunt Margaret had bustled up and declared her desire for a "ladies only" table. Without giving anyone time to protest, she'd collected Rose and whisked her safely out of his reach.

It was then that Sin realized that his troublesome great-aunt was involved in Rose's defection.

Aunt Margaret smiled at him now. "So, Sin, what do you wish to talk about? I've only a few minutes before I need to oversee the decoration of the luncheon tables."

"It's about Miss Balfour."

"I thought so. While you're talking, would you please hold Randolph?" Aunt Margaret shoved her pug into Sin's arms and then pulled a ribbon from her pocket and began to fix it about the pug's fat neck.

Sin looked at the ribbon with the same disgust that was plainly registered on the dog's face. "Why are you putting a ribbon around his neck?"

"I'm putting them around all of the dogs' necks, so they'll match the luncheon decorations. The servants are tying ribbons around the corners of the tablecloths to keep them from being tossed about in the wind. There. Doesn't he look handsome with his ribbon? Just like Beenie here."

"I thought one of them didn't like ribbons."

"Poor Meenie. MacDougal kindly offered to keep her in his room until after lunch. She likes it there, for he allows her to sleep on the foot of his bed." Aunt Margaret took the pug from Sin's arms and placed it on the floor, pausing to adjust the bow. "You look very handsome, my little man," she crooned, and then scooped up another pug, this one silver with a bent ear, and loaded it into Sin's arms.

"Aunt Margaret, what did you say to Miss Balfour?"

She took another ribbon from her pocket and began to tie it about the pug's neck. "What did I say to her about what? Our many conversations have covered almost every topic imaginable."

"Aunt Margaret, you said something to her. We both know it. Miss Balfour won't speak to me at all, and I know it is your doing."

"My dear, stop exaggerating. She speaks to you all of the time: at dinner, in the library, while riding—"

"She does in public, yes, but she will no longer speak to me in private."

Margaret finished tying the ribbon about the little pug's neck and then put it on the floor with a scratch on its chin. "Judging by the outcome of your private speeches with Miss Balfour, perhaps that's best for you both."

Sin glowered. "What has she told you?"

"Everything, I believe. Well, everything that decency allowed her. A few days ago, I was in the library when Miss Balfour came in off the terrace. One look and I could see that she was upset, so"— Aunt Margaret fixed a stern gaze on Sin—"I decided it wasn't wise for you to see her alone anymore."

Sin's jaw tightened. "She's neither a child nor an innocent, but a grown, capable woman. We've done nothing that she didn't encourage."

"Which is why I agreed to help her. You are a very difficult man to say no to, even when one knows one should." She cast a hard look at him. "That's all I'm going to say about the matter. If you have more questions, then I'd suggest you speak with Miss Balfour."

"You're interfering with—" He'd been about to say "my plans," but the sudden martial light in his aunt's eyes made him stop.

"I don't interfere," she said loftily, shoving another pug in his arms. "I *assist*. And only when asked."

He cocked a brow at her. "You've been watching us."

"Who hasn't? It's far too diverting to ignore. Charlotte and I have been watching the two of you since the day you both returned from your ride soaking wet."

"We fell into the river."

"*You* didn't fall into the river."

"Fine. Miss Balfour tricked me into riding onto some poor ground where my horse stumbled, and *then* I fell into the river."

"And afterward?"

"I threw her in as retaliation."

"That's unworthy of you."

He ground his teeth. "Damn it, just leave us alone. Every time I turn around, you are interfering!"

Aunt Margaret kissed the pug as she removed it

from his arms and said in a baby voice, "Who looks adorable now, Weenie? You do!" She placed the dog on the floor and then handed Sin yet another, this one brown with a silver-tipped tail. "Hold Teenie tight while I tie this last bow. He's a jumper."

As if to prove this, the dog scrambled to get out of his arms.

Sin snapped, "Hold!" The dog stopped squirming and Margaret rapidly tied a bow around it.

The dog stared up at Sin as if transfixed, his tail wagging steadily. It was so ugly that it was actually cute. Sin lifted a brow at the dog.

The dog leaned up, his whiskers quivering as he sniffed Sin's chin.

Aunt Margaret beamed. "He likes you."

The dog sneezed in Sin's face.

"Oh, for the love of—" Sin dumped the dog into her arms, pulled out his kerchief, and wiped his face. "Blasted animal."

Margaret kissed the dog's forehead. "Does poor Teenie have a cold?"

Sin stuffed his handkerchief back into his pocket. "You haven't answered my question."

"I'm sorry. What were we talking about again?"

"Why are you meddling in Miss Balfour's and my relationship?"

She sighed. "Sin, I never meddle. How many times do I have to tell you?"

"Of course. You *assist.*"

"Yes, or give a nudge where it's needed, but I never meddle."

"And just who do you think you were assisting when you advised Miss Balfour to avoid me?"

Aunt Margaret set the dog on the floor. "I assisted both of you. When I spoke to Miss Balfour, I realized how difficult things had become for you two."

"Difficult? Things weren't difficult."

"You'd both been here barely a week and you couldn't come into contact with each other without exchanging heated words."

And heated kisses. And I'll be damned if I'll give those up. "We would have worked things out by now if we'd had some time to discuss things." Things like how much he loved to see her come alive under his touch. And how often he'd remembered the feel of her against him, her body perfectly fitted to his. And how—

"You can discuss things with her now, but in the safety of society."

Like hell. "What exactly did you say to her?"

"I told her that I was certain she didn't want to repeat the mistakes of the past."

He groaned. "Aunt Margaret, no!"

"And that it seemed as if you and she were well on your way to doing so." Aunt Margaret paused. "I also told her that if anything happened under my roof, I'd know whose fault it was."

"You can't blame her for—"

"Not her," Margaret corrected him. "*You* are the one attempting to seduce an innocent. She is merely guilty of succumbing."

"Let me put your mind at ease on that head, at least. I've never wished to or attempted to seduce a virgin, and I never will."

"You don't know what Miss Balfour is or isn't," Aunt Margaret said tartly. "It's not proper for the two of you to meet in private, and you both know it. This is safer for everyone involved. There's only a week until the Winter Ball, and after that you and Miss Balfour are free to do whatever you wish . . . under someone else's roof."

A week. The word hit him like a cannon shot. *Bloody hell, I have only one short week before Rose is gone. Perhaps forever.* Urgency gripped him.

Aunt Margaret picked up her extra ribbons. "Now, my dear, if you'll excuse me, I need to see to our luncheon. If you're not going to join us, why don't you take a nap instead? Maybe that will improve your disposition." She sailed off, beribboned pugs snuffling along in her wake.

One ribbon remained on the floor and Sin absently picked it up. It was a silky cornflower blue, the exact color of Rose's eyes.

He curled his hand about it and, with a muffled curse, spun on his heel and left.

Fifteen

From the Diary of the Duchess of Roxburghe
The battle lines are drawn, and the enemy is surging at the gates. But Charlotte and I have girded our little warrior princess for battle.

God knows what Sin has planned, for he's as moody and unpredictable as the sea, but the real battle is about to begin.

Rose stood before the mirror in her room, her breath held as she ran her hand over the soft blue round dress of India muslin. The gown was embroidered along the bottom with superb needlework depicting flowers of soft green and lilac. Small rosettes of matching colors adorned the lace at the neckline. "Oh, Annie, it's gorgeous."

At Rose's feet, Teenie wagged his silver-tipped tail. The little brown pug had followed Annie into the room when she'd come in carrying the armful of gowns that the duchess had sent to Rose, begging her to make use of them.

Rose hadn't wished to, but Annie had been insistent and now, wearing the prettiest of them, Rose couldn't help but be glad. None of her gowns were nearly so finely made.

Annie walked slowly around Rose, stepping over the dog. Head tilted to one side, she pursed her lips and nodded her head. "Och, 'tis weel enou'."

"Well enough? Annie, it's perfect!"

Annie chuckled. "I tol' ye tha' if we'd but take off a flounce or two and add a wee tuck at the sleeve, 'twould fit ye as if made fer ye."

Teenie wagged his tail in approval.

Rose smiled at him. "Annie is very good with her needle, isn't she?"

Teenie's tail couldn't wag harder, so he placed his chin on Rose's slipper and beamed up at her.

She laughed. "We must get you back to the duchess. She'll be worried."

"Och, no, miss. He wanders off all o' the time and her grace ne'er notices."

"I'm glad. I'd hate to give her grace more cause for alarm." Rose regarded the gown in the mirror, unable to believe that she was the woman wearing it. The gown made her look feminine and sophisticated, neither being words she would normally use to describe herself. She wondered if Sin would think it made her look different—

You must stop that. For the last five days, she'd done nothing but wonder what Sin would think of this or that, of how he'd mock the Misses Stewart for their belief in séances, of the way he'd look disgusted at one of Mr. Munro's obviously false tales of his past prowess in the hunting field, and at the way the vicar hid cards while playing whist when he thought no one was looking.

She couldn't seem to stop wondering about Sin's reactions to every moment of her day. Though she had been the one to decide to avoid Sin, not having him to share smiles with left her feeling deeply bereft, further testament to how fast she was falling under his spell.

It was sad evidence of her state of mind, and proof that the duchess was right about the danger of continuing their fascinating flirtation. She sighed, then squared her shoulders—what had to be, had to be. She'd always be glad that she'd found the duchess in the library after leaving Sin that day.

Rose had been so upset that she'd needed a cooler, calmer head to show her the way things had to be. Not that she regretted any of it; she would never regret anything that had happened between her and Sin. At least, not if she stopped things now.

Rose couldn't remember much of the conversation, for she'd been too embarrassed at being caught weeping. But one thing the duchess said had stuck in her head: "I do hope that you and Sin won't repeat the same mistakes that led to such a distressful situation in London. It was very difficult for Sin. More than he lets on." Concern had darkened the duchess's gaze. "I couldn't bear for him to go through that again."

Rose's heart had ached at the words and she realized that the duchess was right; she and Sin were dangerously close to causing another public scene. What was it about the two of them that made them push each other into more and more outrageous behavior every time they were together?

Whatever it was, it was time for it to stop. Though it had cost Rose far more than she'd expected it to, she'd made certain that she and Sin were never alone again.

Rose caught Annie's curious gaze in the mirror and realized that she'd been lost in her own thoughts far too long. "I'm sorry. I was just thinking of . . . all sorts of things." She forced a smile. "The gowns that the Duchess has given me are very finely made. My sister Lily would be in raptures."

"If she's like me own sister, ye'll ha' to take care tha' she dinna steal them once ye return home." Annie stood back and eyed the gown a bit more. "'Tis guid that her grace is no' one to follow fashion, but instead finds gowns as fit her figure."

Surprised, Rose blinked. "This isn't the newest fashion?"

"Nay, miss. The gowns ye see the Misses Stewart wear are the newest fashion. This design would ha' been three, mayhap four years ago. But her grace makes her *own* way and when she sees somethin' she likes, she's no' shy about keepin' it."

"She's a very intelligent woman."

"Ye ha' no idea. Ye're fortunate that ye're close in

size. She's a mite taller than ye but jus' as thin, so 'tis a guid fit."

"It's beautiful, but . . . why would the duchess give all of these to me?"

"I'm sure she's makin' room fer new ones. Her grace's maid, Mrs. Dennis, was told to clean oot the wardrobe and give ye the gowns that are ne'er worn, and tha' is what Mrs. Dennis did. The duchess also said to tell ye tha' if ye dinna wish t' keep the gowns, they go into the rag bin."

Rose gasped. "She wouldn't."

"'Tis what her grace ordered."

"But couldn't someone else wear them? Some of the other maids, perhaps?"

"Och, miss, there are no' maids at Floors thin enou' to wear these." Annie grinned and patted her own girth. "We eat far too well belowstairs fer tha'. Rest assured tha' her grace willna give away anythin' she dinna wish to give. She's a canny one, she is. Usually, when she gives ye somethin', ye can bet there's a re—" Annie paused, her brow lowering.

"What is it?"

Annie just looked thoughtfully at Rose.

Rose waited. "Yes?"

She shrugged. "I canno' remember. All of the excitement o' the dresses and then— Teenie, stop licking the miss's shoes!"

Rose looked down and found the pug licking the edge of her slipper. At Annie's soft admonition, he stopped and looked up at her in the most adorable way. "You silly dog." She bent and scratched his chin.

"He's a mess, he is. I'll go fetch yer shawl." Annie crossed to the wardrobe and returned carrying a rose-colored cashmere shawl.

Rose took it, chuckling when Teenie tried to bite it as it swept past. As she lifted the shawl out of his reach, she caught sight of the clock. "Oh dear. I must go now."

"Nay, we've still an hour before dinner."

"I know, but I told Miss Isobel that I'd seen a book in the library that she expressly wished to read." *And if I don't go now, while I know Sin is dressing for dinner, I might not be able to fetch the book until tomorrow.*

Annie eyed the stack of books by Rose's bed. "Does she read as much as ye do, miss?"

"I don't know, but Lord Cameron recommended this book at lunch today, so she's in a tizzy to read it. If I fetch it now, I can take it to dinner with me and give it to her there."

"Very good, miss. I'll start hemming yer other gowns. When I'm done with them, ye're goin' to look like a princess."

Rose laughed. "I fear it will take more than a gown to do that, but thank you." She bid the maid good-bye and then went to the door. The little pug rousted himself, stretched, and then ambled out with her.

As she closed the door, Teenie continued down the hallway and around a corner, leaving Rose alone.

"Well," Rose said to the empty hallway. "Good-bye to you, too!" With a rueful shake of her head, she made her way to the library.

Rose looked up at the rows of shelves, trying to remember where she'd seen the book Lord Cameron had mentioned. *"A Study of Roman Battles,"* she murmured to herself. "Where did I see that title?"

She crossed to the ladder and, bracing herself against it, rolled it to the place she thought she might have seen the book. Then, her skirt carefully lifted so she wouldn't step on the hem and rip it, she climbed the ladder. When she reached midway, she stopped and began searching the shelves.

After a moment, she sighed. *I don't see it.* She hooked her arm through the ladder and looked around, her gaze examining each shelf. *Perhaps it's by the windows, where I found the book about the rivers of Africa.* She climbed down and tugged the ladder toward the windows. It slid along until she was almost there, then just stopped.

She looked up at the shelves, expecting to see a book had fallen down and was blocking the way, but she could see nothing to keep the ladder from moving. Sighing, she gathered her skirts and climbed up to the very top. Once there, she looked at the wheels that rolled the ladder about the room on the narrow railing, but they, too, seemed fine.

Well, there was nothing for it. She'd have to try to jar the ladder into moving. As she started to descend, her gaze fell on a row of books a shelf over. There, in the center, was the book she'd been looking for.

She hooked her arm about the side of the ladder, and leaned as far as she could. Her fingers brushed the book, but try as she would, she could reach no farther. *Blast it!*

Her gaze narrowed. If she moved to the outer side of the ladder and hooked her leg about the side rail, then she could lean out and get the book.

She hooked her arm around a rung and then, with a little hop, hooked her leg around the rail until she had a foot on each side. The position felt far more precarious than she'd expected, and the ladder felt as if it were tilting to one side.

She cautiously leaned toward the shelf and to her relief easily grabbed the book. "Now I have you!"

Glowing with triumph, she turned to right herself on the ladder. She was almost there when a loud pop broke the silence and the ladder lurched to one side, hanging from the railing by only one wheel.

Rose clung frantically as the ladder dangled like a drunken sailor.

"Oh no!" She glanced at the open door. "Help!" she called. "MacDougal! Anyone! Please!"

Sixteen

From the Diary of the Duchess of Roxburghe

My mother was a great woman. It was she and not Father who ran our household. It was she who tucked us into our bed at night. She selected our governesses, oversaw our wardrobes, and disciplined us for bad behaviors. She also encouraged our efforts, and gave praise only when it was due so as not to cheapen it.

My mother also gave me the best piece of advice I've ever received, advice so brilliant that I had it engraved on a locket.

"Margaret," she told me time and again, "you may be anything you wish, so long as you're never boring."

It took me almost thirty years to figure out what she meant, but I finally did.

I will never be boring.

After talking to Aunt Margaret, Sin had taken a very long ride, at first too furious to think. But eventually, he was able to consider all that she'd said. It was then that he discovered a very shocking fact: his desire to be repaid for his humiliations from that night long ago had been replaced with a bigger, more complex desire. He wanted Rose Balfour.

He didn't want her "because of," or "in order to," or for any other reason than the fact that there was something about this stubborn slip of a woman that set him afire. She challenged him as no other woman ever had.

He'd be a fool not to enjoy her while he was here; they were both adults and there was nothing stopping their mutual pleasure. When their time here came to an end, as it inevitably would, then they'd leave each other with no more regrets.

Somehow, Aunt Margaret had taken that idyllic concept and twisted it about. Of course they had to be circumspect, but not all sensual pleasures resulted in ruin. If that were true, no one in the *ton* would still have an intact reputation.

He and Rose were adults and could take care that they weren't discovered. All he had to do was explain this to Rose.

It was time to take back the reins of their relationship. Voicing a protest about Rose's avoidance would be tacitly allowing her to win her point, but he was willing to accept a small defeat in exchange for a more sensual kind of victory.

He reached the empty hallway outside the sitting room and paused to adjust his cuffs. Perhaps he would have a glass of port while wait—

"Help!" Rose cried. Sin was in the library before he had time to think. She was hanging precariously from the side of the ladder while it slowly rocked back and forth, one lone wheel holding it in place. At any moment, either the ladder or Rose or both could come tumbling down.

He'd just reached her when the ladder gave a loud *crack* and the wheel popped off the railing. As the ladder went tumbling to the rug below, Sin caught Rose.

She buried her face in his neck and held on to him as if her life depended on it. Her eyes were squinched closed, her thick lashes crescents on her cheeks, and she held a book against her as if releasing it would send her tumbling anew.

"Rose?"

She slowly opened her eyes and blinked. "I'm not dead?"

"Not yet, although I am beginning to think that ladder is cursed where you are concerned."

Rose gave a shaky laugh and it was all Sin could do not to hug her tightly.

She gave him a rueful look. "It's not the ladder; it's just me. I wanted to get this book but the ladder wouldn't roll, so I climbed to the outer edge and when I leaned in to get the book . . . You know the rest."

Sin slowly set her on her feet. Her thick black

hair, soft as silk and curling with a life of its own, was already falling down on one side. He kept an arm about her waist, her hair clinging to his arm as if to hold him in place.

"Sin, you can release me."

He could hold her forever.

"Sin?"

He started. "Of course." He removed his arm and she put a respectable distance between them. "We'll tell MacDougal about the ladder on our way out."

She nodded and, after an awkward pause, said, "Thank you for catching me."

"The pleasure was all mine."

She smiled, fingering the froth of lace that decorated the neckline of her gown.

It made him wonder about the treasures hidden under the foamy whiteness. "It's rather fortunate I wasn't, say, avoiding you. Had I been, I wouldn't have heard your call for help."

She flushed and turned toward the door like a deer in flight.

He stepped forward, blocking her way. "No, damn it. Don't rush away. I wish to speak to you."

"I don't think that's wise."

"Then be unwise for a moment. Regardless of what my aunt says, there's no reason for us to avoid each other. We're wasting precious time that we could better spend together."

"Sin, we should never have tempted fate the way

we did. Had someone caught us . . ." She shook her head.

"Tempting fate?" His gaze swept over her. "Oh, Rose, we were tempting much more than fate."

"You didn't enjoy being the center of a scandal before," she retorted. "What makes you think you'll enjoy it now?"

"Perhaps I've found something that is worth risking such an occurrence."

Rose could only blink. "You mean *me*? That *I'm* worth taking a chance on?"

"Who else?" He came closer, moving with that lethal grace that made her mouth go dry. "Rose, I want to see what this attraction is that plays between us. I want to see where it takes us, and I want us to enjoy it while it lasts."

He'd had her, right up to "while it lasts." The words doused her with the cold water of reason. "No." She walked to the door.

She was almost there when he said, "What's wrong, Rose? Afraid to go exploring with me?"

The way he said "exploring" sent a shiver of anticipation up her spine, as if they were on a hunt for a buried treasure. The way his touch affected her, it was an apt description. "No. I'm not afraid of you, Sin." *I'm afraid of me.*

He followed her to the door and placed his hand on her cheek, her skin soft and warm beneath his fingers. "Do you feel that, Rose? How your body reacts when I touch you?" He bent, his mouth beside her ear. "It's the same for me. Every time you're close, I feel *this*." He ran his thumb over her soft lips.

She sucked her breath in, but made no effort to move away. He knew why, too. She could no more say no to their passion than he could. His body was afire, aching, yearning. God, he wanted her.

If he were to have her, he'd have to show her what he meant. Even if Aunt Margaret threw water on their passion with her chilling words, he knew how to kindle it back to a flame—with actions.

He slipped a hand about her waist and pulled her close. "Rose, being fearful of a new moment isn't the worst thing that can happen. The worst thing is missing that moment, of letting it go by. Those moments may never come again."

He bent to capture her lips when she raised her hands between them. "Sin, what are you doing? What do you want?"

"For us to enjoy each other and take this passion wherever it goes." He sank his hand into her hair and tilted her face to his. "Come and enjoy life with me, Rose. Stop worrying about what may happen or not happen. You and I have already had too much of that in our lives."

She met his gaze directly. "And then?"

He shrugged. "Then we go our separate ways, happy to have shared our lives for a short time." He smiled down at her. "You must admit that's a much better ending than the one we had before." He bent and nuzzled her neck, tasting the sweetness of her. At the touch, his body roared to life, but she was pushing him away once again.

"No, no, *no*." She spun away and began to pace the carpet. "This is exactly what I feared would happen."

He watched her hips sway under her gown. "What is?"

"Sin, don't you see what's happening? Every time we're together, we fall into this—this mad way of doing things that rushes us toward a bad ending."

"Being attracted to each other is bad? Enjoying the gifts life has given us is mad? If that's madness, then I welcome it."

"But you and I aren't the only ones involved." She was becoming more and more agitated, waving her arms as she talked. "We've got to control this, stop it. We lived through the outcome of this before and neither of us should have to go there again."

"At one time, I thought the same."

"At one time?" She stopped pacing to stare at him, her eyes narrowed. "You thought that very thing the day I arrived!"

"I've changed my mind. Now I want—"

"Oh, shush."

He blinked. She'd *shushed* him. Never, in all of his days, had anyone shushed him. He didn't know what to say.

"Six years ago," Rose said, "my impulsiveness led to a kiss, that much is true. But it was *your* unchecked passion that made it so . . ." She shook her head. "I still feel that same shock when you kiss me today. You and I are like kindling. One touch of a match and we burst into flames."

"Which is good—"

"Which is *bad*. Do you know how short of a time kindling burns? I don't want that, Sin. I don't want that sort of relationship with anyone."

He hadn't really thought about their having a "relationship." His smile slipped.

"Furthermore," she continued, "you've made my life awkward and uncomfortable."

"How so?" he demanded.

"Because . . . things have changed because of you. I don't even know if I can go back to Caith Manor and be happy again." Her smile wavered. "I used to read and ride horses and do the accounts and help my father with his horticulture. Now all I do is think about you."

He didn't know what to say.

She saw his indecision and her lips thinned. "Your aunt was right: engaging in such shenanigans with you is fool's play, and I'm the fool. Well, from now on I won't think about you *at all*. Good-bye, Sin."

She spun on her heel and marched from the room like a victorious general, leaving him. Yes, leaving *him*. If fury were a color, the entire room would ooze red.

Without knowing why, he reached for her, catching her wrist and spinning her back to face him.

Her back stiffened. "Let me go."

"No."

Her eyes flashed, but just as quickly, she appeared on the verge of tears, which made his heart feel as if it had been stabbed. "Sin, what do you want?" she asked.

Damn it, he didn't *know* what he wanted. He only knew he didn't want to see her walking out the door. Yet his pride wouldn't let him say that aloud. He'd be damned if he'd be that vulnerable to anyone, especially her.

And why should he? She was the one threatening to leave, not him. "You and I began this with two wagers: one on a horse race, which you won by cheating, and one on an archery contest, which I won by talent."

Disappointment flickered over her face and she pulled her arm free of his grasp. "We are done with that."

"We're tied, Rose. We need one more wager to break it." He wasn't certain what that one more wager would accomplish, but at least it would give him more time.

"No."

He stepped between her and the door. "You can't leave. Not until we have a resolution."

Her eyebrows lowered, and she attempted to walk around him.

Sin took a step toward her. He wasn't planning to do anything rash; he just needed to get closer to her in some way. To *show* her.

Her lips firmed into a line and, with a muttered curse, she slipped past him and behind a chair. "Stop right there. I am done talking."

He wasn't sure what he was going to do, but b'God, he was going to do *something*. "Well, I'm *not*."

She gripped the back of the chair and eyed the doorway, obviously measuring her escape route.

He picked up the chair and tossed it aside, ignoring the crash of crystal as it struck a side table and sent it and a candy dish toppling.

Rose gasped and whirled to run . . . but she made it only two steps before he caught her, swooped her up, and tossed her over his shoulder like a sack of flour.

Seventeen

From the Diary of the Duchess of Roxburghe

I vow, I cannot seem to walk past a window without seeing my great-nephew carrying Miss Balfour somewhere. All great romantic poems have such scenes where the hero, in a fit of passion, sweeps the heroine off her feet. Sadly, it appears that Sin's technique is questionable.

I'm surprised that, with all of his supposed experience with the gentler sex, he doesn't realize that women do not like to be carried in a way that musses their hair and leaves them with unattractively red faces.

Sadly, yet another conversation I shall have to have with that boy.

Rose grabbed at his coat with both hands. "Put me down!"

"No."

"How can you— Don't you— I'm going to— How *dare* you!" She beat on his back with her fists as he crossed the room and threw open one of the terrace doors. "Sin, no! You can't take me outside like this; someone will see us!"

"One benefit of my aunt's guest list is that none of them can see a thing at a distance. Their hearing is equally poor, so feel free to yell for help." As the cool evening air enveloped him, a drop of wetness fell on his face. He rested his hand on her backside, holding her in place when she began to kick.

"Let. Me. Down. *Now.*"

As he crossed the terrace, he lifted his face to the misty rain. He could feel her gown dampen as it thirstily soaked up the droplets. "Rain is good for the soul."

"But not for my good shoes!"

He looked at the silk shoes, pulled them off her, and tucked them into his pockets.

"Sin—"

"Shush." Damn, that felt good.

She gave a screech of fury and pounded on his back.

He didn't give a damn. His temper had risen from slow simmer to boiling until he was left with one desire: he wanted Rose to be every bit as upset as she'd made him. This time *he* would be the one laughing, not her.

As he reached the end of the terrace, his gaze fell upon the small punting boats beside the lake. He smiled grimly and strode toward the water.

Rose was still struggling to free herself, so he rested his arm more tightly across her legs. "Stop squirming or I'll drop you."

"Fine!" she snapped, squirming all the more.

He smacked her bottom with a firm hand.

"Ow!" She stiffened and then pounded on his back with her fists. "Don't! You! Dare!"

He chuckled, careful not to slip on the wet grass. Something moved against his coat and he looked down to find one of her curls twined about the breast pocket. Two weeks ago, he'd have sworn that Rose wasn't a beauty in any sense of the word, but he was finding certain things about her appealing.

He was especially fond of the impertinent curls that clung to his coat even now, made him yearn to touch them. He knew they would be deliciously soft, and lively, far from the tepid silkiness of other women's hair. Rose's hair had a life of its own, especially now that it was damp from the misting rain. It frothed and clung, curled and twined, as if trying to tangle him up with its mistress.

She turned this way and that, trying to see where he was headed. "Where are you going? Sin, this isn't funny! I'm going to—What are you doing?"

He'd reached the lake. With a quick heave, he bent and dumped her into one of the punts that was half in the water, the long pole held loosely in place by a large metal ring on the bow.

She scrambled for balance in the bobbing vessel, finally grabbing the sides and holding herself upright. "What are you—"

He placed his boot upon the bow and shoved the punt into the water.

"*Oh! You*—" She glared as the boat scooted into the lake, raindrops pattering like tiny explosions all about her.

"You'd best grab the punting pole."

She looked around. "The what?"

"The punting pole. It's—" The pole fell from the ring that held it in place and dropped into the water.

Rose was now adrift in a punt, no pole in sight. The rain was quickening, too, and her gown was soaked at the shoulders. "You can't do this."

"I can, and I did. And now, I believe I'll join my aunt and her guests for dinner."

She muttered something under her breath and then scrambled to the front of the boat, where she cupped her hands and tried to paddle. But the flat-bottomed punt only turned slowly in place.

"You're wasting your time."

She kept paddling and the punt began to move backward a bit, away from the shoreline.

She dropped back to her heels and scowled at him, panting. "Fine. You've made your point."

"Which is?"

She opened her mouth and then closed it. "I have no idea."

He crossed his arms. "You blame me for your own lack of self-control. For every kiss you've gotten, I've gotten one back. It's a two-way street, my love. And you are not alone in fighting this attraction that flows between us."

She met his gaze for a long moment, the only sound that of the plop of the rain upon the lake. Finally, she said, "I suppose you're right. I don't like feeling so . . . vulnerable." Rain had thoroughly wet her hair and now it frothed and curled about her head like a halo.

I don't like feeling vulnerable, either. "Perhaps we both feel that way at times."

Her gaze sharpened. "Perhaps. I must admit that you've been honest about your desires."

He lifted a brow. *"And?"*

"Oh, for the love of—" She pressed her fisted hands to her eyes. "Fine!" She looked up. "I shouldn't blame you for all of our kisses. Some of them were my fault."

"Another home truth. A pity it had to be wrested from you." He started to turn back to the house.

"Sin, you can't leave me floating here!"

"Why not? You once ran me and my horse into the river, and I didn't even have the luxury of a boat." He rocked back on his heels. "If I were you, I'd sit back and enjoy the solitude."

"The duchess will miss me at dinner."

"Not after I pass on your regrets. Headache, you know. The kind only a good sleep will cure."

Her lips thinned. "You wouldn't."

"Wouldn't I?"

Her gaze flickered across him, the lake, and then her boat. Suddenly her lips quivered and she chuckled. "We are fools, Sin."

Her smile softened his irritation.

"Maybe we deserve each other." She shook her head. "I don't know, but you've made your point."

"Trying to bamboozle me, sweet?"

"No. Just agreeing with you. I'm stuck here, so I might as well enjoy it." She reached into the pocket of her gown and pulled out the book that she'd gone to such lengths to retrieve from the library. "At least I have something to read."

"I'll leave you to enjoy it."

As he turned, she opened the book. "I hope this mist won't get the book wet."

He kept walking.

She said loudly, "It's your uncle's book and such a beautiful one, too. Leather and quite old. And look! There's even an inscription to him from— Heavens, is that from the king?"

Sin stopped and turned.

She ran her hand over the book, which was beginning to shine with dampness. "I daresay your great-uncle prizes this book. Your aunt might, as well. I do hope I don't drop it in the lake." As she spoke, she held the book over the water.

"You little minx."

She put a hand to her cheek and looked so pretend-shocked that he seriously thought about stomping through the water and tipping her over. Without the book, of course.

She looked at him. "Would you like to have your uncle's book back? We all know how he loves his library."

He had to give her grudging respect. "You are the cheekiest woman I've ever met—even while floating in the middle of a lake in a rudderless, paddleless boat."

"I'm also wet and getting hungry, and I've no wish for my new gown to get ruined." She lifted her brows. "I don't suppose you'd be willing to trade? The book for a pole so that I may rescue myself?"

He glanced up at the sky. The drizzle had stopped for now, but it might come back at any moment. "Fine." He removed a long pole from another boat. "Grab the end and I'll pull you closer."

Soon, she was within the pole's length from the shore. "Hold tightly to the end of the pole," he ordered.

She did so and he released it. "Now, throw me the book."

She tossed the book, which landed far behind him in the yard.

"Now we're even." She sat down to thread the pole through the metal ring that would hold it in place. "Thank you for the lovely boat ride. I only wish it had come after dinner. Without rain, of course."

"Just for the record, we still have matters to discuss."

"No, we don't. We won't meet alone again."

"We will. Before you leave this house." With that, he bowed, scooped up the book on his way, and continued on to the house.

As annoying as it was to admit, thanks to his temper, he was back to step one with Rose. Pushing her out into the middle of a lake in a paddleless boat would hardly make her trust him again.

He absently looked down at the book in his hand, opening it to the inscription. *Roxburghe, this is to replace the one I lost. Cousin Harry.*

Sin stopped. Why, that little . . . She'd said it was inscribed from the king! He turned and saw her tying her boat to the dock. With an efficient dusting of her hands, she began to walk up the lawn. Seeing the book open in his hands, she grinned and waved.

Sin clamped his jaw together and continued toward the house. As soon as his back was toward her, though, a faint smile slipped through. He never knew what would happen with Rose Balfour. Perhaps the time had come for some surprises of his own.

Feeling more hopeful, he entered the castle, informing MacDougal that Miss Balfour had been taking the air and might now need an umbrella.

Eighteen

From the Diary of the Duchess of Roxburghe
My uncle used to say that regret is a bitter spice best served with warm bread. I have no idea what that means, but every time I've repeated it to someone, they always look much struck, as if the saying is both profound and pragmatic.

I wonder if this advice would be helpful to my great-nephew? I must find something to urge him onward . . .

Dunn held up Sin's Hessians and eyed the mud caked on the heels. "Has the duchess taken to serving dinner in the middle of the wet woods?"

"That happened before dinner, when I went hunting," Sin said, stretching his feet to the fire.

"Ah. Hunting. Before dinner, no less. As I don't see a bruise upon you, I assume Miss Balfour didn't accompany you."

"Oh, she was there."

"Of course she was. I shall put your boots in the hallway and have them cleaned."

Sin nodded absently. If their little trip to the lake had done nothing else, it seemed to have cleared the air between him and Rose. She'd arrived twenty minutes late to dinner, claiming issues with a hem. Usually a stickler about dinner times, Aunt Margaret had taken Rose's tardiness with amazing calm and had kindly offered the use of her dresser for any further repairs Rose's wardrobe might need.

And for the first time since they'd arrived at Floors, Rose's seat wasn't at the far end of the table, but a mere two places from his. Not close enough for conversation, but several times they'd found themselves sharing an amused glance over something their companions said. Often that glance turned into a smile. And with every smile came a memory of a kiss or a touch. At least it did for Sin. For her part, other than looking slightly flushed, Rose seemed far less affected.

Truly, this was the oddest flirtation he'd ever indulged in; it was more of a trial by fire.

Dunn returned and went to the fire, where he'd hung a small brass pot. He used tongs to lift it from the fire and to open the lid.

The scent of cloves and rum tickled Sin's nose. "Your hot toddies are magical, Dunn."

"So I've been told, my lord." The valet poured some into a cup and handed it to Sin.

"Thank you, Dunn. You're a good man."

"Thank you, my lord. May I inquire as to your plans tomorrow, so that I can lay out your clothes?"

"There was talk of a game of pall-mall, but you know how I detest that."

"Yes," Dunn said drily. "As much as you hate archery and whist."

"That borders on impertinence."

The valet hid a smile, but bowed.

Sin had made certain Aunt Margaret knew his feelings on the subject of pall-mall. He'd hoped they'd planned something that would allow him to spend some time with Rose now that their silence was at an end. But the Misses Stewart seemed enthralled with the idea, as did Mr. Munro, so there was little Sin could say to turn it. "I may ride while the others are playing that infernal game."

"Yes, my lord." Dunn busied himself while Sin sipped his toddy.

Today hadn't turned out as he'd hoped, but at least he'd made some progress in thawing Rose. It was irritating that he had only a week left. It would be nice if he could get Rose away from the house on another ride. But how? His options were growing less by the day. Perhaps it was time he stopped being so proud. Even though he'd told his great-aunt that he didn't play—

A noise sounded in the hallway. "Dunn, did you hear that?"

Dunn, folding small clothes by the wardrobe door, frowned. "Did I hear what, my lord?"

"Never mind. I must have . . ." He frowned at the door and then stood and crossed to it, but by the time he got there, the faint noise had abated.

Holding up a hand to indicate silence, Sin pressed his ear to the panel and listened, his hand about the doorknob.

After a few seconds, he stepped back and yanked the door open with a jerk. He'd thought to surprise whoever had been lurking outside his door, but the hallway was empty.

He frowned. How odd. *I know I heard something. I—*

His gaze fell on his boots sitting out in the hall to be cleaned. "Bloody hell, you little sneak! Don't chew on my damn boots!" He lifted a small brown pug by the scruff and scowled at it.

The dog dropped his ears in placation, its tiny tail spinning. Sin's irritation softened instantly.

Dunn picked up the boots, his mouth tight with disapproval. "The left tassel is torn, and it appears the right tassel has been eaten." Dunn glared at the dog. "Shall I take this filthy creature to the kitchen, my lord?"

A door down the hallway opened and Aunt Margaret's dresser stuck her head out. She looked up and down the hallway until she spied the pug. "Och, there he is! Her grace has been lookin' fer the wee thing all evenin'." Mrs. Dennis came to collect the animal, cooing, "Aw! Such a precious puppy ye are! Thank ye, Lord Sinclair, fer findin' him."

"I didn't," Sin said. "He was wandering the halls."

"He dinna usually do tha', me lord, but he's taken to hiding in Miss Balfour's room." The maid glanced at a door just two down from his own. "The precious puppy loves her dearly. I daresay her door was closed and he couldna get in, and so he came to yers."

"Pardon me, madam," Dunn said in a frosty voice, "but your 'precious puppy' has eaten one of Lord Sinclair's tassels and mauled another."

"Och no!" She looked at the pug, a horrified expression on her face. "He dinna!"

"Yes, madam, he did."

She hugged the dog. "The poor little pup! I do hope it doesna make him sick."

"Poor pup? What about poor Lord Sinclair? The tassels were *gold.*"

Mrs. Dennis's mouth thinned. "I'll be sure to tell her grace tha' ye want yer tassel back." She lifted her brows. "I suppose we can set a footman to lookin' fer it."

"No, no," Sin said hastily. "That won't be necessary." He took Dunn's elbow and pushed the man back into his room. "Good night, Mrs. Dennis. Convey my compliments to my aunt."

"Aye, yer lordship." Mrs. Dennis bobbed a curtsy and Sin closed the door.

Dunn held the boots to the light. "Impertinent

woman. If she knew what these boots cost, she'd have taken a different tone."

"We can get more tassels," Sin said absently, feeling elated. *So that's Rose's bedchamber.* Smiling, he returned to his seat by the fire and stretched his feet toward the blaze. *Thank you, dog. That information is well worth two gold tassels.*

Late the next day, Rose stepped outside and tightened the ribbons on her poke bonnet to keep the wind from stealing it. She took a deep breath of the scent of warm grass and sunshine. It was late afternoon, when the sun slanted at a deep angle, tossing a final golden glow over the world before it faded away. Her favorite time of day.

And it had been a good day. She and Sin had reached an accord and he'd been very polite to her, talking to her with such ease that several times she'd been betrayed into a genuine laugh. Those moments had been bittersweet, though, since she still felt a deep longing for him.

A cacophony of barking made her look across the lawn and she saw the pugs, happy to be outdoors as they tumbled over one another, moving toward her like a swarm of bees.

Followed by a harried-looking footman, they arrived at her feet in a pile of wiggly pug noses and twirly pig tails. She laughed when Teenie ended up sitting on Meenie's head, refusing to move until Meenie squirmed out from under him.

"I'm glad I'm not one of your littermates," she told Teenie, who looked unrepentant, panting with his tongue hanging out one side.

Beenie barked, his tail twirling so fast it looked like a blur. Grinning, Rose bent to pat them all, scratching ears and bellies until the arrival of Lady Charlotte and her fascinating bag of yarn sent them all racing to the terrace.

Chuckling to herself, Rose walked down the lawn to where MacDougal was overseeing the footmen as they put up hoops for a game of pall-mall.

MacDougal smiled as she approached. "How does it look to ye, miss?"

She eyed the course. "The final two hoops are a bit close."

"Do you think so, miss?" MacDougal took a mallet from the leather holder and measured. "Aye, ye've the right of it." He gestured to a footman. "Davies, be a guid lad and move that second hoop. 'Tis a bit close."

The footman bent to fix the hoop.

"Ye play often, miss?" MacDougal asked politely.

"Oh yes. My sisters and I frequently play." And Rose almost always won, much to Dahlia's chagrin. Lily wasn't interested in playing unless there was a prize at stake. If there was no prize, she was frequently distracted from the game and had to be constantly reminded when it was her turn.

But Dahlia . . . Rose smiled. She loved her youngest sister's sense of competition. No one had a fiercer desire to win. Well, except Rose.

She wandered to the mallets and selected a bright red one.

"A poor choice," said a deep voice.

She turned, surprised to find Sin standing slightly behind her; the thick grass and the deep brim of her bonnet had hidden his arrival. "Why is red a poor choice?"

"It's unlucky. Surely you've heard that."

"Actually, I've heard that red is the luckiest color of all," she countered.

He was dressed in his riding clothes, which explained where he'd been all afternoon. His smile glinted. "Green is the best color but, unfortunately for you"—he leaned past her and took the green mallet— "someone already has it."

Her heart trilled. "*You're* playing? The man who just last night called the game 'childish' and 'a bore'?"

"I was just trying to scare off the competition. And I believe I was successful, for it appears we will be the only two on the field. All of our competitors have bowed out." He smiled down at her, and the afternoon sun made him look like a lion, all gold and powerful. "It appears that it's just you and me."

Just you and me. There was something about the way he said the words that made her smile. "How did you manage to get the others to resign?"

"With great cunning and trickery."

She laughed. "I see."

"Actually, all I had to do was point out that you were the best representative of your fair sex, while I was the best representative of mine. After I put it that way, they were content to sit back and allow us to fight an epic battle on our own."

She pretended to consider him, looking him up and down, trying not to linger on certain areas. "I suppose you'll make a decent replacement player. It will certainly mean less work for the footmen, as Miss Isobel always shoots wild. She hit a tree yesterday."

"From here?" He shaded his eyes and looked toward the stand of trees near the lake. "That's impressive. It's a wonder no one was killed."

"I think her grace feared for the windows."

"And with reason, apparently." He gestured to the opening hoop. "Shall we?"

They strolled across the lawn, a rare and warm intimacy between them. Rose sent him a glance from under her lashes. "I must say, this is far more pleasant than my punting expedition yesterday."

He pulled to a halt. "Perhaps I owe you an apology for that."

"And perhaps I owe you one for treating you as if you had the plague." She turned to him. "I've been meaning to have a word with you about our conversation in the library."

"Are we about to have another argument? For if we are, I'd feel better if we weren't carrying weapons."

She laughed. "I took a vow to never use my mallet as a weapon, so you're safe with me."

"I shall take a similar vow, then." He held up his hand and mumbled something that included "mallet" and "forever."

"There." He dropped his hand. "You are now safe from a violent death."

"I'm relieved," she said, trying to keep the laughter from her voice. "As I was saying, I allowed your great-aunt's fear to lead me too far down the path of caution. She was right that we should be more careful, but I should have come to you and said that. Instead, I just avoided you. It was cowardly of me."

"Perhaps. Or perhaps it was very smart." He slanted her a glance that was as hot as a coal. "I would be lying if I said I didn't want you in my bed, for I do. And it would be a lie if I said that I would stop attempting to win you there, for I won't." He leaned down, his voice intimate. "I can promise you one thing, Rose Balfour: one day you will accept my invitation."

As Rose looked into his eyes, a sweet, urgent yearning swept through her. If she closed her eyes, she would know exactly where he was from the tug her body felt from his presence.

She wanted desperately to answer that call. To be honest, she would have been painfully disappointed if he'd stopped attempting to seduce her. It was quite heady having a man pursue one so single-mindedly. "Perhaps I am thinking the same thing."

Sin looked at Rose in surprise, the light in his eyes telling her he wanted to kiss her.

Rose had to fight the urge not to throw her arms about his neck. *Why is it that good things end so quickly, while the bad and mundane seem to march forever?* And he was part of something good—not something permanent, but a part of her life she'd never regret.

Sin tilted his head to one side and the wind ruffled his hair, while the sunlight made his eyes seem almost golden. *I only have one more week of freedom. One more week of being only Rose and not Rose-the-housekeeper or Rose-the-sock-mender or Rose-the-chaperone. I have to take advantage of this opportunity. If I don't, I'll regret it for the rest of my life.*

Over the thud of her heartbeat, she heard herself say, "We *could* make this match more exciting. I believe we owe each other a tiebreaker."

"Yes, yes—a thousand times yes! And the forfeit?"

"Whatever the winner wishes."

He bowed, looking into her eyes the entire time.

Rose had never felt so alive. She gestured to the opening hoop. "Shall we play, then? Just to pass the time until we're ready for . . . other things."

"If we didn't have an audience, I'd show you how ready *I* am for other things, as well."

"Audience?" She followed his gaze to the terrace, shading her eyes. "Oh dear. The duchess and Lady Charlotte, Mr. and Mrs. Stewart, and Lady McFarlane, too. Even the vicar."

"Yes, we are this afternoon's entertainment. I feel as if we're on a stage."

"I'd offer to sing, but it would only upset any nearby cows. I shall have to astonish them with my superior pall-mall skills, instead."

"Superior? Compared to what? I was quite good as a child."

"I'm sure you were quite good . . . as a child. Now pray just stand back and watch how an adult plays." She bent, lined up her mallet, and—*whack*—sent her ball rolling.

Sin's brows rose. "Not bad." He placed his ball, lined up his shot, and followed suit. It rolled to within a foot of hers.

"Not bad." She sent him a mischievous look. "But not good enough, either."

"I'm only warming up, Miss Balfour. I find that it's important to save one's strength for the finish."

"A good credo, if one were a horse." They played on and two shots later, she misjudged a dip in the ground and her ball went to one side. "Blast it!"

From the terrace, Lady Charlotte cupped her mouth and yelled, "*A bit more to the left!*"

Rose turned an amazed gaze toward the house while Sin chuckled. "My, such vigor from a woman sitting in a chair and knitting."

She pulled her gaze back to him. "Fortunately, I can't lose; I have the lucky red mallet."

"And I have the lucky green one. I fear one of our mallets is bound for disappointment."

She kindly patted his arm. "It won't be mine." She went on to make her point by outshooting him at the next two hoops.

Sin badly wanted to win, and not just for the prize. With Rose, nothing else was good enough. He concentrated on his shot and managed to beat her to the next hoop.

And thus it went for the next half hour. Every shot she made, he either matched it or came close. But try as he would, he couldn't pass her. Their audience on the terrace continued to yell comments, most of them useless and all of them irritating.

Finally, they reached the final four hoops. Rose aligned her mallet. Before she could hit the ball, Lady Charlotte yelled from the terrace, *"Not to raise the pressure on you, dear, but we have a lot of pin money riding on this."*

"Wonderful," Rose muttered.

"But don't get nervous," Lady Charlotte yelled. *"Just play as you normally do."*

"Only better," the duchess shouted.

"Yes, a little better," Lady Charlotte continued. *"Play on, Miss Balfour!"*

"They're worse than my sisters," Rose said under her breath. The wind had picked up a bit, so she had to watch her skirts as she lined up her shot. If the wind puffed just as she swung, her skirts could tangle with her mallet.

She waited until a breeze had passed and then took her shot. It rolled straight and true through the hoop.

Applause erupted from the women on the terrace, accompanied by groans from the men.

Sin grinned at their enthusiasm and took his shot, which followed hers almost perfectly. The applause erupted again.

Rose and Sin stopped at the final hoop. The sun was almost down and there was only enough light for a few more moments. "It's a bit rocky in this part of the lawn," Sin said.

"It's going to be tricky."

"Good God, will someone play?" Mrs. Stewart yelled from the terrace. *"I have twenty quid on the gel and it's almost naptime!"*

Rose laughed and peeped at Sin from beneath her bonnet. "Our last shots. May the best pall-maller win."

"To the best." Sin stood to one side and watched Rose prepare for her turn. She lifted her face to the wind and judged it, eyed the rough grass, and then gripped her mallet, a determined expression on her face.

She bent her head to make her shot. Her sweet neck was exposed between her bonnet and the neckline of her gown, and he was suddenly aflame with the desire to press his lips to that spot and feel her shiver against him.

He moved a bit closer, his eyes locked on the spot.

If they weren't being watched so closely, he would have kissed her tender skin right then and there.

Rose swung her mallet back and—

"*Ow!*" Sin grabbed his shin and hopped. "Damn it!" he said through gritted teeth. From the howls of laughter from the terrace, Sin gathered that everyone had seen Rose's shot. Half of them were cackling and crowing while the other half whooped. The sound was as demonic as his shin felt.

Rose was looking at him, her eyes wide, her hand over her mouth.

"Not your fault," he said through gritted teeth. Though his leg still throbbed, he released it and straightened. After a few deep breaths, he was able to say in a relatively normal voice, "Just take your turn. If you don't, those hyenas on the terrace will never quit."

She glanced at the terrace and nodded. She turned and made her shot. Her ball hurdled straight to the pole, easily knocking his ball out of the way.

"*Good play!*" the duchess called.

"*One for the ladies!*" Lady Charlotte said, clapping.

"*And a jolly good blow to the shin, too!*" Mrs. Stewart added. "*An excellent strategy!*"

Sin, who could feel the knot rising on his shin, snarled, "Vultures, the lot of them."

"They're not being very kind," she agreed.

"Well, I have one shot to best you and I'm going to take it, pained shin or not." He eyed the distance with a considering gaze and then limped over to line up his mallet.

He bent to shoot, then stopped and looked up at her. "You're in the light."

Rose moved to one side. The evening wind was rising and she had to keep her hands down to her sides to keep the wind from whipping her skirts too much.

Sin began his swing. Just as he did, a strong wind rippled across the lawn, sending her skirts flapping despite her efforts.

Sin caught the flutter of her skirts out of the corner of his eye just as he swung at the ball. His gaze immediately turned her way and as he looked, so went his mallet. Instead of hitting the ball head-on, he clipped it and it spun into a small dip beside a shrub.

"Damn it!" he snapped.

"Another one for the ladies!" Lady Charlotte called from her knitting. *"Thank you, Lord Sinclair! I just won two shillings from the vicar!"*

"As did I!" called the duchess.

The vicar was staring bleakly at them. "Oh dear," Rose said. "I hope he didn't also wager with Mrs. Stewart. She gloats horribly."

Sin didn't answer.

She turned and saw that the green mallet had already been returned to the leather case. Sin was gone, his broad shoulders catching the final rays of the sun as he headed for the stables, limping.

Nineteen

From the Diary of the Duchess of Roxburghe
I've never heard a vicar speak like that. Had I
known he could curse in such a superior fashion,
I might have listened to his sermons more closely.

Dinner that night was lively. Rose was feted by the
game watchers, toasted as the Queen of Pall-Mall, and
given a crown made of silver paper. Lady Charlotte
and the duchess were giddy and couldn't stop talking
about the game. Even Mrs. Stewart, who was usually
asleep by the second course, had been so enlivened by
winning a shilling from the vicar that she managed to
stay awake for the entire meal.

As dinner progressed, Sin heard such exaggera-
tions about the game that he began to wonder if he'd
attended the same one. But the worst of it was the
mockery he had to endure. He had thought that at
least Mr. Stewart would show some restraint, but
the elderly gentleman had made such comic faces
while telling the story of Sin's injured leg that Lord

Cameron and Mr. Munro had been sent into gales of laughter.

Rose occasionally sent him commiserating glances, which he appreciated, but they did little for his wounded pride.

By the time the gentlemen were having port, Sin was eager to escape. He wouldn't have a chance to speak with Rose this evening since she was the center of attention, so he sent the duchess a message that he was retiring early and left for the quiet of his bedchamber.

Once there, he tossed off his coat, waistcoat, and boots, then stood for some minutes at the window watching the moon spill over the lake. Then he'd found a book, settled in the chair by the fire, and tried to read. Instead, he promptly fell asleep.

He awoke hours later to a dark room, a streak of moonlight limning the room in silver-gray. The fire was almost out and the house was cloaked in silence. Rubbing sleep from his face, he placed his book on the table beside his chair, and then, yawning mightily, went to the window to close the curtains. The full moon washed the castle lands with a gleaming light, while an evening breeze made the grass look like a rippling silver loch.

The beauty of it held him for a long moment before he turned to retire. But just as he turned, a movement caught his eye. On the black ribbon of the drive, a horse cantered along, ridden by a slight woman in a cloak. Sin cursed under his breath. *Rose.*

And it wasn't just any horse, either, but a huge, bruising monster of a mount. Rose looked like a doll perched upon its back, at risk of being thrown at any moment. No groom followed her; she was alone.

Rose cantered down the end of the drive and turned eastward on the stage road.

Cursing, Sin threw on his coat and boots and ran out to the stables. A single lantern hung at the far end of a row of stalls. "Hello?" he called.

A burly groom came around the corner and eyed Sin with distrust. "Aye, me lord?"

"I'm the Earl of Sinclair, her grace's great-nephew. Did you saddle a horse for Miss Balfour?"

"The lass is no' in danger," the groom said sullenly.

"I saw that bloody horse you gave her, and I know he's a handful."

"He can be. But if Pronto gets resty, she'll pull him up. I made certain she could handle tha' horse afore I let her take him."

"I'm sure you both think she can handle that horse, but I'd rather she didn't discover that you were both incorrect while she's out cantering alone in the dark." Realizing his hands were fisted at his sides, Sin forced himself to relax them and say in a level tone, "Find me a horse that can keep up with Miss Balfour's mount."

"Ye might be oot there, me lord." The man smirked. "There's only one other horse as can keep up wit' Pronto and tha' is Thunder."

"Then saddle him and be quick about it."

The man jutted his jaw and crossed his big arms. "Thunder is his grace's favorite horse. Only Roxburghe rides him and no other."

"I don't give a damn whose horse it is—just *saddle* it."

"I canna'—"

Sin slammed the man up against the wall of the stable and hissed through gritted teeth, "Miss Balfour could get injured riding such a brute at night. If anything happens to her, you will bear the brunt of my anger. Do you understand?"

The groom's eyes were wide. "Y-y-yes, me lord. But ye dinna need to worry aboot Miss Balfour. She's a guid rider and 'tis bright as day oot there, with the moon—"

Sin let the man's feet touch the ground. "And if a cloud obscures the moon and the horse stumbles on a rut? Or a rabbit runs across the horse's path and sends him into a frenzy? What then?"

The man gulped. "Aye, yer lordship."

Sin helped gather the saddle and bridle to speed the process. "Is this the first time Miss Balfour has ridden out at night?"

"She's ridden these past few nights, as the moon's been so bright. Afore tha' she came at dawn. Her grace tol' us to gi' her whatever she wished."

Sin leveled his gaze on the groom. "From now on, she's not to go alone. Come morning, I'll have my aunt inform you of that herself."

"Aye, me lord. Should I come wit' ye this evenin'?"

"No. I'll fetch her."

Sin swung up on Thunder and then he was on his way, cantering down the wide, smooth drive. There were clouds here and there, which meant it could easily go dark very quickly. Even more dangerous was if Rose's horse became spooked, and it took very little to do so—a few leaves blowing across the road, a low-hanging branch, or even the whisper of the clothes of the person riding the animal.

Sin tried to banish the chilling thoughts as he reached the end of the drive and turned down the road Rose had taken. Then, eyes straight ahead, he began his search.

Rose lifted her face to the moon and breathed in the cool, moist forest air. For the last quarter of an hour, she'd let Pronto have his head.

He loved the night as she did, the coolness and silence. Every once in a while he let out a whicker and tossed his head, which made her grin. She relaxed in the saddle and looked at the silver spill of moon that lit the road before them. Staying on the main road wasn't as freeing as a ride on the familiar paths at Caith Manor, where she knew where every loose tree root or slick rock might be hiding, but for tonight it was enough.

Her nightly rides calmed her tumultuous thoughts better than anything else, and lately she'd needed that peace of mind.

Most of her unease had to do with a certain tall earl with blond hair and light brown eyes who seemed determined to win their every encounter. Though he might not know it, each time that they spoke, every smile he glinted at her, was winning him yet another piece of her foolish heart.

There wasn't a lot left that was just her own. And yet, she couldn't stay away from him. She'd tried, but each time had left her with a painfully hollow ache and she never wanted to feel that way again. But she suspected that was exactly how she'd feel once she returned to Caith Manor in only a few days, leaving the magic of Floors Castle and Sin's smile forever.

Suddenly a noise intruded on her thoughts. Were those hoofbeats?

She glanced over her shoulder and saw another horse on the road behind her, coming fast. Who else would be out at this time of the night? It looked like . . . Sin!

She grinned and slowed Pronto to a walk. Perhaps she could entice Sin into a little race. The road ahead was straight, wide, and even, and there were no trees to block the moonlight. It ended at a high wooden gate set in a stone wall that marked the Roxburghe lands.

She listened as Sin approached and then, just as he came onto the same stretch of road, she gathered Pronto and sent him into a gallop. The horse responded immediately.

She heard Sin utter a curse, and then the thunder of hooves as he came in hot pursuit.

Rose laughed as she bent low to Pronto's neck, excitement thrumming through her veins as an exultant flood of happiness lifted her. Pronto could feel it, too. He lowered his ears and put his heart into the race as they thundered down the road.

Behind her came Sin and his mount. Heart beating in her throat, Rose bent closer. Her hat had come dislodged and was long gone but she didn't care. The scent of the cool, misty air mingled with the wind rushing over her face and wiped away her thin hold on the civilities.

Pronto whinnied his joy and Rose laughed. She felt as if she could hold her arms out to her sides, and she and Pronto would lift into the air and sail away on the breeze like dandelion fluff. She chuckled and murmured encouragement, her knees urging the horse onward as she heard Sin right behind her. She knew from the sound of the hooves that if she looked over her shoulder, she'd see him coming abreast.

She couldn't let him beat her. The gate was getting closer and oh, how she dearly wished to win. She'd have traded her best gown for a few lengths to leave him behind in the dust, where he belonged.

Sin's horse inched forward and she could see him just over her shoulder now.

He was bent low over his horse's neck. He wasn't wearing his riding clothes, which was odd, and his face was set with concentration, his hands sure on the reins.

He saw her head was turned his way and he yelled something, but it was lost over the thunder of their horses.

The urgency in his tone set her heart pounding even faster and she redoubled her efforts, promising Pronto treats untold if he got them to that wall first. They'd jumped it many times before, but never had she wished to win so badly.

Sin, meanwhile, thought a madness had possessed Rose. But she was a marvelous horsewoman and he knew that she wouldn't take a wall that was too high or deep for their mounts. He'd have to trust her—and he realized, to his surprise, that he did. He would follow her wherever she went.

And then they were at the wall, Rose and her horse slightly ahead. He had a perfect view as Pronto bunched and then lifted, sailing over the gate with an inch to spare. Sin followed, his horse clearing the gate top.

Rose was waiting for him on the other side, her eyes shining, and laughter bubbling in her voice. "I've missed that so much!"

"What? Riding madcap down a deserted road?"

"It's an excellent road and oh, what a glorious moon!" She waved her arm in an arc as if trying to engulf the moonshine.

"You shouldn't be out at night. There could be strangers, or the horse could spook or draw up lame . . . I nearly had an apoplexy when I looked out my window and saw you riding off to God knows where."

"I've ridden this road every day for two weeks. I might risk my neck to ride wildly, but never a horse's." She grinned. "You sound like Mr. Stewart, who thinks the new style of phaeton is a dangerous mode of travel. Next you'll be warning me to wear wool in the winter, and to be sure I button my pelisse in the rain."

Sin glowered. "I'm not acting like an old man." He'd been worried sick, thinking her injured or dead, while she'd been acting as pragmatically as she always did.

"No? Then what are you acting like?"

"Like someone who—" *Cares.* The word stuck in his throat. *Bloody hell, where did that come from?* But of course he cared about Rose; there was nothing surprising in that. She was sunshine and warm days. She was unconventional and impulsive and a hundred other things, all of them good.

He no longer thought of her as the woman who'd humiliated him, a selfish witch who'd embarrassed him for spite. If there was one thing he now knew about Rose, it was that she didn't have an ounce of spite in her body. If anyone could be accused of that, it was him.

Rose twinkled up at him, her smile wide and unguarded. "So, Sin, I win again."

She had. And he found that he didn't care. He liked seeing the sparkle of triumph in her eyes, and he realized that he'd give up a thousand wins just to see her joyous for one moment. "Yes, you win. That's two today."

"And you owe me for both." To his surprise, she sent him a hotly passionate look that made his heart lurch. "I'm glad you came out. Our time at Floors is almost over, but at least we'll have the memory of our moonlight ride."

Two and a half weeks had never passed so quickly. Sin managed a faint smile. "Of course."

She waited and he knew she wished him to say something more, but he couldn't. *Only a few more days.* The words rang with ominous darkness. Once the ball was over everyone would leave, one carriage at a time, until the castle was quiet and—without Rose—achingly empty.

A pained smile flickered on Rose's face. "Shall we ride?" Without waiting for an answer, she turned her horse.

They rode back to Floors in silence, but for the sounds of the horse's hooves. The beauty of the night, the freshness of the air, the scent of heather that rose as they passed the fields all paled before the fact that they were almost out of time. By the time they arrived at the castle, an unfamiliar gloom had settled over Sin.

The groom met them at the front of the castle and led the horses away.

And they were alone. Sin turned to Rose, bereft of words. "I . . . I will be sorry to see you leave—"

She threw her arms about his neck and kissed him, pressing her body to his so urgently that he staggered a bit. But he recovered quickly, his body answering hers immediately, as it always did. He wanted her so badly that in his muddled mind, wanting her and breathing no longer differed.

He clutched her to him, lifting her to plunder her mouth with kiss after kiss after heated kiss. He couldn't taste her enough, touch her enough . . . the more he had, the more he yearned for, until he ached with it.

He soaked in the feel of her firm, strong body under his hands, of the taste of her lips on his, of the scent of her hair—

She broke the kiss, her forehead coming to rest against his shoulder as she panted. He slowly slid her down so that her feet were once again upon the drive.

She held him tightly still, her body trembling. He tried to calm his own breath, but it was impossible. He ached for her, burned for her, wanted her so badly that he couldn't think of a single thing he wouldn't give up for just one hour—one *minute*—of her under him.

"Come." Her voice was husky and aching. She turned away, her hand slipping into his. She led him inside, through the dark foyer to the stairs, and then up into the dark upper hall.

Sin followed, feeling as if his entire life had just turned into a dream. She took him down the hallway and past his bedchamber, and on to hers. At the doorway, she looked up at him. Her eyes seemed huge, her lips swollen and trembling. "Sin, I want more than a moonlight ride to remember these few weeks by." She stood on tiptoe to cup his face. "Just one more memory. That's all I ask."

The words burned into his mind.

With a lingering glance over her shoulder, she went into her bedchamber, leaving the door open behind her.

Twenty

From the Diary of the Duchess of Roxburghe
Love cannot be contained.

Rose stood beside the bed, holding her breath. Would he follow her? She prayed that he would. Life had been unfair to them before. They'd met when she'd been too young and he too full of himself for their passion to be fulfilled.

Now they'd met again and all that they thought they'd known about each other had been torn away, leaving a roaring passion that was ready to consume them. And she was ready to sate this desire that left her weak every time his gaze met hers.

She heard the door close and the scrape of a key in the lock.

Her body trembled, her breasts aching, her thighs damp from the boldness of her own actions. He came closer and captured her shoulders from behind. Without a word, he bent and pressed a hot kiss to her neck.

She moaned and leaned back against him, feeling the hardness of his body, the strength of his arms. His hands slid down to her stomach to pull her close and she could feel his cock pressing against her back. Rose gasped as he slid his hands up and caressed her breasts, his thumbs pressing on her nipples. She shivered and pressed against him, giving him access to whatever part of her he wished to touch.

Sin groaned as she rubbed against his groin; she was so responsive. Her small breasts filled his hands sweetly and he burned to see her nipples harden for him so quickly. Would she moan when he took them in his mouth and—

He suddenly stopped, then set her away from him.

She faced him, surprise and disappointment on her face. "What's wrong?"

"If I stay here, I'm going to do much more than caress you."

Her brow lifted and she smiled. "Who's afraid now?"

The soft words sent Sin's senses into a spiral of desire.

Rose's gaze locked with his, their breaths ragged and quick. She reached up and undid her scarf, and then, with fingers that were already trembling, she unbuttoned the short jacket of her riding habit and tugged it off. Underneath, she wore a white cambric shirt that was ruffled at the neck and wrists. Her gaze still on his, she untied the shirt, tugged it free and pulled it over her head, and tossed it on top of her jacket.

She was left with her full skirts tied at her waist, and only a lace chemise covering her breasts. He could see her dusky-colored areolas through the lace, her nipples hard and beckoning.

He instantly wanted his mouth over those delicious mounds of temptation, and he growled with sensual hunger.

Rose's entire body thrummed with his reaction. "It's your turn, I believe." Was that her voice, so husky and sensual?

He didn't hesitate, swiftly removing his coat and yanking his shirt over his head, revealing a broad chest covered with tantalizing golden hair that narrowed and then trailed down his muscled stomach to disappear at his waistband. As her gaze followed the path, she saw that his manhood was already straining against his breeches. Instantly she felt an answering heat.

She met his gaze and reached for the ties that held her skirt, but his warm hands brushed hers away. In an amazingly short time, her skirt dropped to the floor, her petticoats with it. Cool air brushed over her. All she wore now was her chemise, stockings, and riding boots.

Sin's gaze roved over her, lingering on her breasts, her hips, her thighs . . . He drew a ragged breath. "It's my turn again." He took off his boots and reached for the waistband of his breeches, but she grasped his wrist.

"Allow me."

His eyes gleamed and he lifted his hands out of her way.

She began to work on the fastenings, instantly distracted when her fingers brushed his warm, taut stomach and he gasped. Smiling, she undid his breeches and his cock sprang free.

Rose reached out a trembling hand to touch it, barely grazing the turgid head.

He moaned and pressed her hand onto his cock, wrapping her fingers about it firmly. Her cheeks flamed, but she held her hand there, tightening her grip when his released her.

He gasped, and his cock hardened yet more beneath her fingers. Suddenly, he let his breath out in a whoosh. "Enough! I can't—" She reluctantly removed her hand, and he picked her up and carried her to the bed.

"You don't need this anymore." He slipped her chemise from her shoulders and tugged it off.

She reached for her boots, but he caught her wrist. "Leave them."

He kissed her, his warm skin against hers, his rigid cock pressed against her hip, his large hands sliding over her stomach to her breasts as he traced his warm mouth over her neck, her shoulder, down to her breasts.

He flicked one of her nipples with his tongue and she gasped.

Her thighs were slick, her heart pounding, her nipples swollen with her need. She grasped him and tugged impatiently. He smiled at her eagerness, and rolled between her thighs. His cock pressed against her and she moaned, planting her boots on the bed and lifting her hips to meet him. He slipped inside her a little, moving slowly to prolong the moment. The tight heat that surrounded him sent his blood pumping.

She grasped the sheets at either side, her head thrown back as he pressed farther inside. She growled deep in her throat and released the sheets to grasp his shoulders, her legs locking behind his back as she pressed herself against him.

His last shred of control disappeared and he arched against her with a force that shocked them both.

He felt the give of her virginity just as she cried out and clutched him closer.

His eyes flew open but she never stopped moving, her leather boots tight about his hips. He knew he should stop, knew something wasn't quite right, but his blood-addled mind could only think and feel the tightness of Rose as she rocked her hips against his, taking her pleasure from him, demanding he do the same from her.

He answered her demands, filling her over and over. She answered him stroke for stroke, her legs holding him locked in place, her boots abrading his hips sensually.

As Sin's passion built, he fought to hold it back,

gritting his teeth against the need for release. At the edge of that precipice, Rose grasped him desperately and arched beneath him as she went over the edge of passion, taking him with her.

Neither moved. Their bodies were damp from exertion, their breathing so ragged and uneven that Rose was light-headed. Nothing had prepared her for the exquisite feelings she'd just experienced.

Sin regained his breath first, slowly rolling up on one elbow.

Still panting, she looked over at him. "That is a memory I will always cherish."

"You were a virgin."

There was accusation in his words. Her smile slipped. "Yes. Not that it matters—"

"Not matter?" He rolled away and climbed from the bed. "I was certain that you weren't."

Her heart, so euphoric a moment ago, sank. "Why were you certain? We never discussed it."

"The way you move and kiss, and how you allowed me to touch you—" He raked a hand through his hair. "I was certain of it," he repeated hollowly.

Rose sat up, tugging her sheet over her, her nakedness suddenly wrong somehow. "Like I said, it doesn't matter."

"But it does." His gaze had darkened and he looked at her with a stern expression. "Rose, why did you push me into the fountain all those years ago?"

"What does that have to do with—"

"Answer the question," he snapped.

"The kiss overwhelmed me. I'd never kissed anyone before, and—"

Inwardly, Sin groaned. "That was your first kiss."

She nodded. "When you kissed me back with so much passion and desire, and then you ran your tongue over my lips in such a— It scared me. I enjoyed it, but I panicked . . . and—well, you know what happened then."

He closed his eyes. He could see it all now. She'd been so young, with passions she couldn't yet understand. And then she'd shared that passion with a man too jaded to recognize that she was a true innocent.

And now, six years later, he'd committed the exact same mistake. He walked to the window and stared sightlessly into the night.

"Sin, what's wrong?"

He gave a bitter laugh. "What's wrong is that I've ruined you."

"Nonsense. No one knows what we've done. And I refuse to regret it. I wanted you to touch me. I wanted you to be with me. I'm not sorry." Rose's heart ached. She'd thought their passion was so beautiful, simply incredible. Yet there stood Sin, head bowed, a scowl on his face.

"Rose, this changes everything."

"No, it doesn't."

"Yes, it does." His face was bleak, his jaw set,

though when he met her gaze, he tried to smile. "I will get a special license and we will marry in two weeks' time. It won't be anything special, but later on, we can have another ceremony for our families."

She waited, her breath caught. But he said nothing more. She let out her breath. "Sin, I won't marry you."

His stiff smile disappeared. "What?"

"I refuse." She scooted to the edge of the bed and wrapped the sheet about her. Making sure his back was turned, she swiped away the beginning of her tears. She'd never felt so empty or alone in her entire life as she did at this moment.

"Rose, you have to—"

A sound came from the hallway. Rose sighed. "That's one of the pugs. He's been visiting me at night." At least the pug would be glad to see her. She went to the door.

"Rose, don't—"

She'd already unlocked and opened the door, her gaze on the floor. A pair of pink slippers peeked out from a silk robe. Astounded, Rose followed the robe all the way up to Miss Isobel's shocked face.

The woman's eyes flickered from Rose's sheet-clad body to where Sin stood naked by the window, fully exposed by the moonlight.

Isobel's eyes widened and then she screamed.

Twenty-one

From the Diary of the Duchess of Roxburghe
The number of people wandering the halls of
Floors Castle in the middle of the night is appalling.
The next time I invite guests, I shall put rat traps in
every corner. Perhaps that will teach them.

The duchess placed a cold cloth over her brow, her
red wig precariously perched over one eye. "Well."

Lady Charlotte nodded as if that one word covered
it all.

Rose sat on the edge of her chair. "So that's what
happened."

"You've told us everything?" her grace asked.

"Yes. All of it." Rose's cheeks couldn't be hotter.

Lady Charlotte clicked her tongue. "And Lord
Sinclair hasn't said anything since Miss Isobel interrupted your, ah, meeting?"

"Nothing." Rose squeezed her hands tightly, her
nails biting into her palms. The pain kept her from
crying as she said, "I think I should leave. Not only

did Miss Isobel see us, but Lord Cameron did, too. He came charging out of his room when Miss Isobel screamed."

"I see."

"After that, everyone came. Isobel's parents and sister, and then Mr. Munro joined them and—" She tried to swallow, but couldn't. "I'm well and truly ruined this time."

The duchess said, "To be honest, I'm surprised Sin didn't ask you to marry him on the spot. He knows what's due his name."

"He'd already asked me, but I had refused him."

Two pairs of eyes locked upon Rose. The duchess sat up very slowly. "Why did you refuse him?"

"He . . . I don't know if I should say anything else. This affects him, as well."

"Good God! There are too many damned secrets in this house!" Enraged, her grace balled up her kerchief and tossed it on the floor. "Rose Balfour, you listen to me. I'm here to help you, but I cannot do so unless you tell me everything—and I mean *everything* that happened."

Rose nodded uncertainly and looked away. "I don't know if it's important, but once Sin—Lord Sinclair found that I was a—a virgin, he said that we should marry."

"Said?"

Rose nodded. "He just . . . said it."

They were silent a long moment.

Finally the duchess said in an amazed voice, "He said you should marry him, but he didn't say one word about love or loyalty or trust, or call you beautiful or—"

Rose shook her head.

"That numbskull! I don't blame you for refusing him. What did he say after you did so?"

"He was angry. We were arguing when I heard the noise in the hallway and thought it was Beenie." She looked at the pug now sleeping with his chin on her slipper. "I wish it had been."

"So do we all," Lady Charlotte said, her knitting needles flying.

"And after Miss Isobel's scene? What did my numbskull great-nephew do then?"

"He ordered MacDougal to take some smelling salts to Miss Isobel's parents' room, as that's where Lord Cameron had carried her. Then he told Mac-Dougal to go to each room and see if anyone wished for a night draft to help them get to sleep again. He was very thoughtful to everyone, but—" Her voice broke.

Lady Margaret's frown deepened. "But you."

Rose nodded miserably. "I can tell that he w-w-wishes we'd never met." Her words ended on a wail, causing Lady Charlotte to drop her knitting and come to sit beside Rose.

"There, there, child."

"That fool!" The duchess's fingers tapped impatiently on the arm of her chair. "I fear this calls for drastic measures."

Lady Charlotte turned to her friend. "You have a new scheme!"

The duchess nodded. "And to begin with, I think Miss Balfour is right: she should return home."

Rose hadn't thought she could feel any worse, but she did. "Y-yes, your grace." She wiped her eyes with her handkerchief and stood. "I'll pack now."

"I'll send your maid up to help. Can you be ready in thirty minutes?"

Not trusting herself to speak, Rose nodded.

Lady Charlotte stared at the duchess. "Really, Margaret, don't you think we should arrange for Sin and Miss Balfour to speak?"

"No. Sin's made his choice. Let him stand by it. Miss Balfour, I'm sorry to send you home, but as you can see, I have no choice."

"Of course. Thank you for—" Her voice broke.

Her grace's expression softened and she came to give Rose a swift hug. "I want you to know that I do not hold you responsible in any way for what happened." She took Rose's hands between her own. "You are not to blame for any of this. Once this has all blown over, I look forward to having not only you but your sisters, as well, here at Floors Castle. I promise to invite a livelier crowd, too."

"That will make them very happy, your grace. Thank you for that."

The duchess patted Rose's hands and released her. "I shall have MacDougal call round the carriage."

Rose turned to go, but then stopped. "One more thing, your grace. If . . . if you don't mind, I don't want Lord Sinclair to know the direction to Caith Manor. It's better we just stop this now and . . ."

"Say no more, child. I'll protect your location with my life."

Rose managed a weak smile and curtsied. "Thank you."

As soon as the door closed behind her, Charlotte turned to Margaret. "I've never been closer to calling you something less than a lady."

Margaret chuckled. "Don't give up quite so quickly, Charlotte. I may be old, but I still have one or two tricks up my sleeve."

Sin stood in the library with a glass of port. He'd spent most of the day riding aimlessly, mulling over the events of last night, tiring himself and his mount, and arriving home when everyone was at dinner. Not feeling hungry, he had dressed and gone to the library to help himself to some port and await the rest of the guests.

He'd just poured his second glass when he was joined by Mr. Stewart, Lord Cameron, and Mr. Munro. They all looked startled to find him awaiting them.

He inclined his head. "MacDougal selected an excellent port. It's one of the better ones in the cellar."

Mr. Stewart, all fuming outrage, glared at him.

Lord Cameron offered a stiff smile. "Excellent. It was a very quiet dinner and some port would be most welcome." He poured three more glasses. "Munro?"

Munro came to take a glass, his gaze locked on Sin. After a few gulps, he asked, "So . . . you and Miss Balfour, eh?"

The meaning was unmistakable.

Sin swirled the port in his glass, but said nothing.

Mr. Stewart continued to glare.

Lord Cameron cleared his throat. "Munro, that was quite a good roast her grace served tonight, wasn't it?"

Munro tossed back a few more swigs, his gaze still locked on Sin's. "Tell us, Sinclair, what was she like, our little Rose? Such a tease."

"Munro, really," Lord Cameron said desperately. "Stop."

"And here I really believed her an innocent. But you saw right through her little act, didn't you, Lord Sin?" The man's laugh was ugly. "Tell us, was she as tender as she look—"

Sin punched him in the nose, sending him reeling back so hard that he hit a chair and flipped over it.

Mr. Stewart gasped.

Fists clenched, Sin headed for Munro, but Lord Cameron grabbed his arm, "Sin, please. He deserved it, but don't make things worse by causing a scene."

He gripped Sin's arm tighter. "Please. We must remember the ladies."

As if on cue, the door opened, and Lady Charlotte entered with Mrs. Stewart leaning on her arm. They stopped at the sight of Munro struggling to get up, blood running from his nose.

"Don't block the doorway," Margaret said, pushing past and taking in the situation in a glance. "Mac-Dougal, bring more port and some sherry for the ladies. We've had a stressful day. And have some footmen remove Mr. Munro from the room. I won't have him bleeding all over my good rugs."

Mr. Stewart gaped. "Your grace, you don't understand what happened!"

"Oh, but I do. Mr. Munro clearly made an ass of himself by saying ugly things about Miss Balfour without truly understanding the circumstances, and Lord Sinclair set him right." She cocked a brow toward Sin.

He returned her look sullenly, his mouth white from holding back his fury. At his side, Lord Cameron nodded. "Yes, your grace. That's exactly what happened."

"I thought so. MacDougal, once you've removed Mr. Munro, assist him with his luggage. I'm certain he has no wish to remain under my roof after being so rudely handled. I'm sure there's room in the Stag's Head, which is but four miles from here. I stayed there once when my carriage broke down during a rainstorm, and it's not a bad little inn."

There was a bustle of activity as the footmen rushed in and did as they were bid. Lord Cameron finally released Sin, who, after sending a scathing glare at Munro, retreated to the terrace window to stare out into the night. Though Mr. Munro murmured a woozy protest, he seemed glad to be taken out of Sin's presence.

It wasn't until the sherry and fresh glasses had arrived that Margaret found herself facing Sin.

"Where is she?" His voice was hoarse with anger.

Margaret didn't pretend she didn't understand. "You're just now noticing that she's gone?"

"This is no time for games. I was out all day and I assumed she was here with you. Has she gone to her room with a headache?"

"No." Aunt Margaret watched Sin over her sherry glass. "She's gone, Sin. She left this afternoon."

A pang went through Sin, so sharp and painful that he felt his head might split open. "She didn't tell me."

"She didn't wish to make any bigger a scene than had already been made. But she's gone. Because of you."

"Nothing happened between us that she didn't actively enjoy."

Aunt Margaret's blue eyes blazed. "Miss Balfour's willingness to participate in your tryst does not diminish the fact that you did nothing last night to alleviate that poor girl's embarrassment."

"There was nothing I could do."

"Oh?"

He flushed under her glare. "You don't understand the entire situation."

"I know that you asked her to marry you once you'd discovered your error in thinking her one of your usual flirts."

His jaw worked. "I am sorry I made that assumption. I told her so, too."

"Yes. You told her you were sorry you thought so ill of her. But did you ever tell her why you wanted to marry her?"

"No."

"Why did you wish to marry her? Do you even know?"

"I was doing the honorable thing."

"If you'd been interested in doing the honorable thing, you'd have never seduced that gel to begin with."

He glowered.

Her gaze narrowed. After a moment, she sat back, a stunned look upon her face. "You don't know, do you?"

"Know what?"

"Why you asked Rose to marry you." She leaned closer. "You *didn't* offer to marry her to save her reputation, because until she opened that door, her reputation was still intact. What's the *real* reason you asked her to marry you, Sin?"

"Because I had to," he said stubbornly.

"And that's the only reason?" Aunt Margaret's gaze bored into his.

Through a welter of hurt, and whatever other hell churned inside him, he sneered, "Yes, damn it. That's the only reason." Then he walked away.

Twenty-two

From the Diary of the Duchess of Roxburghe
Stubborn, proud boy. Silly, proud gel. The very
thing they have the most in common—pride—is
now keeping them apart.

I've never found a less enjoyable irony.

"Yer grace?" A cacophony of barking answered
MacDougal's knock. He tried again, knocking a little
louder. "Yer grace?"

"Wait a demmed minute, will you?" Margaret
snapped from where she'd just risen. She slapped a
nightcap over her iron-gray braid, swooped up her
robe, and marched to the door. She yanked it open
and found an apologetic MacDougal standing in the
hallway.

The pugs leapt joyfully, mauling his breeches and
shoes.

"Stop it, you ingrates!" she ordered.

The pugs stopped jumping, but continued to sniff
the butler's shoes.

"I'm sorry, yer grace." The butler wrung his hands. "I know 'tis late, and ye're weary, but 'tis Lord Sinclair."

"My nephew? He returned?" After their argument in the library he'd ridden off, and they hadn't seen him in two days. Margaret tried to pretend she hadn't been worried, but she couldn't keep a note of alarm from her voice just now.

MacDougal's expression instantly calmed her. "He's here, yer grace. Unfortunately . . . he's demanding to see Miss Balfour."

"But he knows she's gone. I told him before he left."

The butler grimaced. "He's oot of his mind, then. I didna wish to wake ye, but I was afraid one o' the other guests might come and . . . Well, we've already had enou' scandal fer one month and I thought . . ."

"MacDougal, either you will speak a straight sentence and explain what's going on, or I'll fetch the fire poker and whack the facts out of you."

The butler blinked, and then gave a weak grin. "Aye, yer grace. I'm sorry fer bein' a bit put aboot, but Lord Sinclair's set me on edge, bangin' on the doors and demandin' 'his Rose.' "

" 'His Rose?' Is that what he said?"

"Aye, yer grace. I finally got him into the library and tried to tell him, but he wouldna hear me. Yer grace, I canno' do aught wit' him. Ye'd best come, though I warn ye tha' he's proper shot in the neck."

"Ape-drunk, is he?"

MacDougal nodded.

"That boy will be the death of me." Margaret returned to her bed and stuck her feet into her slippers and then snatched up her shawl from the chair by the fire. She swung the shawl about her shoulders, the fringe swinging madly as she walked past MacDougal, the pugs trotting behind her. "Fix some tea and toast and bring it to the library," she ordered over her shoulder.

"Aye, yer grace, but he's in no shape to eat."

"He will be by the time I'm through with him," she replied grimly. "We'll also need some water straight from the pump—icy cold."

"Yes, yer grace. I'll bring it with a washbowl and towel."

"Bring it in a bucket with a blanket." She reached the bottom of the stairs. "The water first, the tea second."

"Yes, yer grace." MacDougal hurried to open the library doors.

She entered the room, the pugs trotting after her as MacDougal closed the doors.

The room was dark, the only light coming from the fire in the grate. Sin was pacing wildly, his hair mussed as if he'd raked his hands repeatedly through it, his face covered with several days' worth of stubble. His clothing was mussed, his cravat twisted to one side, his coat and waistcoat open. He looked as far from the fashionable rakehell who'd entered her house three weeks ago as was possible. *Ah, how the mighty do fall.*

His gaze locked on Margaret. "I want Rose. I thought MacDougal might know where she is, but he won't tell." Sin's words were slurred, his eyes red. "You know where she is."

"So I do." Margaret walked to the fireplace and held out her hands to the welcoming blaze. "I promised her I wouldn't tell you."

He looked as if he'd been punched in the stomach. "She asked you that? Not to tell me?" Sin stalked away and back, pacing like a wild lion in a cage.

Margaret's throat tightened at the raw emotion in his eyes. She had to take a moment to harden her heart. "Miss Balfour needed to leave. Had you wished her to stay, you would have done something about it."

Sin's shoulders slumped as if he were about to collapse. "Damn that woman."

"That hardly sounds like a man desirous of winning a woman's affections."

His mouth pressed into a thin line. "I can't want what's not there to give."

Margaret came to stand by the fire, wrinkling her nose as she caught the smell of stale ale. "You smell like a tavern."

His lips twisted into a sneer. "Behold Sin!"

"Behold Foolishness is more like it," she said in a sharp tone. "You're drunk."

She took the chair closest to the fireplace and sat.

"Well, Sin? What brings you banging on my door in the middle of the night, soaked in gin? After the last time I saw you, I'm surprised to see you crossing my threshold."

"Aunt Margaret, I'm sorry for—" He raked a hand through his hair and laughed shakily. "God, I'm sorry for so many things."

"Oh?" She reached down and scooped a pug into her lap, patting it as it settled across her knees, warmer than any blanket. The others settled before the fire, plopping like fat snowballs onto the hearth rug. "You may be sorry for many things—God knows we all are. But I suspect that only one of those things is what's bothering you now, and I don't think it has to do with me."

"I don't know what you're talking about."

"You're drunk, disheveled, and you haven't slept since, hmmm, I'd guess it's been two days?"

He shook his head. He'd tried to sleep. God, he'd tried. But every time he closed his eyes, he saw Rose. He saw her laughing up at him as he attempted to beat her at pall-mall, and became so enthralled with the nape of her neck that he got in the way of her mallet. He saw her sputtering as he "rescued" her from the river, and the humorous smile she gave him when he'd slipped into the woods while she was searching for a lost arrow and he had kissed her breathless.

If he closed his eyes right now, he'd see her again. "What I would give to undo those few minutes . . ."

He sighed and dropped his head. "But I can't, can I? Aunt Margaret, I—I don't know what happened to me. But Rose . . ." He rubbed his forehead. "Damn her for coming back into my life."

"You can't blame her. She tried to avoid you, but you would have none of it."

He scowled. "She's the most impertinent, demanding, mocking, infuriating—" His voice broke and he clenched his fists before he finished with a husky whisper, "dear."

Margaret's eyes widened. "'*Dear*'?"

Sin rubbed his neck, his entire body aching from exhaustion. "This whole thing is my fault. I didn't mean to embarrass her—"

"Poppycock," Aunt Margaret said. "You planned to do just that from the very beginning."

"But not after . . ." He gestured.

She leaned forward. "Not after *what*, Sin? Say it, demme you."

"Not after . . ." He splayed his hands, trying to find the words. "Things changed."

She sighed. "That's the best you can do? 'Things changed'?"

"Yes. They changed because I realized that she wasn't what I'd thought at all. All this time, I thought I knew her and I hated her."

"And then you met her."

"And she is passionate and impulsive, full of laughter and curiosity. She can't say no to a challenge, nor can she admit defeat." He gave a sudden, rueful laugh. "We are quite alike, we two."

"You no longer blame her for your reign as Lord Fin?"

"That was my fault, too." He raised red-rimmed eyes that were wet with tears. "I love her."

Margaret almost gave a whoop. There it was. *Finally.* "It's about damn time you realized that."

"You knew?"

"Everyone knows except you and Rose."

"I tried to tell her, but she wouldn't have me. I told her that I wouldn't allow her to be a ruined woman. That I wanted to marry her and—"

"Oh, for the love of—" Aunt Margaret's voice dripped with disgust. "Of course she wouldn't have you if you said it like *that*."

"How should I have said it?"

"Obviously you didn't use the word 'love.'"

"No. I thought I'd save that for later. When things weren't so tense."

"Which is exactly when you *should* use the word. If you want Rose back, that word is crucial. No woman worth her salt would listen to a proposal without the word 'love' in it. And I think Miss Rose Balfour is worth her salt."

He sighed. "So do I." He rubbed a hand over his face as if to clear cobwebs. "The real irony is that I'd changed my mind about enacting my vengeance and ruining her."

"And then you proceeded to do it anyway. Fool."

"I—I—I don't know what it was, but I couldn't leave her alone. I just couldn't *not* touch her." He rubbed his chin, befuddled and oddly lost. "Aunt Margaret, am I going mad?"

She gave a bark of laughter that made the pugs jump to their feet. "Lud, no. If anything, you're finally coming to your senses. You're in love, boy! Head over heels, by the sound of it."

"I don't understand how it happened."

"None of us do. Even under the best of circumstances, it can sneak up on you and smack you over the head."

He sat and leaned forward, his elbows on his knees. "So what do I do now? Ride up to her house on a white steed, throw her over the back, and ride away?"

Aunt Margaret drummed her fingers on the arm of her chair. "No. I don't think that would suit Miss Balfour. She strikes me as a practical sort of woman. I don't think she'd like being thrown over a horse under any circumstances."

He considered this. "You're right; she wouldn't appreciate it at all."

They fell silent a moment, and then Aunt Margaret straightened, an awed expression on her face. "Sin! What if I convince Rose to attend my Winter Ball? You could speak to her then."

He blinked. "Do you think you can?"

"I can try." Aunt Margaret set Meenie on the floor,

the other dogs immediately standing and stretching. "And while I'm doing my part, you be sure to do yours." She swept to the door, the pugs bounding after her. "I expect you to be on your best, most princely behavior. More to the point, I expect you to leave your pride at the door and tell that girl what you think about her, and to do it with prettier words than 'must' and 'have to.'" She stopped and looked back at him. "It's time we were done with this nonsense. Six years is long enough."

Sin couldn't help but gape. "You think I've been in love with her for six years?"

"It certainly appears that way to me." Her gaze narrowed. "So go get some rest, and for the love of God, shave that blasted face of yours. It's a disgrace."

He rubbed his chin, the scruff making a raspy sound, and had to laugh. "You always make me feel like I'm five years old."

"That's about the age you've been acting, tossing that poor gel into a river, and trying to race her over hill and dale, leaving her adrift in a punt, and trying to get her shot with an arrow—"

"*I* was the one who got shot."

"I'm only surprised you didn't dip her hair into an inkwell. The time has come for you to grow up, my dear, painful as it may be."

"I'm ready," he replied, surprised that her speech didn't make him angry.

"So are we. Your mother, in particular, will be glad

to know that. Now, if you'll excuse me, I must get my beauty rest. Roxburghe returns soon, and I've some scheming to do if we wish to see Miss Balfour gracing our ball in two days."

"I will owe you for this, Aunt Margaret."

"Repay me by naming your first daughter after me. I've never wished to have a namesake, but it will irritate your mother, so I'm certain to enjoy it." She sent him a wink. "Get to bed, you scamp. I'll see you at the ball in two days' time. Be there by eight."

For the first time in two days, Sin smiled.

Twenty-three

From the Diary of the Duchess of Roxburghe
I find that being a godmother is quite an amusing, though exhausting, hobby. And I must say that I seem to have quite a knack for it.

"Rose, that's enough."

Surprised at the irritation in Dahlia's voice, Rose looked up from her sewing. The two sisters were working on a pile of darning in the former nursery since the small room could be warmed with very little coal.

"That's enough what?" Rose asked.

"Enough of this—" and she gave a long, mournful sigh to illustrate.

Rose's face heated. "I'm sorry if I was sighing and it bothered you. I didn't hear myself."

Dahlia looked concerned. "We've all been hearing it since you returned from Floors. Rose, what happened? *Please* tell me!"

"I've already told you everything."

"No, you haven't. Lily and I are worried. Even

Papa has noticed a difference, and he never notices anything."

"I'm just tired. All of the dinners and punting and horseback riding and archery contests and midnight rides . . ." *All of it with Sin.*

She bent her head over her work so Dahlia wouldn't see her tears.

Dahlia sighed. "There you go again."

A shout came from below, and after sharing a startled glance, Dahlia and Rose hurried to open the casement window.

Lily stood in the courtyard below, jumping up and down in excitement.

Dahlia leaned out the window. "What is it?"

Lily looked up. "It's a trunk! Right here, beside the door. Someone must have brought it while I was gone!"

Rose poked her head out beside Dahlia's. "Is there a note on it?"

"I don't think so, but it's far larger than Father's usual flower samples. Oh, wait. There is a note: I'd just missed it." Lily removed a small envelope that was attached to one handle by a string. She scanned the envelope and looked up, surprised. "Rose, it's for you!"

Dahlia turned wide eyes in Rose's direction. "What is it?"

"How would I know? I didn't send it to myself."

Dahlia leaned out. "Lily, we'll meet you in the sitting room. Fetch one of the stable boys and have him carry the trunk inside."

"I'm not waiting for a stable boy. Come down and we'll carry it ourselves."

Dahlia and Rose hurried downstairs.

Moments later, panting and puffing, they all stood in the sitting room staring down at the trunk.

Dahlia gave a little hop. "Rose, open the trunk!"

"I don't have the key!"

Lily dangled a small golden key before her. "It was on the string with the envelope."

Rose stooped and tried the key in the lock. Who would have sent her something? "Blast it, I can't get this key to—"

"Oh, let me." Lily stooped beside Rose and began to wiggle the key in the lock.

Rose stood and straightened her gown.

With a triumphant cry, Lily turned the key and the latch fell open. Dahlia pushed past Rose as Lily raised the lid.

Rose lifted on her tiptoes, trying to see over Dahlia's head. "What is it? What's in the trunk?"

Lily lifted a startled face to Rose. "It's a *gown!* Oh, Rose, you have to see this!"

"I would, except Dahlia's head's in the way."

"Oh dear. I'm sorry." Dahlia moved out of the way and Lily held up a shimmery confection of a gown that made Rose gasp.

A celestial blue satin slip trimmed in a heavy band

of white lace peeked from beneath a long polonaise robe of white gossamer net. Short full sleeves set off the neckline, while blue satin knotted beading decorated each cuff and banded about the high waist to tie under the bosom.

"It must have been made by a French modiste," Lily said in awe as she gently stroked the silk. "I've never seen anything like this."

"Me, neither." Rose's curiosity was growing by the second. "Was there no marking on the trunk as to who sent it?"

"No. And the letter only had your name, nothing else," Lily said.

"Rose!" Dahlia's voice was hushed with reverence. She held up a pair of the most beautiful shoes Rose had ever seen. They were of delicate kid leather painted with a dull gold varnish so that they seemed almost made of glass.

Rose reached for the shoes, but Dahlia pointed into the trunk. "What's that under the tissue paper in the corner?"

Rose peered inside and saw a Grecian scarf of dull gold silk that matched the shoes and offset the blue-and-white gown to perfection. "Oh, that's lovely."

"And gloves!" Lily dove into the tissue paper and pulled out a pair of elbow-length white gloves of French kid. "Rose, I know just how you should wear your hair! You should put it up in the Eastern style and blend in a few flowers and—"

Rose gave a breathless laugh. "Lily, please, all of this cannot be for me. There must be some mistake. There must be a note in here. Help me look through this tissue paper."

"Here it is!" Dahlia held a missive sealed with a seal that Rose instantly knew.

Lily watched as Rose took the missive from Dahlia. "You know who sent it?"

"It's from the Duchess of Roxburghe."

Dahlia crowed, "Aren't you glad you attended her house party now?"

"You must read the note and see why she sent you such a lovely gown," Lily said, ignoring Dahlia's outburst. "Hurry! I'm dying to know what she says."

Rose opened the missive and turned toward the window to read it.

My dear Miss Balfour,

I write this note with a heavy heart. You were not treated well in my house and it pains me greatly. I'm an old woman, not well at all, and you would do me a great favor by accepting this small token of my affection and attending my ball tomorrow evening.

My nephew's rash actions may have started some gossip that may now be spreading. But as you know from the unfortunate incident six years ago, running away is the worst way to deal with gossip. Your presence at my ball, along with my visibly warm welcome, will squash any rumors, as no one would believe that I'd welcome one of my nephew's flirts into my home. Difficult as it may be, you owe it to your sisters to face down the rumor-mongers with a smile upon your face.

There is only one other reason I can think of that might keep you away from my ball—concern that A Certain Person might be present. Allow me to plainly state that Sinclair will not be at my ball. He and I had quite a row upon your leaving, and I vow upon my aunt Agatha's grave that he will not be present.

I hope to see you tomorrow. I will send a coach for you at five.

> Sincerely,
> Margaret, Duchess of Roxburghe

Rose bit her lip and reread the letter. Sin had been so bitter when she'd last seen him, so angry with her for wanting more of him than he had to give. She blinked, trying to stanch the tears before they came.

Lily murmured softly and a kerchief was pressed into Rose's hand. She wiped her tears. "I'm so sorry, I didn't mean to turn into a watering pot, but I didn't expect to see— Lily! Dahlia! You *wretches!*" Her sisters had their heads together over the duchess's letter.

Lily, her lips moving as she silently read, held up a hand as if demanding silence.

"Dahlia," Rose said. "Stop reading at once and—"

"Who is Sinclair?" Dahlia asked.

Lily's eyes were wide. "Rose, it's not the earl from—?"

Rose snatched the note back. "I didn't give you permission to read that."

"Never mind that," Lily said impatiently. "Tell us about Sinclair."

Dahlia, clutching the beautiful shoes, sat on the edge of the settee. "Yes, please tell us."

"There's nothing to say."

Dahlia gave an inelegant snort. "There's a lot to say, beginning with why you left there so abruptly."

Rose sighed. "There's not much to tell. Lord Sinclair and I met at his grandmother's, and I discovered that he was still incensed at my behavior all those years ago. In retaliation he was going to . . ."

"Going to what?" Lily demanded.

"He said he was going to seduce me."

Dahlia leaned forward. "Rose! Did he *succeed*?"

"Of course not." The more she thought about it, the less sure she was about who had seduced whom. "The trouble is that I started to care for him. Much more than he cared for me." Her misery caught her by the throat. "I worried I might make even more of a fool of myself than I had, and so . . . I left."

Dahlia nodded, but Lily gave her skeptical look.

Rose looked at the gown and sighed. "Which is why I must give these back."

Dahlia hugged the shoes. "No!"

"Rose, you're going." Lily stood and began collecting the items from the trunk. "When that carriage arrives, you will be wearing these gifts. You can't let the duchess down; this is her way of apologizing. How can you refuse her that?" Lily shrugged. "Besides, if this Lord Sinclair isn't going to be there, what excuse can you have not to attend?" Lily locked her gaze with Rose. "Or is there more you're not telling us?"

Rose managed to stifle a grimace. "Of course not." Her gaze fell on the letter, and she reread the lines about facing down the rumors. *I must do this for Dahlia and Lily. They will be the ones who will be the most hurt by my errors.*

She had no choice. "I'll go."

Dahlia gave an excited hop. "I'll fetch pen and paper, and we'll send a note to the duchess right now!" She was gone in a trice.

Lily patted Rose's hand. "You're going to be glad you went. Wait and see."

Twenty-four

From the Diary of the Duchess of Roxburghe
Just as I'd feared, it's much too warm for ice sculptures. Fortunately, Charlotte and I found an acceptable decorating alternative . . .

The carriage pulled up to Floors Castle. Clad in the beautiful gown, roses threaded through her hair, Rose had avoided looking out the window for fear of being struck with memories. Now, as she took the footman's hand and stepped out, she gasped.

The castle blazed with light. Candles had been placed in every single window, surrounded with mirrors that multiplied their flames.

MacDougal stood by the door. He smiled on seeing her awed expression. "Ye should see the ballroom and gardens, miss. Her grace outdid herself, she did."

"I can't wait," she replied seriously. The foyer had been transformed into a hothouse, rows and rows of exotic flowers upon every surface, their rich scent filling the air. More candles had been added, too, which made it seem as if they were in a magical garden.

MacDougal escorted her to a place near the stairs that had been set up for a receiving line. "If ye'll wait here, miss, her grace is on her way down. She was jus' puttin' the dogs away. We dinna want the wee things trampled by a carriage."

"Thank you, MacDougal."

"There you are, Miss Balfour!" The duchess, dressed in a resplendent gown of red silk that clashed with her wig, sailed down the stairs. "Ah, my dear, that gown looks beautiful on you!"

"Thank you. It was too generous of you."

"Nonsense. I am glad you came. Roxburghe sent word that he won't arrive until eleven, so I'm glad to have you with me."

"I'm very happy to be here."

"Good. We two have work to do tonight. Charlotte will relieve us in the receiving line in an hour, after most of the guests are here. After that, all you must do is mingle and appear to be enjoying yourself. Are you ready?"

"I think so."

"Not everyone knows about what happened. The rumor is a new one and no one knows you, which is good. Had you been a personage of note, people would have talked more. There is more of a curiosity about you. All we have to do is show the world that you are a lady of refinement, and the rumor will die a quick death."

Rose took a steadying breath. Some people would stare, or whisper, or laugh, but she would ignore them. The duchess was right; if not addressed, the rumors would only grow.

Outside, a carriage rolled up, followed by another and then another.

Rose lifted her chin. "Your grace, let's grab this lion by the mane and ride it to perdition."

The duchess smiled. "Well said, Miss Balfour." She offered her arm to Rose and they went to the head of the receiving line.

It was much worse than the duchess had predicted. Rose could only suppose that while people didn't recognize her name, they were quite familiar with Sin's. Though Lady Roxburghe's presence at Rose's side kept anyone from saying anything directly to her, it didn't keep them from staring at her with disdain when her grace's gaze was turned elsewhere.

Everywhere Rose looked, people seemed to be staring at her, talking behind their hands and fans, some of them giggling or sneering. It took all her strength to keep a smile on her face, but she managed, aided by the duchess's support. When the hour had finally passed and Lady Charlotte arrived, the duchess took Rose's arm and they entered the ballroom.

The room was draped in blue, purple, and rose

silk, all tied back with gold cords. Golden lights shone here and there, and candles danced in mirrored splendor on every table. "Oh, Lady Roxburghe, it's *lovely*."

Her grace looked around with an air of satisfaction. "It's well enough, though there's not much that's wintry about it."

"It looks like a starry night."

The duchess smiled. "That's exactly what we were trying to create." She patted Rose's hand. "Come. Let me introduce you to some of Roxburghe's friends."

Rose obediently walked with the duchess, pretending not to notice the looks that followed her.

A half hour later, the dancing began. Her grace smiled. "And now I'll have the pleasure of seeing you dance. We had so few at our house party that dancing wasn't feasible, but there are so many young people here." She patted Rose's hand. "You'll have a partner before this dance even finishes."

But again, the duchess's enthusiasm went unrewarded. No one asked for Rose's hand for that dance. Nor for the next dance. Nor the one after it. Nor the one after that.

Finally, a handsome, fashionable gentleman approached. The duchess coolly introduced him as Viscount MacRae, a neighbor. When he asked if her grace's "lovely friend" would care to dance, the duchess hesitated, but Rose quickly stepped forward with a breathless "Thank you." Perhaps now the duchess could sit down and enjoy the ball instead of fretting over her.

It proved to be a country dance, which allowed for occasional conversation. They went down the line, talking of the weather, the number of candles used to light the castle, the beauty of a famed waterfall.

Lord MacRae said in a teasing tone, "Miss Balfour, I must say that you are quite the topic of conversation this evening."

Her face heated. Perhaps if she feigned ignorance, he would take the hint and change the topic. "My, it's certainly a full ball, isn't it? There was a line of carriages all the way down the drive to the main road."

His gaze narrowed, but to her relief, he smiled and began to converse on the size of the crowd, wondering if it would cause a press at supper.

She assured him that the duchess had everything set, despite the large crowd, and she had the pleasure of having a conventional conversation without feeling the weight of someone's knowing gaze.

She was just beginning to relax when they danced by the terrace window and MacRae, tucking her hand in his, broke out of the dance line.

She frowned. "Lord MacRae, what are you doing? We shouldn't leave the ballroom."

"When the duchess has gone to such lengths in lighting the gardens?"

Rose had forgotten that. Now that she looked, several other couples were walking out to see the lighted paths. She laughed at her overly cautious behavior. "You're right. I would love to see them."

They walked to the doors and he gallantly held one open. Refreshing air came sweeping in. "Perhaps you'd relish a cooling stroll under the moonlight?"

She looked over her shoulder, catching the hostile gaze of at least two young ladies whom she'd never before met. Suddenly, the coolness of the well-lit terrace held even more relief, and she nodded. "Yes, let's take a walk."

She walked through the door, Viscount MacRae following.

A few minutes later, MacDougal announced in a loud voice, "The Earl of Sinclair."

Margaret frowned as Sin joined her. "Where have you been?"

"I had some unavoidable business to attend to." He frowned, looking about the room. "Where's Rose?"

Aunt Margaret gestured toward the dance floor. "She's dancing with Viscount MacRae."

Sin's jaw tightened. "That bounder? How could you allow her to dance with him?"

Margaret gave him an exasperated glare. "Because he was the only one who asked her. People are talking far more than I expected."

"Not more than I expected," he said, his voice dark. "Munro has been wagging his tongue all over town. I shall have to speak to him again."

"Please do. Poor Rose has been very calm in the face of it, but I can see that she's hurt. And then, when no one would ask her to dance—"

"Where is she? The set has gone around twice and I don't see them anywhere."

Margaret's brows snapped low. "I just saw them a few moments ago. Surely he didn't—"

But Sin had already left. He'd walked only a few feet when he heard a frightened yell. The ballroom came to an abrupt standstill, while people stared at the terrace doors.

Sin ran as fast as he could, only vaguely aware that others followed. All he cared about was Rose.

Rose shook her hand and hopped on one foot. "Ow, ow, ow!" she said through clenched teeth.

Viscount MacRae, his hands over his nose, managed to say through a nose already swelling closed, "You bern't even indured!"

"I am too injured! I bruised my knuckles on that rock you call a nose."

"You shouldn't hab hit me!"

"And you shouldn't have tried to kiss me! That was very improper."

Viscount MacRae looked sulkily at her, his hands still over his nose. "You knewb I was goinb to kib you."

"No, I did not. Why do you think I jumped when you tried? You scared me to death!" She eyed him with disfavor. "You, sir, are no gentleman."

"Why do you think I asked you oub on the terrace to begin wib?"

"Because you wished to see the lights in the garden, which is what you said, you idiot. I'll never forgive you for— Oh, do stop dripping blood everywhere. You're making a mess. Here." She pulled a kerchief from her pocket and held it out to him.

"I cannob let go ob my nobe or it bill bleed more." He sat heavily upon the edge of the fountain. "You'll hab to hold it ub while I releab it."

"*I* have to hold it up— Oh, you really are a pain." She bent down and tried to peer under his hands. "Blast it, I can barely see in this light." She dropped to her knees. "Lift up a bit."

He half stood, half crouched.

"When I count to three, lift your hands and I'll press the kerchief to your nose."

"Dank yew," he said meekly.

"You're welcome. Now—One. Two. Thr—"

Sin burst into the clearing, his furious eyes seeing only two things: Rose was on her knees, and the viscount seemed to tower over her.

He stalked up to MacRae, grabbed the bounder by the lapel, and drew back to strike the man.

Rose grabbed his fist. "Sin, no! What are you doing?"

"I heard you yell, and now I'm going to send this despicable blackguard to hell!"

"You can't hit him! Just *look* at him."

Sin forced his gaze to the viscount. The man's hands were tightly covered over his nose.

"You can cover your nose all you want," Sin ground out, "but I'm going to break it."

"Too late," Rose said in a chilly voice. "I already did it."

Sin blinked. For the first time, he noticed the blood on the viscount's chin and cravat. "Oh." Sin set the viscount back on his feet and turned to Rose. "But . . . I heard you yell."

"No, you heard Viscount MacRae yell."

Sin tried to remember and realized that it had been a man's yell, but in his concern for Rose, he hadn't stopped to question it.

Suddenly, he became aware that they had an audience. A quick glance confirmed the worst. Every pathway was filled with curious faces.

He scowled and turned to Rose. "What in hell were you thinking, coming outside?"

He didn't mean to snap at her, but he'd been trying to rescue her and it seemed that all he'd done was make things worse by causing yet a bigger scene.

"I came outside because it was hot inside. The garden is well lit and there were a lot of people about. But then as we walked, everyone disappeared and . . ."

A murmur from someone in the crowd made Rose stiffen, and suddenly she was aware of all the eyes upon them.

Sin saw her face go pale. He stepped forward, "Rose, don't worr—"

She whirled on him, her eyes blazing. "That's *it*. I tried to make things right. I tried to put up a brave front so that my sisters could have a decent chance, but—" A sob broke her voice and she turned, ready to back out of his life.

Sin caught her and lifted her into his arms.

She fought, as furious as a cat in a wet bag. "Let me down!"

"No. You're going to listen to me." But she wouldn't stop struggling. Frustrated, he looked around, and then smiled. He strode to the fountain, stepped over the edge, and strode to the middle, the water up to his thighs.

She grabbed her skirts, trying to keep them out of the water. "What are you *doing?*"

"Making sure you will at least listen to what I have to say."

"Put me down this instant!"

"No. You'll get wet."

"I don't care. I don't want to hear anything from anyone!"

"If you won't listen to me here, you'll listen to me at your home, or in the stables when you go out for a ride, or somewhere else. If I have to chase you from one end of this earth to the other, I will."

Rose's gaze locked on his eyes. He was deadly serious. It showed in the steady line of his jaw, in the way he stood, feet planted in the fountain.

She cast a glance around and realized that the crowd had grown. At least fifty people were crowded about the fountain, listening to every word.

Her chest tightened and she cleared her throat. "Sin, just . . . put me down." Her voice broke and she looked up at him, tears in her eyes. "Please," she whispered. "I just want to leave."

Sin leaned forward and pressed his lips to her forehead. "I can't let you go, Rose. I've tried and it kills me."

She stared at him. "I don't understand."

"Losing someone you love does that to you." He set her on the marble pedestal under the statue.

"Sin, what are you—"

He dropped to one knee and looked up at her. "Rose Balfour, will you do me the very, *very* great honor of taking my hand in marriage?"

Rose swiped at her eyes, unable to believe her own ears. "Did you just say . . . that you love me?"

He reached up and took her hand between his. "Rose Balfour, you are the most frustrating, most argumentative woman I've ever—"

"This isn't sounding a bit romantic."

A smile lit his eyes. "Let me finish. Rose Balfour, you are the most frustrating, most argumentative woman I've ever met, *and* the most cherished and loved of all women ever."

"Ever?"

"Ever. I've loved you since the first time I saw you,

a naïve girl of sixteen, and I've been running away ever since. I finally ran right into your arms, and I'm never leaving."

"Never?"

"You can try to make me, but of course you won't succeed."

"He's stubborn," came the duchess's voice. "Like a mule. So you'd best save us all time and trouble and just say yes."

Rose had to laugh. "Yes, Sin, I will marry you."

Sin's smile made her think of a sunrise. He stood, swooped her up, and kissed her thoroughly.

Rose kissed him back with equal passion. Her gown was trailing in the water, her shoes ruined, but she didn't care. She was finally where she belonged: in Sin's strong arms.

As the crowd applauded, Margaret wiped a tear from her eye. "Charlotte, I hope they name their first daughter after me. I deserve it after all I've been through."

Epilogue

Several weeks later, Margaret watched as a carriage decorated with flowers pulled away from Floors Castle. Rose leaned out, a garland in her hair, and waved to the small group gathered under the portico to see them off.

Margaret's heart swelled with pride as Sin leaned out the window beside his new bride. He sent Margaret a wink and a smile of pure happiness that quite made her eyes tear up. Then he slipped an arm about Rose and gently drew her back into the carriage.

The curtains on the carriage closed.

"Won't they get hot with the curtains closed?" Rose's sister Lily asked their father.

Sir Balfour, mopping his eyes with his handkerchief, appeared flustered as he tried to come up with an innocuous explanation.

"I'm sure the other curtain is open," Margaret said, which seemed to satisfy Lily.

MacDougal announced from the top step that a light luncheon had been placed upon the terrace, and the small crowd began to meander in that direction.

Margaret stayed to watch the coach disappear down the drive, her spirits leaving with it. After the ball, the last few weeks had been a flurry of preparations for the wedding. And now that it was over, she felt oddly listless.

Charlotte threaded her arm through Margaret's. "I'll never forget how he looked at her in that fountain."

Margaret managed a smile. "He is head over heels, isn't he?"

"Yes, and just didn't know it. It's a good thing you showed him." Charlotte pursed her lips. "Forgive me for saying this, but something has been bothering me about the entire situation."

"Oh? What's that, my dear?"

"Miss Isobel Stewart. Why was *she* in that hallway outside Rose's bedchamber that night? Her bedchamber wasn't even on that floor. And yet there she was, in her dressing gown and slippers. If I didn't know better, I'd have said that she was the one involved in a tryst."

"Yes, those details did get overlooked, didn't they?"

Charlotte looked at her friend. "You're not surprised."

"Lord Cameron and Miss Isobel have wished to marry for over eight years now, but her parents aren't amenable for he has no property and, thanks to his wastrel brother, is greatly in debt."

"Oh my! I never knew."

"I must give Lord Cameron credit for being so persistent. It seems that his affections remain unchanged."

"Did you plan for Miss Isobel to find Miss Balfour and Sin together?"

"Lud, no. I didn't realize that Miss Isobel and Cameron had, er, sealed their relationship, as it were. It just happened that way, that's all."

"But you knew why Miss Isobel was in the hallway. You could have used that to scotch the scandal about Sin and Rose."

"I could have, if Sin hadn't angered Mr. Munro so. After that . . ." She shrugged. "But this way Sin and Rose had to come together to fight the scandal. Nothing binds a couple better than a little adversity."

Charlotte shook her head. "You are amazing, my dear. What a lovely day, and such a beautiful wedding, too."

"It was, wasn't it?"

"Sheer perfection. Everyone is so happy . . . Well, except poor Sir Balfour." Charlotte sighed. "The poor man. A widower, you know, and you can see he's worried to death about his daughters, as he should be. Two lovely girls, and no prospects whatsoever."

Margaret looked thoughtfully across to where Lily and Dahlia stood to one side, looking out of place among the guests. "Those poor, motherless girls."

"Yes. I'm sure their mother would wish someone to assist them in finding good husbands. I do hope they have a kind aunt somewhere."

Margaret straightened. "Charlotte, I never thought of it before, but now that Rose is off to the continent for an extended honeymoon, Lily and Dahlia have no hopes of meeting eligible men."

"None. It's so sad."

"Tragic!"

"I know. I can see why Sir Balfour is so despondent."

"He would probably be happy if someone—say me, as the girls' godmother—were to offer to assist him."

"Margaret, what a lovely idea! You are so generous."

"Perhaps another house party for Lily. But no archery. Poor MacDougal still gets the shudders if one but mentions it."

"I can't blame him," Charlotte said. "Shall we make a list of whom to invite? If we don't hurry, all of the young men will have gone to London for the season."

"Lud, yes. We must set to work immediately!"

"Lily will need clothes—"

"And dancing lessons, too."

"And a new hairstyle, perhaps something with ringlets."

"Oh dear, there's so much to do!" The duchess beamed.

Charlotte smiled serenely. "I can see we're facing a very busy month."

"Or two. It could take longer."

"However long it takes."

From the Diary of the Duchess of Roxburghe

I'm not the sort of person to get involved in the lives of others—live and let live, I always say. But how can I ignore someone who is so plainly in need of help as Sir Balfour? Only I have the connections necessary to find suitors for fashion-mad Lily, and then shy Dahlia. So help him, I must.

And I think I know just the hard-hearted bachelor to woo Lily . . .

Read on for a preview of the next novel

in the Duchess Diaries series by

Karen Hawkins

Coming soon!

Kelso, Scotland
June 10, 1813

The carriage creaked to a stop beneath one of the towering oaks. The old woman pushed back the curtains with a hand heavy with jewels and looked at the thatched cottage with disbelief. "*This* is it?"

"What? You do not like it?" Piotr Romanovin, the royal Prince Wulfinski of Oxenburg, threw open the carriage door and called to the coachman to tie off the horses. "It is charming, no?" Grinning, the prince reached up to help his grandmother to the ground.

His Tata Natasha, a grand duchess in her own right, looked at the cottage and noted the broken shutters, the half-missing thatched roof, the front door hanging from one hinge, and a profusion of flowering vines growing across the windows. "No," she said bluntly. "This is not charming. Come, Wulf. We will go back to the house you bought and leave this silliness to the wilds."

"That is a castle. *This* is a house. And here I shall live."

"But the roof—"

"Can be fixed. As can the shutters and the door and the chimney."

"What's wrong with the chimney?"

"It needs to be cleaned, but otherwise it is strong. The craftsmanship is superb. It just needs some care."

She eyed her grandson sourly. The prince was a big man, larger than all of his brothers, and they were not small men. At almost six foot five, he towered over her and all nine of their guards. But large as Wulf was, he was her youngest grandson and the most difficult to understand, given to fits and starts that were incomprehensible to all and left his parents in agonies.

Take the simple matter of marriage. His other brothers had fallen into line and found matches among Europe's royal families, but Wulf refused every princess who came his way. Be they short or tall, thin or fat, fair or not—it didn't matter. With only the most cursory of glances, he'd refused them all.

Tata Natasha looked at the cottage and shook her head. "Wulf, your cousin Nikki, he was right: you have gone mad. You purchased a beautiful house—" At Wulf's lifted brows, she sighed. "Fine, a castle, then. With twenty-six bedrooms, thirty-five fireplaces, a salon, a dining room, a great hall, and more. It is beautiful and fitting for a prince of your stature. But this—" She waved a hand. "This is a hovel."

"It will be my home. At least until I've found a bride who will love me for this, and not because I can afford a castle with more chimneys than there are days in a month." He took his grandmother's hand, tucked it in the crook of his arm, and pulled her to the cottage door. "Come and see my new home."

"But—"

He stopped. "Tata, it was your idea for me to meet the world without the trappings of wealth."

"No, it was *your* idea, not mine. I only offered to travel with you."

"Fine. Then travel with me a few steps further." He pushed the crooked door to one side.

"Why must you make everything so difficult?" She tugged her arm free so that she could hold her skirts out of the dirt. "Why not marry a princess? They are not all horrible people."

He shrugged. "I didn't see one that I liked."

"What *do* you like, Wulf? What sort of a woman do you wish to meet?"

His eyes grew distant as he raked a hand through his black hair. "I want one who will treat me as Piotr and not as a bag of gold. One with passion and fire. One who will marry me because of me—not because of my title or wealth."

"You cannot deny your birthright."

His jaw tightened. "No, and for that reason, I will not hide that I am a prince. But I will not admit to my wealth."

Tata sighed. "I wish your father had never passed that blasted law allowing you and your brothers and sister to marry as you wished."

"He married for love, and he wished us all to have the same luxury."

"He married my daughter, who was a crown princess of Bulgaria!"

"Because he loved her and she loved him. Not because he had to. He knew he was fortunate in that."

Tata threw up a hand. "Love, love, love. That is all you and your father talk of! What about duty? Responsibility? What about that?"

He crossed his arms over his broad chest and smiled indulgently. "Rest assured, Tata. I will marry a strong woman, one who will give me many brave and intelligent sons. Surely that is responsible of me?"

Tata wished she could smack her son-in-law. What had he been thinking, to free his children to marry commoners? It was ridiculous. And now look what it had led to. Here they were, she and her favorite grandson, looking for a wife among the heathens that populated this wild and desolate land. "If you will not believe in the purity of bloodlines, then how will you know which woman is right for you?"

He didn't even pause. "I'll know her when I see her."

She ground her teeth. "Why did we have to come to this godforsaken part of the world to find this woman? Scotland isn't even civilized."

He sent her a humorous glance. "You sound like Papa."

"He's right in this instance! For once." She scowled.

"Tata, everyone knows me in Europe. But here . . . here, I can be unnoticed."

"Pah! As usual, you take a good idea and carry it too far. No one would know you in London, either, and we'd live far more comfortably there."

Wulf grinned but paid her no heed as he looked about the small cottage. "My little house is more spacious than you thought, no?" It was, too, for he could stand upright, providing he didn't walk toward the fireplace. There the roof swooped down to meet it, and he'd have to bend almost in half to sit before it.

Still, he looked about with satisfaction. The front room held a broken table and two chairs without legs. A wide plank set upon two barrels served as a bench before the huge fireplace, where iron hooks made him think of fragrant, bubbling stew.

Tata scowled. "Where would you sleep?"

"Here." He went to the back of the room, where a tattered curtain hung over a small alcove. A bed frame remained, leather straps crisscrossed to provide support for a long-gone straw mattress. "I will have a feather mattress brought down from the castle. This frame is well made and I will sleep like a baby." He placed a hand upon the low bedpost and gave it a shake. The structure barely moved.

Tata grunted her reluctant approval and looked around. "I suppose it will make a good hunting lodge once this madness of yours is gone."

"So it will. I'll have some of my men begin work on it at once. I'll wish it cleaned and stocked with firewood."

She shot him an amused glance. "You'll still let your men do the work?"

"I will help, of course, but I've no experience with thatching. I'd be foolish to try now when the rainy season is about to begin."

"At least you are keeping some good sense about you."

"I'm keeping all of it." He held out his arm. "Come, Tata. I'll take you home for tea."

"Not the English kind. It's so weak as to taste like hot water."

He chuckled. "No, no. I will get you good tea from our homeland. We brought enough for a year, though we will only be here a month or so."

Tata paused before she walked out of the doorway. "Wulf, do you not think a month is too short a time to persuade a woman to marry you? One who thinks that an empty title and this"—Tata waved at the cottage again—"is all you possess?"

"Yes."

"Then you are as arrogant as you are foolish."

His smile faded, his green eyes darkening. "Tata, I told you of my dream. That is why we are here."

"Yes, yes. You dreamed of Scotland, of a woman with hair of red—"

"Red and gold, with eyes the color of a summer sky."

She paused thoughtfully. "The dreams of our family have always had meaning."

"This one especially. I've had it four times now—the exact same dream. And every time, it is the same woman who—"

A scream rended the air.

Wulf spun toward the door. "Stay here."

"But—"

But he was gone, shouting at his guards to remain until he needed them.

Lily slowly awoke, her numbed mind creeping to consciousness. She shifted and then moaned as every bone in her body groaned in protest.

A warm hand cupped her face. "Easy, Moya," came a deep, heavily accented voice. "The brush broke your fall, but you will still be bruised."

I must still be unconscious to hear such a delicious voice. And what is he talking about? Did I— Oh yes. I remember now. She'd been riding through the forest by Floors Castle, where she'd been staying as a guest of her godmother, the Duchess of Roxburghe, when a fox had leapt from the bushes and caused her horse to rear. Lily had been caught unawares because she'd been admiring the flowers growing alongside the path. She was glad her sister Rose hadn't been nearby, or she would have gotten a scolding for the lack of attention to her riding.

Lily cautiously opened her eyes to find herself staring into the deep green eyes of the most handsome man she'd ever seen. *He's not a dream.*

The man was beyond large; he was huge, with wide, broad shoulders that blocked the light and hands so large that the one now cupping her face practically covered one side of it.

She gulped a bit and tried to sit up, but was instantly pressed back to the ground.

"Nyet," the giant said, his voice rumbling over her like waves over a rocky beach. "You will not rise."

She blinked. "Nyet?"

He grimaced. "I should not say 'nyet' but 'no.'"

"I understood you perfectly. I am just astonished that you are trying to tell me what to do. I don't know where you are from or who you are, but I am perfectly fine and well able to handle this situation myself."

His expression darkened, and she had the distinct

impression that he wasn't used to being chastised. She stirred restlessly, suddenly uneasy. "Please, Mr.— I'm sorry. What's your name?"

"It matters not. What matters is that you are injured and refuse assistance. That is foolish."

She glared at him and pushed herself up on one elbow. As she did so, her hat, which had been pinned upon her neatly braided hair, came loose and dropped to the ground behind her.

The man's gaze locked upon her hair, his eyes widening as he muttered something in a foreign tongue.

"What's wrong?" she asked.

"Your hair. It is red."

She gave an exasperated sigh. "No, it's not. It's blond with a touch of red when the sun— Oh, why am I even talking to you about this? You still haven't told me your name or why you're here or—" She eyed him with suspicion. "I don't know who you are."

"You will."

He said the words as if it were a fact.

"What do you mean?"

Slowly, he shook his head. "It is nothing, Moya. Nothing and everything."

"Look, Mr. Whatever Your Name Is, this is *not* amusing. I'm going to get up and leave, and you are going to stay here."

"You think so, eh?"

"I *know* so. For if you don't, I will scream, and the groom who was with me will hear and shoot you dead."

She was bluffing, for there was no groom. She should have taken one with her, and had been informed that she should, but the day had been so pretty and the summer breeze so gentle and the horse seemingly so mild-mannered that she'd never thought she'd actually need a groom. Now she wished for nothing more.

The stranger's brows rose. "Ah. You think I am being too—what is the word? Forward?"

"Yes, forward."

"But you are injured—"

"No, I'm not."

"You were thrown from a horse and are upon the ground. I call that 'injured.'" His brows locked together over eyes of the deepest green she'd ever seen. "Am I using the word wrong?"

"No, but—"

"Then do not argue."

"Of all the nerve! I'm bruised, but no more." To prove her point, she sat upright, even though it brought her closer to this huge boulder of a man. "See? I'm fine."

"Ny—No. You will stay where you are until one of my men brings the doctor."

"One of your men?" *So he has "men," does he?*

His gaze grew shaded. "They are my companions. Nothing more."

"Ah. Then you are a groom of some sort?"

"No. I am not a groom. I am Piotr."

She waited, and when he said nothing more, she sighed. "That's it? Just Piotr?"

"Piotr of Oxenburg. It is a small country beside Russia."

She wracked her brains. The country's name seemed familiar. "There was a mention of Oxenburg in *The Morning Post* just a few days ago."

"Hmmm. Whatever you read could not be about me. No one knows I'm here. My cousin Nikki, he is in London. Perhaps he is in the papers." He rocked back on his haunches, the golden light filtering from the trees dancing over his black hair. "You can sit up, but not stand. Not until we know you are not broken."

"I'm not broken!" she said sharply. "I'm just embarrassed that I fell off my horse."

A glimmer of humor shone in the green eyes. "You fell asleep, eh?"

She fought the urge to return the smile. "No, I did not fall asleep. A fox frightened my horse, which caused it to rear. And then it ran off."

His gaze flickered to her boots, a frown marring his amazingly handsome face. "No wonder you fell. Those are not good riding boots."

"These? They're perfectly good boots!"

"Not if a horse bolts. Then you need some like these." He slapped the side of his own boots, which had a thicker and taller heel.

"I've never seen boots like those."

"That is because you English do not really ride, you with your small boots. You just perch on top of the horse like a sack of grain and—"

"I'm not English; I'm a Scot," she said sharply. "Can't you tell from my accent?"

"No."

She opened her mouth to respond and he threw up a hand. "Do you never just say yes to one single thing? Is that because you are a woman, or because you are a Scot?"

She frowned. "You don't need to be insulting."

He grinned and stood and held out his hand. "I apologize, Miss—?"

"Lily Balfour." As she reached up to place her hand in his, one of her red-gold curls fell to her shoulder.

Her rescuer froze, an odd expression on his face as he reached past her hand to grasp her hair. Slowly, he threaded it through his fingers, his gaze locking with hers.

Her heart leapt as his hand grazed her cheek and she had the oddest sense of breathlessness, as if she'd just run up a flight of stairs.

Cheeks hot, she tugged her curl free from the stranger's grasp and repinned it with hands that seemed oddly awkward. "That's— You shouldn't touch my hair."

"It is not permitted."

"No."

"It should be." He sighed regretfully. "Come. I will take you to your home."

Relieved to hear that was his intention, she brushed some leaves from her skirts just as he bent and scooped her up as if she were a blade of grass.

Before she could do more than gasp, he began striding through the woods.

Lily had little choice but to hang on as best as she could, uncomfortably aware of the deliciously spicy cologne that tickled her nose and made her long to burrow her face against him. "What are you doing?"

He looked down at her, surprised. "I'm carrying you."

"You can't just carry me off like this!"

"But I have." There was no rancor in his voice, no sense of correcting her. Instead, his tone was that of someone patiently trying to explain something. "I have carried you off, and carried off you will be."

She scowled up at him. "Look here, Mr. Piotr—"

"Romanovin."

She paused, interested in spite of herself. "Mr. Piotr Romanovin, then."

His grinned, his teeth white in his black beard. "Yes, I am Piotr Aleksander Romanovin of Oxenburg."

Though she hardly knew him, his relaxed grin was reassuring. He looked like many things—handsome, exotic, overbearing, strong—but he would not harm her. Her instincts and common sense both agreed on that. "Why were you in this forest?"

"Ah, I brought my—how you say, *babushka*? Ah yes, grandmother. I brought her to see the house I have just purchased."

She must be safe, then, Lily decided, for no man would invite his own grandmother to a ravishment.

The amazing green eyes now locked with hers. "You will meet my grandmother soon, but not today. I think you will like her."

It sounded like an order.

She managed a faint smile. "I'm sure we'll adore each other. But really, I doubt we'll meet."

"No? I think you are a guest of the Duchess of Roxburghe, no? These are her woods."

"How do you know the duchess?"

He shrugged, his huge shoulder moving against her cheek. "Her grace knows my grandmother. They've known each other since they were schoolgirls, although I do not think they were fond of each other."

"Ah. Yet they are fond enough now that the duchess invited your grandmother to visit?"

"Of course. A rivalry is no reason for rudeness. It is the way of the world to have rivals, no?"

"I suppose so. I just— Look, I really should wait here for the duchess's men. Once the horse returns to the stables, they will come looking for me. And if they don't find me, they'll think something horrible has happened."

"I will send my men to wait for the duchess's servants, so no one will be left untended."

"Your men?" She frowned. "You said that before. How many men do you have?"

His gaze slid away. "Enough."

"Then you're a military leader." That explained his boldness and overassuredness.

"Yes."

"What are you? A corporal? A sergeant?"

"I am in charge." A faint note of surprise colored his voice, as if he were irritated that she should think anything else.

"You're in charge of what? A squad? A battalion?"

"Of course not." He looked a bit insulted. "I am in charge of it all."

She blinked. "Of the entire military of Oxenburg?"

"I shall tell you, because the duchess will soon say it anyway. I am not a general. I am a prince, which is why the duchess has asked that my grandmother and I attend her events. I had not thought to accept her invitation, but now—" He grinned down at her, his teeth flashing. "Now, I think I will agree."

"Wait. You're a *prince*?"

He shrugged, his broad shoulders making his cape swing. "I am one of six."

She couldn't wrap her mind around the thought of a room full of men like the one before her now: huge, broad shouldered, bulging with muscles and lopsided smiles, their dark hair falling over their brows and into their green eyes . . . She couldn't picture it. She fixed her gaze on his face. "If you're a prince then you must be fabulously wealthy."

He looked down at her. "Not every prince has money, Moya."

"Some do."

"And some do not. Sadly, I am the poorest of all my brothers."

Her disappointment must have shown on her face, for he regarded her with a narrowed gaze. "You do not like this, Miss Lily Balfour?"

She sighed. "No, no I don't."

He paused and looked down, one brow arching. "Why not?"

"Sadly, some of us must marry for money."

"I see." He continued to carry her, his brow lowered. "And this is you, then? You must marry for money?"

"Yes."

"But what if you fall in love?"

Lily didn't know if it was the shock of her fall or the fact that she felt so safe in his arms, but she heard herself say with completely honesty, "I have to marry a wealthy man to aid my family's situation, and you are the first man I thought was . . . interesting. So yes, I'm sorry to hear that you are not wealthy." She detected the flash of disappointment in his gaze and said quickly, "I wouldn't be looking for a wealthy husband, except that I must. Our house is entailed and my father hasn't been very good about— Oh, it's complicated. But I have no choice. I *must* marry for money."

He seemed to consider this. After a moment, he nodded. "You need funds to save your family home. It is noble that you are willing to sacrifice yourself."

"You think it will be a sacrifice? I was hoping that I might find someone I could care for, too."

"You wish to fall in love with a rich man. Life is not always so accommodating."

"Yes, but it's possible. The duchess is helping me. She's invited several gentlemen for me to meet—"

"All wealthy."

"All wealthy gentlemen." Lily turned her gaze to his and sighed. At one time, a wealthy gentleman had seemed enough. Now, she wished she could also ask for a not-wealthy prince. One like this one, who carried her so gently and whose eyes gleamed with humor beneath the fall of his black hair.

But it was not to be. All she had were these few moments. She sighed again and rested her head against his broad shoulder. *This will have to be enough.*